"You," he whispered with his mouth on hers. "It really was you."

Ignoring shaky limbs that refused to behave properly and his heart's off-beat rhythm, Colton leaned into her. Licking gingerly at her lips, nipping lightly at the corners of her mouth before again sealing his lips to hers, he took her breath into his lungs, and felt that breath warm him.

Had this slight, ebony-haired creature truly fought beside him, placing herself in jeopardy in order to help? Although Rosalind's mouth was momentarily motionless beneath his, Colton sensed with every instinct he possessed how much she wanted to respond.

He wanted her in that moment as much as his beast had desired her in the park. Every inch of him yearned for her, now that he'd been awakened and had captured her in his arms.

One word resonated in his mind, on its own loop, playing over and over.

Mine.

WOLF BORN

LINDA THOMAS-SUNDSTROM

Published in Great Britain 2015
by Mills & Boon, an imprint of Harlequin (UK) Limited,
Eton House, 18-24 Paradise Road, Richmond, Surrey, TW9 1SR

ISBN: 978-0-263-25399-3

89-0215

Harlequin (UK) Limited's policy is to use papers that are natural, renewable and recyclable products and made from wood grown in sustainable forests. The logging and manufacturing processes conform to the legal environmental regulations of the country of origin.

Printed and bound in Spain
by CPI, Barcelona

Linda Thomas-Sundstrom writes contemporary and paranormal romance novels for Mills & Boon® Nocturne™ and Mills & Boon® Desire™. A teacher by day and a writer by night, Linda lives in the West, juggling teaching, writing, family and caring for a big stretch of land. She swears she has a resident Muse who sings so loudly, she often wears earplugs in order to get anything else done. But she has big plans to eventually get to all those ideas. Visit Linda at lindathomas-sundstrom.com or on Facebook.

To my family, those here and those gone,
who always believed I had a story to tell.

Chapter 1

Everyone had demons.

"Some species are just closer to them than others," Colton Killion muttered as he ran beneath the light of a huge Miami moon. For a werewolf like himself, the desire for what the moon offered fit into another category altogether. But now wasn't the time for beastly antics. He'd had an emergency call.

Drenched in moonlight, and in human form, he sprinted over a wide stretch of dirt and grass. The night air, filled with the scent of the ocean and a dozen kinds of Cuban food, burned his throat as he sucked in it, and left a warm sensation in his groin.

Running appealed to his animal nature.

At the moment, though, he couldn't afford to blow his cover. Two other cops were on his heels, running as fast as their human legs would take them. The radio on his shoulder kept repeating directions interspersed with static.

"Officer down. All units on the south side respond to the following address. 521 Baker."

The harsh words wouldn't have been half as bad without the address the dispatcher had given out. Damn if his family didn't live on the same street.

Colton lengthened his stride to reach an area of what in Miami passed for a forest of trees. Liquid moonlight had already begun to move through his veins as if he had injected it into an artery. The phantom sensation of an elongated muzzle made him reach up to check that it hadn't materialized yet.

Those cops behind him couldn't see that. There was no way they would understand having a Lycan in their midst, and that a searing, breath-robbing heat was spreading outward from deep inside his chest where a sleeping beast lay curled, craving the night, awaiting its freedom.

"Killion! Wait up!" Julias Davidson, the officer responsible for this beat yelled, the strain in the man's voice due to him being shamefully out of shape and having to run to the cruiser parked on the street.

Colton didn't care about the identity of the officer loping along in Davidson's wake. He was more concerned that Davidson, usually nosy as hell, hadn't asked why Colton had been passing through this way in the first place when he was officially off duty.

Good thing he hadn't been asked that question, since Colton didn't know the answer. He'd just acted on a feeling that something was up with this park and had dropped by for a look. Most of the time, he paid attention to those little sparks of intuition.

"Hell." In deference to the unanswerable *why* he was here, Colton found himself in a precarious state. With the muscles of his neck throbbing and the skin on his bare arms undulating like disturbed water in a pond, restraining his lupine abilities took every ounce of willpower he possessed.

The moon called to him, but there was also an officer down just two doors shy of his parents' house. And the sudden notoriety of an injured or, God forbid, dead police officer would be unwanted attention for a family like his that had a lot to hide—and even more to lose, if they were identified as Lycan.

"Hellfire!"

The whitewashed oath didn't satisfy him, or take the edge off his anxiety. "I've got a bad premonition about this dispatch to Baker Street," he whispered hoarsely. In fact, his gut told him he shouldn't wait for the others, and that he would get to the crime scene faster if he ditched the limiting human persona.

Too late now. He had company. Turning, he said to a breathless Davidson in a steady voice, "I'll go ahead," as Davidson hit the edge of the trees.

"On foot?" Davidson tossed back.

"I know a shortcut through the park."

"This park's dangerous enough with three of us out here."

"There hasn't been much real trouble since Scott, Wilson and the other boys cleaned it up last year," Colton said.

Key word there: *Other* boys. Capital *O*. There weren't many completely human bones left in the bodies of detectives Adam Scott and Matt Wilson, whose lives had radically changed after receiving rogue werewolf bites less than a year ago, and who now had their own secrets to keep.

"Yeah? Well, suit yourself, Killion," Davidson said. "Some bastard shot a cop, and we need to be there."

Without stopping for anything longer than two quick breaths, Davidson and his partner took off again. Colton watched them go, his own breath regulating now that he was about to be alone.

Or almost alone. That initial spark of intuition nagged at him again. The night had a strange feel to it that was thicker, denser than a normal night. It felt to him like too many unseen things moved through the dark, taking up space and crowding the atmosphere. Notable oddities like these seemed to hint at an unusual kind of energy massing on the park's periphery.

He could taste that wayward energy. The word to describe it was *wild.*

Raising his face to the moon, he absorbed the tingle of light on his skin, and sniffed the air. Most of the scents under the trees were familiar to him. He often worked this part of Miami.

He sniffed again and waited to make sure no intruders appeared, knowing that he had to let the moon have her way this time. He had to let the beast out because of his need to get somewhere fast. Werewolf speed was legendary and what he needed right now was to beat the other officers to the crime scene.

In order to beat Davidson and the others to the crime scene on Baker, Colton Killion, officer of the law, but also much more than his seemingly human appearance or profession, needed to morph into a creature that really wasn't an entity other than himself, but an integral part of him.

Not a metaphorical twin or the symptom of a split personality with an evil side, his beast was something he birthed by merely turning himself inside out to expose what lay beneath the surface of his skin.

All true Lycans, with pure, undiluted Lycan blood in them, were born to this. Lycanthropy, the oldest form of werewolfism, meant housing a rare blood disorder that predated history, escaped explanation and encompassed the strongest, fiercest of the beings falling under the heading of *wulf.*

Man-wolf hybrids. Not wolf, but *wulf.* Royal-blooded werewolves, able most of the time to blend in with human society in a world that had unknowingly absorbed them.

"Okay," he said with calm finality. "Bring it on."

Lupine euphoria hit before he finished the invitation. His body quivered with excitement. His core temperature rose in a lightning-fast ascent, reaching the level of "sizzling" before his next intake of air.

Claws popped from the ends of all ten of his fingertips like spring-loaded blades. Brief, swollen seconds of what felt like dark-dipped madness came and went, a throwback to a state people once called Lunacy. And then the process of a man becoming a werewolf took over.

Bones snapped. Ligaments stretched. The sound of hot, wet flesh tearing echoed in the night as his muscles redefined themselves. Colton's stomach knotted and clenched, doubling him over at the waist for a few more tense seconds as rich brown fur sprouted from his pores.

When he again stood upright, feeling inches taller than his usual six-two, and confined and claustrophobic in his clothes, he opened a mouth full of razor-sharp teeth and issued a low guttural growl that mimicked the sound of distant thunder, a sound that was both a response to the temporary pain of this shape-shift and a keen acknowledgment of being something other than one hundred percent human.

Following that, he belted out a harrowing, piercing howl that rolled through the park's vast emptiness with a feral quality that would have sufficed to make any animal's skin crawl, and was meant to do just that.

But as he gathered himself, ready to utilize the animal's agility and superior speed, Colton's senses suddenly jerked again to a state of full alertness. The feeling of not being alone made a comeback.

And then, out of the silver-coated darkness, came the surprise of an answering howl.

What the hell?

Had he missed something out there?

Colton's fur stood on end. He backed up a step, stunned as another howl followed the first. This one was higher in pitch than his own vocalization and no less menacing. But it was also tantalizing and seductive.

Colton glanced up, thinking that the moon must have been playing a trick. But a third sound came soon after the second, closer this time, and from ground level.

Haunting, preternatural, seductive in nature, this howl originated from the part of the park where he'd sensed strangeness but had seen no one. No human, anyway.

The wulf's immediate natural instinct was to find what had made that sound and mount it, instead of dashing off in the direction he needed to go. The animal's need to chase down whatever had made those wolfish sounds was so strong and insistent that Colton tightened his mental leash on the beast.

Despite the check of restraint that had him frozen to stillness, Colton's insides writhed with the new dilemma he faced due to hearing that answering howl. Should he hurry to Baker Street and see what had happened there, or take the time to find out who or what else roamed this park?

He and his beast weren't completely at odds over voting for the last one. It was, however, an unexpected trip in the agenda when timing might be critical.

Waiting out several more thunderous heartbeats, the blood inside his distended arteries began to burn. Judging by his arousal, he knew that the unexpected visitor was female.

Not just any female, either. Not with a voice like that. This was a she-wulf—powerful, practiced and pure Lycan, or he was a sorry son of a bitch who didn't know a Lycan from a hole in the ground.

Who are you?

Where did you come from?

He hadn't met many purebred female Lycanthropes.

The rarity of full-blooded she-wulfs was the reason true Lycans as a breed were slowly dying out. Females often weren't wired correctly for the transition from human to werewolf, and many of them didn't make it past the Blackout phase of their coming-of-age party for reasons no one actually knew. Special Lycan matchmakers traveled the world to find females to bring home to a qualified clan. He, himself, had been waiting ten years.

And what? One of those rarest of creatures has just announced her presence here in Miami, on the edge of this park? To me?

The acknowledgment of this possibility hit Colton with the force of an oncoming train. His wulf-heavy limbs shuddered. His teeth snapped together, filling his mouth with the acrid taste of his own blood. He grew hotter, and a little confused.

Hell, his human side wanted to chase after whatever had made those sounds as much as the beast did. Finding a *She* fulfilled a powerful need and provided a possible solution to a lot of problems of sheer physical necessity for a male. *Keep the line going. Keep it strong. Choose a mate.*

But damn the timing of finding this female. Not only did duty call, it also called with an overriding personal necessity that meant the possible welfare of his family. He had taken an oath to protect and serve not only the population of Miami but the few Lycans left in his scattered clan. Oaths were binding for werewolves, and lifelong.

In addition to that, he might know the cop who had been shot.

Shit. He visualized the scene. There would be officers, CSI techs and television crews all over the place, knocking on doors.

And a she-wulf appeared now?

Really bad timing. Effing bad.

Worse yet, his beast had already driven him to take a step toward the female's invitation, stretching at its leash.

Colton hauled himself back with difficulty and a barked chastisement. *Can't have this. Get a freaking grip. There's too much at stake.*

Good advice in the best of times, but the beast's needs were elemental and approaching the point of no return. It was hungry to bury its cock in that female's damp, furry, feminine folds, and angered by the restraint.

He had to get away, though leaving this spot would be one of the hardest things he had ever done. He had to ignore this she-wulf, knowing the odds of ever finding another one.

Resolutely, regretfully, he echoed the she-wulf's call with a low-pitched howl that could have been translated as: *You have no idea how sorry I am for having to go.* Though it actually meant so very much more than that, and perhaps even the extinction of his family's line.

Stepping out from under the trees, and filled with regret, Colton took off. Alone. Into the night. Toward the scent of a downed cop's blood in the distance.

Chapter 2

Rosalind Kirk dropped to her haunches and slammed a furred-up fist into the ground to keep herself from following the Were in the park, whose scent was new, feral and overtly masculine.

Her hackles rose with a mixture of curiosity and anger.

That wulf had ignored her invitation.

She stared at the way he cut a smooth swath through the trees, running faster than anything she had ever seen. He was a big werewolf, tall and powerfully built. His brown pelt blended with the shadows. Highlighted by moonlight, it appeared that he wore clothes.

Strange.

Although anger flared over his rude rejection of her call, Rosalind's heart raced as she watched him run. She felt the rhythm of the movement of the brown

Were's legs in her muscles, and heard the harshness of his breathing echo inside her chest. All this made her feel disturbed in a way she'd never experienced before.

Her fur ruffled.

Her chin lifted.

Finding a male of her species hadn't been the reason she had slipped her father's net when he wasn't looking, but suddenly seemed like a bonus.

She'd been homesick for her bayou property, where she could run unhindered. Here in Miami, where her father had accepted an invitation to visit the Landaus—an ancient Lycan line as old as her own—she had been quarantined on the estate's grounds. Her father had forbidden her to go past the expansive property's stone walls.

Right. Like she'd listen to that, or be chained to a ridiculous confinement, however lovingly the directive had been issued by a father who said he had her best interests in mind.

Like she had ever met his expectations.

I'm a woman now.

Even her father, an elegant, intelligent Lycan, had no idea how elevated her metabolism became on a night like this one.

Sure, it was dangerous being out here in wulf form. There were plenty of risks in ignoring the rules and restrictions. It was equally dangerous to expose herself to a member of another pack without being properly introduced. Yet her boundless need for freedom resonated in every bone and cell in her body. The moon's influence blasted through her like some kind of invisible ray, dispersing her humanness almost completely.

She had too much pent-up energy, and her search for

freedom had been interrupted before she'd used it up. Her focus had been riveted to a big brown werewolf sprinting in the opposite direction who hadn't paid any attention to her at all.

Didn't you hear me, Were?

Shaking her head without taking her eyes off him, she leaned forward, into his scent. A series of disgruntled growls rumbled in her chest, registering her displeasure. Maybe Miami Weres held contempt for those outside of their packs, and that's why he had turned from her.

His loss. She was lithe, smart, fast and strong—a worthy mate for a purebred male. In spite of that, she had been shielded from all eligible partners and kept from pursuing any outside company at all, leaving her to wonder what everyone had been waiting for.

She was sick of the tight ring of supervision surrounding her, and ready for her first close-up with a prime example of her species.

Like you, pretty, brown-pelted wulf.

Wasn't finding a mate what she was eventually supposed to do?

Had the brown Were considered her unworthy, when the whispers behind her back at the Landaus' place had described her as special?

Special...

The dreaded Blackout phase wired into her family's line had come upon her at thirteen, instead of the usual age of twenty-one. Surviving her body's internal rewiring at so young an age had caused her to acquire a stellar repertoire of abilities.

Special...

At fifteen, she outdistanced her father in races. By

sixteen, she could painlessly shape-shift in seconds whenever she chose to, with or without the moon. Even her father couldn't do that.

Tonight, at the matronly age of twenty, eight-foot-tall stone walls hadn't stood a chance of containing her. One agile leap was all it took to escape the Landaus' boundaries.

Piece of cake.

In her defense, she hadn't planned on being outside those walls for very long. Merely one good sprint to calm her had been the justification…

Until she felt the ongoing song of this male's Lycan blood as if that song had been written for her. Until she had sensed him in the shadows as clearly as if he'd stood five feet away.

Even now, his earthy, alluring scent pulled her like some sort of unavoidable undertow.

Unsure of what to do next, because she actually was socially inept, and had been more or less a prisoner in her own home all of her life, Rosalind didn't completely understand the feelings of wanting to catch up with the brown wulf in spite of his rebuff.

Seconds ticked past as she stood there, longing to give chase. Her legs trembled with the desire to move. Her dark muzzle quirked at the thought of werewolves having one-night stands in public spaces, and how that would go down.

So, which way to go? Back to her father, or after the rude brown Were?

With a glance over her shoulder toward the Landaus' walled border in the distance, Rosalind straightened to her full five-foot-five-inch height. Her black pelt—thick, rich, shining like polished obsidian in the moonlight—reflected the bright look of rebelliousness in her amber-green eyes as she made her decision.

As Colton had feared, the five-hundred block of Baker Street crawled with people. Too many people gumming up a crime scene always made a bad situation worse.

He hit the side of a building hard with his left shoulder to shock his wulf side back to reality. Closing his eyes, blowing out a breath, he willed his beast into the background and corralled it with a word of promise. *Later.*

The reversal of his shift was equally as hard on his body, but one hell of a lot quicker. Everything rearranged with a soft snapping of ligament and bone. On human legs, Colton cut a path through the hordes of neighbors out in full force behind fluttering expanses of yellow crime tape. But after those few moments of letting the beast out, the sensory bombardment of being near to all these human bodies weighed him down. Fresh from his run, his thermostat had yet to settle. He was damp with perspiration and needed about ten more deep breaths in a quiet place where he could fully recover before showing himself—a luxury he didn't have.

In spite of the distraction in the park, he had beat Davidson to the scene. Six other cruisers were parked along the street. Two emergency vehicles were in attendance with their back doors wide-open. Uniforms moved like an army of ants up and down sidewalks in the dark.

Colton grabbed hold of a blue uniform whose name tag said EMT Smith. "What happened here?"

"Homicide," Smith said after checking out Colton's badge.

"Where? Who?" Colton's voice cracked with emotion.

"Name's Connelly. And one officer was shot after arriving at the scene."

"Connelly." Colton processed the news. "Which Connelly?"

"All of them."

"What?"

"The whole family was killed. Two adults and two kids. It's one of the worst scenes I've been to. Blood and body parts are spewed all over the place. The house looks like a freaking horror movie set. No offense or disrespect, Officer, but I need some air. I've only been on this job for three weeks."

Colton felt a rush of adrenaline returning in a bad way. He knew the Connellys. His parents had socialized with that family on occasion. A year ago he had helped to build their kids' swing set.

But the arctic adrenaline dump jarring him was also an indication that he needed to chill out in public. EMT Smith was still looking at him as if the guy awaited permission to be dismissed, so that he could slink away and hurl his dinner.

"Thanks," Colton said. Staring at what Smith had called a house of horror, he added, "The injured officer? How is he?"

"He's been taken to Miami General. Took a bullet in the upper abdomen, but it looks like the gun might have belonged to one of the other victims, perhaps shooting at whatever moved. I heard another EMT say that if he's in good shape physically, he'll probably make it."

"His name?"

"Don't know. Sorry. Got to go." Smith hurried back to his truck.

Colton looked down the block to where a city streetlight should have been glowing and wasn't. The bad feeling in his gut quadrupled in intensity. His parents' house sat beneath that blown-out bulb. The front windows were dark.

He ran. Ducking under the yellow tape with his eyes locked on his parents' house, he rushed across the lawn and up the front steps. Forgetting himself and his innate strength, he tore the screen door off its hinges and reached for the knob.

He stepped across the threshold, where the brutal odor of blood and exposed Lycan secrets hit him in a moment of monumental frenzy, and the severed head of his proud Lycan father lay on the carpet at Colton's feet.

Stunned by the sight, Colton let out a wail of anguish that nearly buckled him at the knees.

Chapter 3

Rosalind heard the sound of a Lycan's roar and froze midstep. Registering the sounds as pain and loss, the intensity of the emotion in the roar rocked her. Hearing something so personal made her want to run away. Stubbornly, she stayed.

Drifts of a dreadful odor hit her, tearing her from the shadows. *Enemy stink. But what kind?*

After the darkness of the park, the revolving lights on the police cars hurt her light-sensitive eyes. She was in werewolf form and in danger because of it. She couldn't be found like this. She didn't dare follow the big male's muffled howl of pain. She wasn't used to crowds. With so many people around, changing back to her human semblance wasn't an option, since she'd be naked if she did.

Nevertheless, she was drawn to the sound of the

brown Were's pain, and moved through the dark spaces between houses on the opposite side of the street, her black pelt acting as camouflage in the night.

She was stopped by the sight of three human police officers heading toward where she hid.

Time to get away.

She had to leave the wulf and what had happened here, and didn't want to. That sound. The pain in it. *Where are you?*

She had been gone for a long time now. Her father would be frantic. Still, she couldn't dismiss her feelings of connection to this male, or what might have happened here. His pain had become her pain. She hurt, and shared his sorrow.

Hugging the building, she watched the scene with her heart in her throat. *Go, or stay?* For the second time in so very few minutes, the decision of what to do was a heavy weight on her shoulders.

Colton's world began to spin. Walls closed in.

He made himself stand still and forced down another scream, too shocked to regulate his breathing. If this was what was left of his father, he definitely didn't want to stumble upon what might be left of his mother. He couldn't pinpoint her life force amid the carnage when he should have been able to. Her amiable presence didn't call out to him like it always had.

His body wasn't so frozen by shock that he didn't feel his heart break. His insides roiled. His mouth was dry. At the same time, a nagging insistence warned that he had to move, had to take care of this. Officers might knock on the door any minute now. Beyond family, there was a secret to protect.

The cop side of his training began to seep through the sickening whirl, perhaps as a defense mechanism for coping with a loss this great. With that training, one thing became perfectly clear: whoever had enacted this rampage of evil deeds not only knew who the werewolves in this neighborhood were, but how to kill them.

Silver bullets in the chest or a full beheading were the only ways to truly rid the world of a strain of very powerful Lycans. The Killions had been around for more years than a human could count. They knew how to defend themselves and should have scented trouble before it arrived.

Why then, how then, had his parents been taken down in their own home? The answer came to him in the form of a jolt that further messed with his head and equilibrium.

No human did this.

What about the Connellys then who, according to the young EMT, had been slaughtered? Not beheaded, but "slaughtered." Could those poor people have been decoy killings to cover up the murder of his family?

His parents had been down-to-earth in their day-to-day living. His father had been a college professor. His mother had worked in a dress store. They hadn't concerned themselves with their royal genes or the special Lycan blood in their veins that made them honored within their species. They had raised him in the same down-home way, and instilled in him their values.

The Killions were protectors. Had always been protectors…of Lycan secrets, of their Lycan blood, in their low-key relationships with the humans they lived among.

"Not just paranoia," Colton snapped. "There's more here to discover."

He smelled something beyond the cloying odor of Lycan blood. In order to identify this, Colton made himself breathe. Through the forced intake of air he began to soak up anomalies in the environment, realizing that every minute he stood there in a state of silent agony was a minute wasted in going after the monsters responsible for this heinous crime.

"Who were you?" he demanded angrily of the invisible, murderous fiends, tuning in to clues by opening up his senses up full throttle.

"Help me, wulf."

The arrival of his beast's keen awareness came to him like a swift kick in the solar plexus as it melded with his own intuition. Colton glanced up. Hovering near the ceiling lay a subtle scent, hardly there at all, that made him sway on his feet.

"Can't be," he objected. "Look again."

The wulf growled adamantly.

"Christ! Vampires?"

Colton took the sudden weight of his beast pressing against him as confirmation of the deduction being correct. Could it honestly be true, though? "Yes. Hell." Only the dead would stink like old soil and sour, aged, rotting wood. Nothing else could possibly smell like that.

There were vampires loose in Miami, and this was very bad news. The worst kind of news. And a Lycan's age-old enemies had found his family.

Not many humans knew about the presence of werewolves in their communities. If the world wasn't ready for werewolves, how would people feel about a new breed of enemy that amounted to a plague of murderous bloodsuckers in their neighborhoods?

"Shackled." Colton's voice broke. The awful truth was that he couldn't warn the world to be on guard. He couldn't tell anyone what had happened here, or allow this scene to come under public scrutiny. He was therefore virtually shackled to silence.

"Besides, who would believe it?"

If this had been a vampire kill, no evidence would have been left for CSI teams to catch. There'd be no fingerprints or footprints or detectable stray hairs for any system to analyze. For all the advances in human technological wizardry, as far as that technology went, the dead were dead.

Still, other than trained werewolf hunters, only vampires would know exactly how to take a werewolf down. Unlike with human criminals confronting a powerful Were family able to hold their own, vampires couldn't easily die trying to tackle a wolf-human hybrid, since vampires had the advantage of being dead already.

And damn it, if the rumors were true, those fanged children of the night were the fastest creatures on the planet. One blink, and they could be on you, then gone before your last breath rattled.

Reason this out. Why did they strike at us here?

Reasoning was another important part of the cop game, as was following suppositions with hopes of getting somewhere.

It was possible that his parents, with the addition of the Connellys as a distraction for the law enforcement system, had died because of a centuries-old vendetta between species. Vampires and Weres hated each other.

Then again, maybe a vamp had merely stumbled upon his parents somehow and had been hungry.

"No. That's not it," he shouted, because vampires hadn't been here for a drink. Bloodsuckers couldn't ingest werewolf blood of any kind. Lycans were poisonous to them.

"Premeditated strike, then."

If his family had been outside tonight, conversing with the full moon, they would have been ten times stronger and able to withstand an attack. But for some reason, they hadn't made it to the door.

"Hate crime."

The mortal world was filled with such things in this day and age. So was the supernatural one.

The more Colton thought about it, the more likely it seemed that the Connellys had merely been in the wrong place at the wrong time. After the carnage here, it was possible the pale, dead, fanged bastards had worked up an appetite.

Besides all the usual gangsters and gangbangers around, vampires were a horrific addition to Miami's rising crime wave, and what had happened on this block might be an indication of things to come.

As Colton stared down at his father's silver-haired head, he felt the rise of a blazing anger at the atrocity committed to a man he dearly loved. He couldn't stay here to grieve, though.

"They're all gone." He whispered this with a grim finality that made the beast inside him spasm with anger and disgust. He and his wulf shared the agony because they were one, one and the same with the same memories.

With a brief glance to the door, he remembered that

there was a young EMT named Smith outside who had run from a gruesome sight a few houses away. He wondered what the poor guy would think of this.

"No one will know that two sets of murders have been committed tonight," he said. For now, he had to manage his pain so that he could find his mother.

Stepping over the body of his father, he searched the room, then the house. His hopes rose, as hopes always did, despite his inner premonition. Maybe she had been spared. Possibly his mother hadn't been here, which would have been a rare occasion, since imprinted pairs wouldn't tolerate separation.

Colton searched all over again, feeling each agonizing second that hurtled by.

Then he found his mother on the back porch step, half in the house, half out, as if she'd been reaching for the moon. The brutality that had been dealt to her washed over him like an icy wave. Nausea threatened. She also had been beheaded.

"Damn those filthy bloodsuckers!" he cried.

Two members of one of the oldest Lycan families in existence had been taken out. And the stench of the undead hung over the tidy backyard like an insidious vapor.

Despite the gnawing ache growing by bounds in Colton's chest, he'd have to invent a way to cover this up. His pain, great enough to be nearly intolerable, had to be internalized. In order to go on, he'd have to focus elsewhere.

"Vengeance." His whisper fell flat. Vengeance was an emotional state Lycans had tried to outdistance as human populations began to rise and the sheer number of humans forced Weres into hiding. Revenge was a reaction Weres had learned to tamp down in favor of more peaceful aspirations and acceptable coexistence.

Contrary to all that, rage was overtaking him. He felt sick, shaky, pissed off and ready to do something about it.

As Colton lifted his mother's limp, desecrated body in his arms, his beast, tucked inside him, trembled with rage.

Aware of the disturbed emotions surfing the air, Rosalind had to move. She ran past the hordes of cops and stopped when she spotted a house that radiated the familiar scent of Were. Silently, she crept up the steps and through the open doorway.

The front room was dark and empty, but it reeked of both sadness and Lycan damage.

Not just Were. Lycan.

The reality of that turned her stomach. Chills covered every inch of her body. Did the brown Were live here? What had happened in this place?

She rolled a series of throaty growls meant as a warning that if someone was in this house, they now had company.

No reply came.

Exploring on bare, padding feet, she found two bodies on a bed in a small room, and choked back a cry. These were dead Lycans. Someone had placed them there.

The scene seemed insanely surreal, but the room also gave off the scent of the male she had followed. He had been here mere seconds before she arrived. She hadn't missed him by much.

Leaping over the furniture, feeling her anger sift to

the surface of her skin, Rosalind raced for the back door. Then she was out again, in the moonlight, back in the relative comfort of the cover of darkness.

Chapter 4

Vampire tracks weren't easy to follow. Nevertheless, Colton knew a trail of rot when he smelled one.

The alley behind the houses snaked through the neighborhood, eventually leading back to the park. Colton started that way without getting far. An icy prickle at the base of his neck made him spin around. He scanned the dark. This section of the alley seemed too quiet. No one was out. Not one dog barked.

Standing in the open, he allowed moonlight to caress his human hands and forearms as he waited for his senses to skip past the tragedy and delve into the arena of hunter and prey. Red flags waving in his mind told him the vampires had been this way not long before. More than one of them, by the intensity of the odor.

It was no wonder that the neighborhood dogs had run.

Rolling his shoulders helped him to gain control of

his tension, but his nerves felt like long threads of fire. Inching sideways, closer to a fence, he cocked his head to listen for clues. All the while, his beast pummeled at him, wanting to be free, its desire to take over the hunt stirred by a cop's ingrained need to catch some killers.

But freeing his animal side was not doable at the moment with uniforms swarming around a short distance behind. He had to fight the moon and the wulf for the time being and hope he'd win.

"No movement. No sound."

Gazing through the shadows of the alley, Colton felt his knuckles ache from holding back his claws. The sinister stink of these particular blood-drinking intruders was especially bothersome to his beast.

Colton had never seen a vampire up close, yet his soul seemed to recognize them. The wolf particles embedded in his long-term memory knew the smell and taste and feel of an ancient enemy.

"Burned toast," he said, picking a valid description of the sum of all those parts. "Disgusting."

The beast gave a rattle that shook Colton to his boots. The closeness of monsters was luring his animal instincts to a riotous state that messed with his hard-won self-control.

He flinched as the ligaments in his shoulders and knees began to stretch, and exhaled some air as the skin covering his biceps began to bubble. The whooshing sound he heard was a claw bursting through his skin. Another claw appeared. Then more, until all ten fingers were lethal.

Did this minimorph mean that the wulf knew something he didn't? He was willing to bet that it did.

A shout came from behind, untimely as hell because

it came from a cop who had no doubt seen something in the alley. Colton was in uniform, but his body was half in transition and burning badly with the need to chuck the binding accoutrements tying him to a human's sense of justice.

"Hey! You!" the uniform said from the other end of the alley; a cop who couldn't help here or offer moral support. A human, either in or out of uniform, would in fact be easy pickings for any walking undead hanging around.

He had to remove the cop from this equation.

"Killion," he shouted back to the officer, his voice gruff. He coughed, unlocked his throat and added, "Metro PD. I'm on it. All is clear. No sign of anything back here."

"Okay," the cop shouted back.

"Killion?" Davidson's familiar shout followed the other one.

"Yeah. It's me," he said.

"You're one fast son of a bitch. You actually beat me here?"

"Pays to be in shape."

"Not if that doesn't include pizza."

More footfalls, then Davidson's final remark. "We'll go around the other way. The bastards had to come and go from somewhere."

After agonizing seconds spent waiting for the men to disappear, Colton's internal heat finally overwhelmed him, and his clothes ripped apart at the seams.

Rosalind watched the brown-furred werewolf hurdle the wooden fence as if it were nothing as soon as the humans at the head of the alley had gone. She covered the length of that alley in twelve huge strides. One good leap after that, and she, too, was over the fence.

She had seen the beautiful Lycan before and after his shift, but this time she had been close enough to take stock—a second rare occurrence in the highly personal world of werewolves and only, she supposed, because he had been distracted to the point of not recognizing the presence of another wulf in the area.

Her brown wulf had been incredibly handsome as a man. His face was angular. Tanned skin stretched over high cheekbones. His mouth was wide, his eyes deep-set. Dark, slightly wavy hair framed those features, long enough to cover the tops of his ears. Each strand glinted like gold in the moonlight.

The man side of the Were was tall, his physique leanly muscular, with broad shoulders and a narrow waist. He had spectacularly molded thighs that hinted at a Were's hidden strengths. Rosalind guessed him to be in his late twenties, though it was hard to gauge werewolves, especially since she had met so few of them.

This one had been not only beautiful, but naked. Her first naked male of any kind. And he was definitely a perfect specimen that she imagined most women would call mouthwatering.

The skin of his bare back and buttocks had shined with a tanned tautness that suggested he saw a lot of sun without wearing clothes. No white lines traversed the flowing, golden flesh. Nor did he bear tattoos, other than the ring of scar tissue on one upper arm in the shape of a wolf's bite that all true Lycans possessed.

Rosalind passed a clawed hand over her own similar

mark, taking this as a further sign of an unmistakable bond with whoever he was.

She had held herself back so he couldn't see her when he'd turned. She had observed how a light drift of masculine hair ran the length of his powerful chest and over his sculpted abs to become even darker as it nestled between his legs. The feature that had been momentarily displayed between those thighs made Rosalind flush.

And then there was the werewolf.

The beast that unfolded from all that glorious humanness had brown-auburn fur the same color as the man's hair. Denser than his human form, and heavier with tension-loaded muscle, this werewolf was also damn near perfect, and too magnificent to be real.

Rosalind fielded the arrival of a full-fledged hunger for him. Battling sensations that were new, instinctual, primal, she wanted to wrap her arms around him and lick his golden-brown neck.

Her sexual appetite intensified with each ripple of his incredible Lycan muscle. But Rosalind also sensed a pain-filled anger that would prohibit him from shifting in such close proximity to others. His body visibly shook with that anger.

In spite of all the possible repercussions of empathy with a stranger, as well as a fair amount of misplaced erotic hallucinations, Rosalind followed him when he moved, as if she were his shadow.

He had ignored her in the park, not because she was a stranger, she now knew, but because he had been needed elsewhere. He hadn't rejected her out of choice.

Picking up her speed when he started to run, she raced in his wake, keeping back apace, watchful, careful, realizing that she was going to pay for this in one way or another when she got back to Judge Landau's place.

Then again, surely her father would understand the situation once he heard about the Lycan killings, and comprehend her need to help this wronged Were. Maybe she could lead this male to the Landau retreat, where he'd be safe and among friends, even if Were packs were private and didn't usually mingle.

At that moment, she was willing to place her own life and secrets in jeopardy for the chance to offer comfort and support to the first young Lycan she had ever come across, one who made her feel viciously alive.

Silent words tumbled in her throat.

You are not alone.

My strength will come in handy. I give my strength to you.

As Rosalind sprinted after him, she felt the chill of a terrible premonition about what awaited them both in the cover of darkness. The night rippled around them as though tugged by an unseen force.

If werewolves had pockets for cell phones, she'd have sent an SOS to her father. Still, in whatever faced them out there, two Lycans were always better than one.

Pity the poor soul, she growled, *who finds this out firsthand.*

Colton ran like a fiend, working with each stride to maintain enough humanity to keep his reasoning powers functioning. He couldn't afford for Otherness to overtake him completely—or for his pain to overwhelm him.

Once he was through the last of the suburban homes, his vision sharpened. He sped across open ground on the west side of the park, heading for the trees, calculating how many buildings rose in the distance on the eastern and southern sides.

He knew the night creatures hadn't headed toward those buildings, toward civilization. Rationalization told him that perhaps they hadn't been randomly hungry, but on a mission. There had been plenty of opportunities in the surrounding neighborhoods between here and his house for a freak's blood buffet, and yet they had picked his street.

So, where are the murderous vipers headed?

North of the park lay the posh estates of prominent Miami citizens wealthy enough to enjoy the luxury of space and privacy. Big houses protected by security gates. Lycan presence lay in at least one of them. The famous Landaus, head of their own pack. Surely no fanged monsters existed near there.

His knowledge of the habits of vampires was insufficient, and that was a snag. Did they have clans, packs, dens? Did the presence of these few mean, like cockroaches, there were others in the area?

What sort of weapon would de-animate a creature already dead? The mythology listed wooden stakes, exposure to sunlight and beheading. Thinking that holy water could do the trick had, so rumor said, always been a mistake. Garlic as a deterrent was laughable.

The only question remaining was about how many vampires a werewolf could handle at once with his bare hands.

No matter. Have to try.

Finding his rhythm in much the same way that real wolves chased down prey, Colton took in great gulps of night air that were like candy to a beast so hot inside and out. Apprehension was in itself a kind of narcotic.

He ran, driven by what may have been his own kind of bloodlust, able to tell he was getting closer to the vampires. The mood in the park changed, darkened, intensified, along the park's edge.

Movement.

Rustling in the shadows.

Don't vampires know that Lycans can hear?

Colton veered to his right with his nerve endings blazing in time to see an outline of whatever was out there coming on exceptionally fast. A fuzzy blur.

His senses all but exploded. He had time for just one more breath and to bare his teeth. Then they were on him.

Too many of them, maybe, Colton acknowledged as his claws began to swing.

Stunned for a moment by the sight ahead of her, Rosalind slammed to a halt some distance away from the disturbance to get her bearings.

These weren't humans the Were had gone after. She didn't immediately recognize the scent, but the odor of maliciousness these creatures gave off saturated the otherwise spring-flavored night with something similar to the iron-like taint of blood.

They were a kind of creature new to her, and they moved too fast to see details, or get a head count. Ten of them, maybe twelve, she figured. Fifteen?

Dropping from the trees like winged bats falling on an insect, they had either been waiting for some other poor, unsuspecting soul to trespass here, or else they had laid a well-planned ambush for the brown Were, having expected him to pursue.

She gave a soft roar of sympathy as she carefully studied the scene.

The big Were rushed through the blur of monsters. The beautiful werewolf who had been a golden-skinned man not long before this tore into the attackers with aggressive, fluid skills and a look of pure madness on his face.

She caught a word from the brown Were's mind without knowing how she could do that. *Vampire.* That's what this werewolf faced.

Her blood began to pound in her veins. Some distant part of her recognized the concept of bloodsucker even if she didn't fully understand it. What she did realize was that a masterful, powered-up Were didn't stand much of a chance here without the aid of several more like him. There were just too many monsters in this fight.

Also clear was the realization that she truly couldn't leave him to fight alone.

I'm here.

Moving in from the werewolf's left side with the fury of a black tornado, Rosalind plowed through the haze of bodies, wielding her claws like the weapons they were originally intended to be, slashing at everything in her way.

The shockingly gaunt, fleshless creatures targeting the brown Were shrieked when hit, and came back at her baring long yellow fangs. Up close, their faces were spectral and expressionless. Dull red eyes sank deeply into bottomless sockets. They had Lycan blood on their breath.

The brown Were, too busy to acknowledge her help or toss her a look, had felled two monsters by landing well-placed swipes to their necks that cut cleanly through to the bone. When those monsters sagged, their bodies exploded into a rainfall of foul-scented gray ash that drove the remaining creatures into a frenzy.

Only two down—out of too many.

Using the Were's technique as an example, Rosalind aimed for their necks and exploded one bony mass of her own.

Her first kill.

An odd sensation flowed through her, as though she had swallowed the wind and it continued to churn her insides. As gray ash clouded the area, her beast's energy began to blaze. Surging ahead like a caged animal that had finally been freed, she felt a new and terrible energy take her over; it flowed through her muscle like a river of fire, and left an icy residue.

She doubled her efforts.

More vampires came on, each of them fighting with ungodly speed and an unearthly agility of jaws that housed far too many gnashing, needle-sharp teeth.

The new, crazed kind of energy fueled Rosalind's fury. An unrecognizable thrill for battle made her fight on without thinking of the consequences. She was fast, strong and good at fighting. She felt as if she were made for this.

She wanted to kill them all.

Driven by that objective, she whirled, bit and clawed at the corpselike flesh around her. As she took another vampire down, Rosalind howled.

The air trembled with her silent battle cry.

Death comes to all who oppose me!

* * *

Colton fought with all his might. To the right. To the left. Coming from behind. Dropping down from above his head.

He barely heard the sounds over his own rattled breathing. He was moving so fast, he'd lost some control over his actions. His arms were tiring. He'd lost count of how many vampires he'd taken down, but had taken several vicious blows himself.

He smelled blood, and knew it was his. His face was damp, and it wasn't sweat. In five years on the police force, he had garnered a reputation for fearlessness, driven by a werewolf's need to protect innocent citizens and the knowledge of how fast he would heal if he were ever to be injured on the job. But this was no street gang or worrisome mob. This was a nest of particularly bloodthirsty monsters, attacking with intent.

More of them arrived. Each kill was replaced by another set of snapping teeth. Another Were had arrived from who knew where, but he had no idea what was happening to that beast, and had no opportunity to look. He thought he could hear that other Were close by, making growling sounds that mirrored his own. But the fight had gone on for so long, with no end in sight, that Colton wondered if they'd make it out of this one.

He fought with a renewed vigor, bolstered by the thought that someone had come to his aid. He swung his arms, swiped through fetid vampire flesh with his claws, and bit through the bones of several hands and many thin necks. And still the monsters came on; an unending supply of mindless foes animated by something purely evil in design.

God, where did these monsters come from?

I'm sorry, he wanted to say to the Were that was someplace beside him because, too late, he had realized that this may have been a trap.

Rosalind slashed her way through the flood of fanged monsters, determined to beat her way to the brown Were's side. But as she finally reached him and saw the wounds he had already taken, she opened her throat again and let out a howl that rose from the depths of her soul.

Her beautiful Were's face and shoulders had been slashed nearly to pieces. He was covered in blood that seemed to drive the monsters mad. And still, as his limbs moved, weaker now but with whatever determination he had left, the brown Were was a magnificent beast.

Her howl echoed in the park with the effect of a sonic boom, a throwback to ancient times when like called like, and species survival was paramount. The call was answered.

Sounds rose above the fighting, rolling like thunder over the bloodstained grass. She recognized her father's voice, alongside the furious vocalization of another wulf. A third howl arrived, and a fourth. From just past the trees, harrowing werewolf voices lifted in an eerily beautiful Lycan symphony, crowding out the grunts of the remaining bloodsuckers. These were low, aged voices—terrible, experienced and deadly to all that would stand against their song.

Rosalind's big mistake was stopping to listen.

She heard the terrible growling breath that escaped from the brown Were's throat, knowing with a sudden and overwhelming feeling of horror that she had hesitated a mere minute too long.

Chapter 5

Rosalind couldn't stop pacing. Her heart continued to race as she moved back and forth in the hallway leading to Judge Landau's living room. She felt caged, and anxious. The walls were closing in. She needed to be out in the dark, under the moon, where she could breathe… but she couldn't go anywhere.

Her father faced her, sitting on a step, observing her motions in a quiet manner.

"He will heal?" she asked him.

"Not completely, I'm afraid," he replied.

"We always heal, miraculously," she pointed out.

"This is different, Rosalind. He has been torn to pieces by vampires. It's a miracle that he survived at all."

Rosalind shook her head, and continued to pace. Her heart was racing. She hadn't been able to ease the edge of her anxiety since her father and his friends had turned the tide of the fight, and then brought the severely injured brown Were here.

Her brown Were.

"The wounds have ravaged his immune system. If he comes out of this, he will be changed," her father said.

Rosalind paused, every muscle feeling strained. "How, exactly, will he change?"

"We don't yet know the full extent."

"Then how can you predict that he won't completely recover?"

"You saw him not minutes ago, Rosalind. What did you see?"

"He is alive, and breathing much easier than he did two days ago."

"What else?"

"His wounds are already better. Less vivid. Closed over."

"Please state the obvious, Rosalind."

Her father expected a reply. She didn't offer him one.

"His color has changed," her father said. "You saw that. What was he before this happened?"

Her father was in the way. She could have leaped over him, but knew that he was keeping her from going upstairs, to the wounded Were's side.

"Brown and beautiful," she said. "He was brown-pelted, and beautiful."

"And now?" her father pressed.

"His hair is white. His skin is pale. But maybe that will change again."

Jared Kirk shook his head. "White Weres exist only in legend, or so we thought. No one here has ever seen one, and the minds of the Weres visiting the Landaus go back quite a distance."

Rosalind noted how her father paused to allow her time to soak that information in.

"He won't be what he was before this if he heals enough to open his eyes," he continued. "He's a ghost, Rosalind. That's what legend calls a wulf who shouldn't have survived such horrific trauma, yet somehow did."

Trauma. Was that the right word for near total destruction? Rosalind didn't like the description. It left a bitter taste in her mouth.

"If he were to continue to get better," her father went on, "he will likely choose to walk his own path, because he will have one foot in this world and one in the next. He has straddled the fine line at the end of his own existence."

Rosalind ignored the fact that her father was eyeing her closely. She held her breath until he spoke again.

"Ghosts see out of the eyes of both worlds. This wulf was strong, and of royal lineage, but who could be the same after what has happened?"

"He is a wulf, and a cop. He will know what to do," she protested.

"Rosalind. Listen to what I'm telling you. No soul can survive the cost of those kinds of internal damages intact. He wasn't just wounded, he was mauled by vampires. Their blood has mingled with his. This fight didn't kill him, but it has changed him. He has been altered. The white hair proves that. The best healers can't change or reverse the process."

No, Rosalind silently protested. She had just found her brave, lovely Were, and wasn't ready to let him go.

She was eager to find out why she felt connected to him, and why she wished so fervently for him to heal.

She desperately wanted to be near to this wulf—ghost or otherwise. She could feel him upstairs. She wanted to go to him.

"Maybe those are just stories, about the ghost wulf," she suggested.

This strapping Were could not have been broken by vampires. Fate couldn't be so cruel.

"Truth often fans the flames of myth and rumor, as you well know," her father counseled.

"And some rumors are just rumors."

"Werewolves, to the human population, are a myth. But we exist. We blend with humans because we choose to. We keep our secrets because it's better for everyone that we do. A ghost wulf who has had a life here won't be able to blend so easily. What will his friends think when they see him? How could he go back to work, or explain?"

Rosalind stopped pacing and looked at her father.

"He will leave them behind," he father said. "He might choose to live in the shadows, on the fringes, not because he will be forced to, but because he will have to make peace with what he has become."

"Which is?"

"An old legend, made new. A ghost wulf. Part man, part wulf, and for all we know, part vampire."

Her father sighed, as if these explanations were a chore, and painful for him.

"You don't know that. You're not sure of anything," Rosalind said.

"You're right. Time will tell. But the elders who have tended to him have noted that something new has entered his bloodstream, and that out of necessity, this new thing will likely change his soul."

This information didn't sit well with Rosalind. In spite of everything being told to her, she still felt connected to the Were, oddly enough, now more than ever.

She had rushed to his side when the other Weres had arrived. She had seen him close his eyes, and fall to his knees.

She had pressed her mouth to his while the others finished off the vampires, and breathed into him some of her own chaotic energy.

If he was changed, as her father was saying, theirs would be a sympathetic bond. She had been forced to be a loner, almost held captive by her father for most of her life. She could relate to being apart from others, and living on the fringes. She had been called special. Which also translated to mean different.

They were both different.

A ghost and a loner. She and this injured Lycan were perfect for each other.

Her father's voice dropped in tone. "You can't wish him back to normal, Rosalind. You must accept this as fact, just as the Were upstairs will have to accept his fate."

Rosalind squeezed her eyes shut to avoid her father's wary expression. But the thought persisted that he had kept her from all Weres in the past, and that maybe this warning was just another example of her father's overbearing overprotection.

Well, she wanted to say to him, *I can't be kept from this one. I won't be kept from him. Not this one.*

"He's a ghost because of me," she said. "The responsibility is mine."

"Not so," her father countered vehemently. "A vampire attack caused this. You were brave, but also foolish to have joined in such a fight. It's a miracle you weren't hurt equally as badly, and that Landau and the elders were with me, searching for you. You could be lying in a bed upstairs. What would I have done then?"

"Those monsters killed his family. He went after them, just as you or I or Judge Landau would have. He did this alone."

A long pause preceded her father's next remarks.

"Rosalind. It's important that you hear what I'm going to say to you now. You and I will go home tomorrow. You have to let this wulf go. We will leave him in the Landaus' care."

"No."

"I'm not blind or insensitive to your feelings, but this male is not for you. He wouldn't have been compatible before this event, and certainly isn't now. You have no idea what would happen if..." Her father's voice trailed off, then returned. "You have no inkling of what his life might be like if he heals well enough to keep it."

You have no idea what would happen if...

If what? Rosalind wanted to know, picking up on the unsaid portion of an argument and tasting the tang of withheld secrets.

Rosalind chilled up as she stared at her father with a new thought. *Has he been keeping secrets from me all this time?*

"I want to stay with him," she said.

"That's impossible." Her father shook his head.

"Judge Landau will let me stay, if I ask."

"You won't ask. I forbid it."

"Then the wounded Were can come with us."

"You cannot have your way in this, Rosalind. My decision is final. You might be in real danger here, now that vampires have your scent in their filthy noses."

"The bloodsuckers were killed."

"They can transmit signals we have no notion of."

Rosalind stubbornly stood her ground, legs splayed, hands on her hips. "It was my fault he was hurt so badly. My inattention did this. I owe him. Don't you get that?"

"The Landaus are a powerful clan with powerful friends, and are experienced healers. He needs time, and couldn't be in better hands."

"He could be in mine."

Her father got to his feet. "You can't help him. This is a fact. Moreover, you cannot remain near to him. It's imperative that you two are separated, the sooner the better."

The authority in her father's tone had hardened his formidable features. In the firm set of his mouth, Rosalind sensed the gap in his explanations. Her father's secrets were heavy enough to be like the aura of another person in the room.

"Are you going to tell me the real reason he can't come with us, without going around in circles?" she asked.

"It isn't time for that, or necessary."

"I'm not a child."

"I know that. But two such extremes are destined never to meet, if in fact they could exist at all," her father said.

His reply came with a sting. An unspoken message resided in what her father had said a message so terrible it couldn't be spoken. A dark secret?

Extremes, he said.

Two such extremes are never destined to meet. If they could exist at all.

Her father had just called her a freak, without coming right out with the word.

He had uttered this remark as if he'd been near wit's end and it had merely slipped out. Whatever he held inside didn't want to see the light of day; a secret that if spoken, might come to pass all the quicker.

But she couldn't accept that, and needed to have things in the open. Her father was keeping something important from her. And even though knowing he thought his daughter a freak hurt like a knife to the chest, she had to stand her ground. What other option was there?

"Not good enough," she said. "Nothing you've said is good enough to change my mind about this Were."

You aren't the only one with secrets, she wanted to shout.

Separating me from the wulf upstairs will do no good, because against all odds, he and I have already bonded. And bonds between Lycans are unbreakable, except by death.

She had another secret. Her insides ached with longing for the Were upstairs. Her womb thrummed for the golden-fleshed man who had shed his clothes in the moonlight. She hungered for his gaze, and for what hung, hard and swollen, between his powerful thighs.

Instincts trumped innocence here, and she wasn't to have that? Wasn't to see him again?

"I know better than to argue with you," she said.

Indeed, nothing would influence her father once his mind had been made up. Still, she was responsible for the Were's injuries, at least in part. If she had gotten to him sooner, fought harder, not stopped to listen to the calls in the night, he might have been spared some of his wounds.

She looked past her father. The Were upstairs was stirring. She felt this, and her fingers twitched in reaction. Her inner defiance against her father's restraints rose again.

There was more truth she had to hide from her father. Another secret pain that she didn't understand. When she had issued the howl in the park that had brought help, something had happened to her. It was as if restraining straps had been unbuckled, setting part of her free that she'd had no idea existed. Wild. Complicated. New.

God, there was more, yet. *The worst part.*

In hearing her cry, the fanged monsters attacking her had stopped their attack. After that cry, they had transferred all their attention to the brown Were, leaving her alone, leaving her standing there, unheeded, untouched, while her golden-skinned, brown-furred male, heavily outnumbered, was ripped to shreds.

After her call, the fanged creatures had bypassed her as if she no longer existed; as if she had suddenly become invisible to them, and no longer mattered.

I'm not quite right inside. But how do I tell you the extent of this, Father? Your wizened eyes, gazing at me, suggest that you might know the reason for this, and possibly even why those bloodsuckers had left me alone. Freak, is what you were thinking. Not the time for reasons, you said.

Everyone, it suddenly seemed to Rosalind, had secrets. But so many secrets made the world a much darker, more unbearable place. She was going to get some answers. Now.

* * *

Colton wasn't sure if he had died. His first thought was that he must have.

The last thing he remembered was that his heartbeat had slowed to near nothing when the last wave of fangs hit him. He recalled shutting his eyes when the pain had become too great and his limbs had stopped working.

Soon after that, he had fallen into a dark tunnel, listening to the sounds of a continued battle all around him without being able to participate.

As he lay where he was now, wherever that might be—heaven or hell, maybe—his thoughts kept returning to that brave Were who had come to his aid, and was little more than another smudge of darkness in his mind. He had, for the briefest seconds of time before his fall, imagined that other Were to be female. Maybe her lips had touched his, he thought, or else he had been dreaming.

Female werewolves were nearly as able as males, and he had sensed one in that park, earlier. But the werewolf fighting beside him had torn through the vampires like a creature hell-bent on utter destruction. That dark-coated werewolf, merely a blur in the night, had been nothing less than a total fighting machine.

Had he died out there? Was he in shock? There seemed to be a disconnect between his mind and his limbs. It didn't hurt him to think, and his thoughts kept returning to the same questions. If he had died, had the other Were who'd helped him died, as well? Had she whispered something to him out there as his eyes had closed? More important, had those fanged vipers who had stolen the life from his family been defeated?

Colton's pulse gave a sudden kick. He groped for the reason for this sudden alertness.

There was no sense of anything waiting to take him over. No overriding awareness of angels or demons surrounded him. The blanks in his mind were holes occupied by swirling drifts of a silver-gray mist. In that mist, he thought he saw Death's outline hovering. He was almost sure he heard Death's call.

The cop side of him wanted to fill the holes in his reasoning so he could understand his current state. Cops were trained to fill in gaps and connect the dots. But he just didn't seem able to do that.

Pertinent lapses in memory could be his mind's way of reaching for a temporary peace after encountering the rabid side of chaos, he reasoned. Those lapses could just as easily mean that consciousness continued for a time after the body formerly housing it had succumbed to its final loss of breath.

But he hadn't lost his breath.

He was breathing now.

Colton suddenly sensed something else. He reached out to this new presence with his senses.

"Hey."

The voice cut through the swirl of gray. He classified the sound as a word. Beyond it lay a familiar fragrance that was nothing at all like the stench of vampires.

Flowers. Musk and flowers.

Not hell, then.

"Can you open your eyes?" the soft voice asked.

It was an odd request, he thought, since he'd been sure his eyes were already open.

"Can you see me?"

This was said in the slightly husky tone of a female's whisper.

Turning his head took effort.

"I'm not supposed to be here, but I had to see you," she said. "My father will take me away tomorrow."

Father? Some feeling came, centered in Colton's chest. He knew that particular word because he had a father.

Sharp pain struck without warning, as though an arrow had pierced him. It was the arrow of past tense. He'd *had* a father. But not anymore.

"Can you talk? Will you make the effort to speak to me?" the female asked, her breathy voice bringing with it another hint of the taste of a floral bouquet. Roses. Bloodred roses, rich in color and sprinkled with dew.

No. Not dew. These roses were covered in fur.

Black fur.

Memory zigzagged. Colton wanted to slap his head to make things work more smoothly, but couldn't move his arm.

A Were with a black pelt? Had he seen that out there? *Absurd.*

Why should he remember that, when there were no true black-pelted Weres? Dark brown, yes, but not black. The color itself denoted unfathomable darkness. Even black-haired Weres in human form shifted to a different color.

"Yes," she, whoever she was, coaxed. "I'm here. If you open your eyes, you'll see me."

The voice struck a distant chord. It was filled with submerged emotion and as demanding as it was inviting. This voice was the human equivalent of the howl of invitation a she-wulf had issued to him in that blasted park.

It's her.

You.

Wanting nothing more than to see who was near, Colton struggled to do as she asked. His eyes hadn't been open, after all. He opened them, sorry that he had when a glare of hurtful light hit him.

"Wait. I'll dim the lamp," she said. "It's just one lamp, by your bed."

Absorbing the ache that followed so much time spent in darkness, Colton forced himself to focus. His vision took a while to get into working order, and then he found himself gazing into a pair of large green eyes, very near to his.

His insides stirred restlessly.

There was something about those eyes. Not exactly familiar, but…

A surge of heat broke through his numbness. Again, he heard a howl, far away now, but there, all the same. He saw a dark-pelted wulf charge in to help him, and join in the fight.

His nerves began to simmer, then fry, which in turn caused feeling where there had been nothing but a wasteland.

The fire spread.

Hunger came upon him, heated, and with a ravenous need for the *She* with that mesmerizing voice.

His biceps tensed. His toes curled. He heard the crack of his spine straightening as whatever power those green eyes held hurled him toward full consciousness.

The flames tearing through him called up his beast. His wulf unfurled as fluidly and easily as if he'd merely spread his arms, the shift silent and uncommonly fast. It came on in a wave, similar to a smooth ruffle of air between two breaths. No extra pain. No forethought. No moon necessary.

Left panting from a transition that had no right to have happened in the first place, Colton, in werewolf form, squatted on a soft blue cloudlike surface, trembling and in shock. All he saw was the brilliance of the green eyes across from his that had not wavered in intensity or retreated by so much as an inch.

This female wasn't afraid of him.

I know you, he thought again.

His growl was the sum total of his strange new feelings of hunger and longing, and lingered in the space around him.

"I knew it," the green-eyed woman beside him said. "You're still in there."

Rosalind felt the throb of this werewolf's blood in her veins. The erratic rhythm of his heart spoke of the depth of his inexplicable need for her.

There was no second-guessing what this need was. It came across as primitive, hotly sexual, and was, Rosalind would have known without the rapid acceleration of her own pulse, very much reciprocated.

She wanted to be with him. Be like him. She wanted to meet him wulf to wulf. Wanted everything this male had to offer.

Exerting pressure to control herself, Rosalind knew that she had been right. They had imprinted not long ago, without their eyes meeting, a fact as unusual as this wulf's snowy-white pelt. Their hunger was mutual, no matter what shape he was in.

Rosalind was glad she had locked the door. As she stared into his eyes, she could barely keep her hands off the wulf on the bed. Her beast was starved for his beast. She craved his touch, and was left trembling.

"Yes," she whispered. "We have bonded."

Tremors rocked her. Similar tremors moved through the white wulf beside her. He was sharing the effects of their bond. He felt what she felt.

"I don't understand why they would separate us," she said, tilting her head, trying to speak slowly. "You'll need details of what happened, some of which you probably already know."

Rosalind swallowed her beast's needs down and lowered her voice. "You've been badly hurt, attacked by bloodsuckers in the park. The same suckers that killed your family, I suppose. We've taken care of those fiends, got rid of them. My father and the judge brought you to Landau's house. Judge Landau's wife has been treating you."

Placing a hand on her chest, as if that would slow her racing heartbeat, she continued. "These vampires were savages. The Landaus say you've knocked on Death's door and stepped across the threshold, only to be pulled back by the strength of your will."

It was impossible for her to slow down. A deep breath didn't help.

"You're alive, but changed. I don't know how, exactly. I'm not sure what your white pelt means. They won't tell me everything. They never have."

The creature her father had called a ghost remained almost motionless, though his white fur rippled with the force of his pulse.

"I'm Rosalind Kirk," she said. "My father is Jared

Kirk. You'll need to know those things in order to find me."

The white wulf stared at her soundlessly.

She fell silent for a minute, maybe two, noting how the room at the top of the Landaus' house that posed as a one-bed makeshift hospital ward smelled of clean laundry and antiseptic. It was sparsely furnished, with a large bed, one soft chair and two bedside tables. The window in the wall opposite the bed was open. The curtains moved in a faint breeze.

Rosalind had no idea what kind of care they had given this Were, or what those treatments entailed, but he had pulled through. Her actions in the park hadn't killed him.

She blinked slowly to take that in.

On the surface, most of the stink of the vampires had been wiped clean from this wulf, and from the room housing him. Underscoring the room's aura of calm, however, Rosalind still perceived hints of vampire. Black glittering molecules, as shiny and sharp as polished shards of glass, seemed a part of every breath she took.

Wary of this, and mindful of the fact that she had sneaked upstairs when the judge's wife had gone for food, Rosalind went on.

"You're at the Landau estate at the edge of the park. Since you're a cop and a Were, I'm guessing you know Judge Landau and about some of the secrets kept in this place."

The white wulf growled softly, as if trying out his voice through a throat the bloodsuckers had ripped open several times over. It seemed to Rosalind that she might have made a similar sound without realizing it, because her own throat felt raw.

The eyes looking at her were intent, piercing and the palest green. They were ringed by deep purple circles, leftovers indicative of how badly his face and body had been injured.

She didn't want to think of how he had looked when her father and the others had come to the rescue. All that blood. And she had seen glimpses of bone beneath his torn and mangled flesh.

At the time, it seemed that a true miracle would be necessary in order for him to survive. "You look better," she said, hoping this might calm him.

And that was true. He did look better. Already, after just two days, new skin covered bone and sinew, though several patches of fur and flesh were missing from his neck and shoulders, leaving lines of raw, reddened flesh. Red welts lined his face like the stripes of a tiger, but they were no longer oozing blood.

His moon mark, an indication of his superior place within their species, showed through the colorless fur of his left upper arm. It was riddled with tiny puncture holes, as though the vampires had purposefully gone for it with gusto, hoping to tear the mark clean off.

For a Were, removal of a moon mark was a blasphemy. For this big male, it would have been a forced emasculation. But the filthy blood drinkers hadn't tackled this Lycan easily. He'd fought hard before succumbing to the sheer number of attackers. Burned into her mind was the image of the brown Were feverishly taking on the monsters.

"Brown or white, Were or ghost, you are the most

beautiful, the most courageous being I have ever encountered," she said.

And I have nearly caused your death.

"I'm to be taken away," she repeated. "They will separate us, and it will hurt, when you've already been hurt so badly."

Another growl came from him, noticeably stronger, and meaning for her to go on. Coming from this formidable creature who had looked Death in the eye, the sound seemed strangely exotic, and took her breath away.

"I come from the bayou country. I'm seldom allowed out from under my father's strict supervision and rules. We have no modern forms of communication there. No computer, no television, no phones. Only a radio," she said, pausing as the absurdity of these facts registered. "I learn about the world through that radio."

They had, in fact, been living like they were deprived backwoods folk. Compared to the Landaus, they were decades behind the times. Backwoods cousins.

"This is the first occasion the Landaus have hosted us as guests, and I think this was due to an important meeting between Lycan elders. For me, it's a quick visit here, and then back."

They had so little time. She could hear it ticking away.

"Landau's son and some of his pack aren't here, though I've heard them talked about. I've seen no one my age, and only briefly have met Landau and his wife. I don't think I'll be allowed here again after this."

She waited out a span of several shallow, rapid breaths before continuing, needing to get all this out in the open.

"There are other secrets hidden here. I don't pretend to understand what's really going on, only that some of those secrets pertain to me. I can sense being the focus of this meeting, and believe those secrets are why I've been kept away from other Weres, and ultimately why I'll be kept from you. There is, I think, something wrong with me."

Do you want me to go on?

The wulf continued to study her intently. He hadn't moved.

"I understand the pain of loss." Her voice was beseeching. "My mother was killed by hunters. Not vampires, but monsters in their own right."

The white wulf blinked slowly, as if he was riding out a wave of pain.

"My father says that your fur has turned white due to the intensity of the injuries you have sustained. It might also be a physical manifestation of devastation and loss."

She cleared her throat. "I wish I could take away the anguish of that."

It had taken more than a dozen vampires to gain hold of him. This Were had fought like he was the right hand of Death, when even death, as vampires proved, didn't have to be the end.

"I feel your pain. And I am so very sorry."

She was hurting for herself, and for him. In sharing his heartache, she had to let him know how sorry she was that he'd been injured so badly. As much as she could bring herself to confess. When their imprinting was complete, he'd find out her secrets by easily reading her. They would eventually share thoughts.

"I didn't help you enough out there," she said, noting the alertness in this ghost's eyes.

She couldn't go on, was unable to utter the words that might have freed her from the terrible, plaguing guilt. If she spoke the truth in its entirety, if she confessed what she had or hadn't done now, her white wulf wouldn't want her. There was no way he'd come after her, find her, mate with her, when she wanted those things so desperately.

"I—" She paused when the green eyes across from her began to recede, and the white wulf shape-shifted in a slick, soundless, reversal.

"I couldn't leave you to face them alone," Rosalind whispered as the man from the park, who was now just as captivating with his white hair framing his wounded, angular face, reached for her.

Colton jumped to his feet. With both of his hands on Rosalind Kirk's shoulders, he backed her into a corner so quickly that her breath escaped in a startled hiss of surprise.

He gave her no opportunity for further sound or protest. His mouth covered hers as if her breath alone could make him whole again. As if the beating of her heart against his bare chest could jump-start his, and prove finally, absolutely, that he was alive.

His need was all-consuming. His body was on fire.

He drank her in as if his survival counted on those things.

The fragrance of her breath seemed familiar.

Rosalind Kirk was a young, black-haired, oval-faced vision, and slight to the point of an ethereal thinness. Although her mouth was momentarily motionless beneath his, Colton sensed with every instinct he possessed how much she wanted to respond.

There was a possibility, he realized, that she didn't know how.

Her lips were warm, supple, tender, sweet and not in the least bit rigid. In her stillness came a reminder of what she had told him. She had been kept from others. She'd been sheltered from actions like this by an overprotective Lycan father. She had no family or friends. This might, in fact, have been her first real kiss.

He wanted her in that moment as much as his beast had desired her in the park. Every inch of him yearned for her, now that he'd been awakened, and had captured her in his arms.

Had this slight, ebony-haired creature truly fought beside him, placing herself in jeopardy in order to help? Was she the one who had come to aid him in a time of trouble?

"You," he whispered with his mouth on hers. "It really was you."

Ignoring shaky limbs that refused to behave properly, and his heart's offbeat rhythm, Colton leaned into her. Licking gingerly at her lips, nipping lightly at the corners of her mouth before again sealing his lips to hers, he took her breath into his lungs, and felt that breath warm him. One word resonated in his mind, on its own loop, playing over and over.

Mine.

He wasn't dead. This moment was real. Where there was feeling, there was hope, and he desperately needed some.

He kissed her, and the kiss drew a gasp. The raspy sound of Rosalind's breathlessness shuddered through him as the pleasure of being close to her far outweighed the nagging internal pain he harbored.

His captive wore a black shirt he hardly noticed, except that it felt cool and silky against his bare chest. His current impulse was to tear the shirt from her and get down to it, chest to chest, groin to groin. This was his animal side taking over. His beast voted for that.

Injuries be damned! This Were female had a name that rolled easily on his tongue. *Rosalind.* A name as creamy as the sexual act itself.

Her black hair, worn long and straight, spilled over her shoulders in a gleaming cascade. Her face, with its prominent, sharp-edged bones, would suit few people, but somehow suited him. She had a small, tapered nose. Perfectly arched eyebrows looked like dark smudges of paint on ivory skin decorated by huge, penetrating green eyes.

Her shoulders were narrow, her hip bones like blades. Lycan females never had overindulgent curves or ponderous shapes due to their super-revved metabolisms and the frequent nighttime sprints, and Rosalind didn't break that mold.

Small, firm breasts, perfectly proportioned to the trimness of her body, pressed against him through her shirt, begging to be touched, licked, suckled, by someone who would understand what she needed in a mate.

She was no mere pretty young thing. This was a category of female he had never expected: unique, sensual, animal and almost supernaturally beautiful.

Mine.

Colton's wulf roared, possessive and protective of Rosalind Kirk in spite of the fact that she had been a freaking lightning-quick fighting machine in that park.

Couldn't have been her, his mind still argued. The female in his arms had a trembling, succulent mouth. The Were in the park had been lethal, black-pelted and incredibly fast.

Thoughts fled as her lips parted and her tongue, extremely hot and seductively moist, tentatively met his. The action cued something in Colton's body that had long lain dormant. It was a real need for her, having nothing whatsoever to do with the concept of superficial. He longed for closeness and connection. He wanted to hold in his hands something fine and special and long-term. In the face of those needs, self-control was not an option.

The heat of her presence pushed his pain aside. Colton had a sensation of his strength returning by bounds, as if she were the one pulling it back, inch by agonizing inch, and as if the kiss connecting them was drawing his better parts out.

Her arms encircled his neck. Their hips ground lusciously together. Through the silky cloth of her shirt Rosalind continued to radiate the kind of enticement that he imagined would be similar to getting too close to the sun. *Pure, radiant fire.*

He groaned when her hands touched the nape of his neck, and he repeated the sound when her fingers moved upward into his hair. She grabbed hold of a handful of strands and tugged, trying to pull him closer. But the only way they could have been closer was for him to be inside her. And there was no way to describe how much he wanted that.

His body responded to hers as if he hadn't been hurt. His erection was proof that a Were's ability to heal was indeed nothing short of magical.

Rosalind's touch made illness seem distant and irrelevant. The swift return of his libido told him that if his body wasn't fully recovered, he was well enough to oblige the desire to claim her, and to enter the blistering heat he knew would be waiting for him if he did.

"Ties that bind. You and I, Rosalind," he whispered to her, allowing her only a very small breath.

It seemed to him that the female whose tongue now swept boldly across his had somehow created an energy flux that encompassed them both. Maybe it was only a male-female attraction that had made him get up from that bed, because hell, he didn't know how he could be standing up when he had only opened his eyes a short time ago. He wasn't entirely sure what had happened to him out there in the dark.

Nevertheless, there was healing in her fingertips. Her breath rammed a steady stream of energy into him as she willed him to take her, and urged him to hurry.

She was a fast learner, an apt pupil. Already she kissed him back with enough fervor to melt away the doubts.

Oh, yes. One of his dreams lay within his grasp. All he had to do was what came naturally to them both.

But, his mind nagged, *they are going to take her away.* Away from him. This seemed a ridiculous impossibility, now that he had found her.

Dampness broke out on his forehead. Rationality warned that they were guests in someone else's house, and that the door might open any minute. Rosalind had mentioned the name Landau.

Still, Rosalind's fingers moved like little bolts of lightning across his upper back, scorching his tender skin, making him wince from the sheer intensity of the pleasure. She was exploring him, as well as the other way around, and she liked what she found.

He seemed to hear her whispering to him, though his mouth on hers left her no ability to do so. "Now," she was thinking. "Seal our fate."

Chapter 6

Reluctantly, Colton pulled his lips from hers to gaze at her flushed face. How far would she go? How far would she let him go? The she-wulf was looking back at him. Their gazes met, held.

He had a sensation of falling, though he was on his feet. His body imploded with the desire to have all of her; every last bit. Wrapped in her heat, he could almost forget the vampires and what they had done. He stood a chance of sidelining his need for vengeance.

When he tore at her jeans, neither of them spoke or moved apart to make access easier. Rosalind's palms were like burning coals when she placed them on his chest.

With ease, he lifted her from the ground, turned and threw her on the bed where he'd been tended. Rosalind was, he noticed, barefoot, her feet delicate, her toenails unpainted.

Her jeans were discarded in seconds. The blue underwear beneath them was destroyed in less time than that. She lay half-naked on the bed, her hair and her silk shirt glistening in the light from the bedside lamp. Her eyes told him that she anticipated what might come next.

Colton crawled up to arch over her on his hands and knees, so that the only thing between them, below the hem of her shirt, was his thrumming cock—the dusty, unused body part of a werewolf who had been too long without.

"Mate," she said huskily through pink, swollen lips, her eyes wide and as brilliant as emeralds.

"Yes," he growled.

Her hips rose to meet him when he slid both hands beneath her slick, bare buttocks, buttocks that were as sleek as her shirt. Her legs were endlessly long, and stretched out beneath him. Her thighs were shaped with lengths of strong, lean muscle.

"Some other time and place," he told her, "this would take much longer and move much slower. Hours. Days. Weeks."

"Find me. Promise," was all she said in return.

Somehow, Colton knew there was no time for foreplay and that the needs driving them ruled out any effort at further restraint. With trembling fingers, he explored the spot he needed for entering her body. Although she might have been kept from this in the past, Rosalind was more than willing. Between her thighs, behind a wedge of dark fur, she had dampened. With his fingers pressed against her, she growled low in her throat.

When her legs opened for him, he forgot everything else. Time, and all that had gone on before, seemed to slip away.

Easing the tip of his cock inside her, Colton closed his eyes. He didn't want to move, wanted to linger and soak up this wicked heat, but he had to continue. His body demanded satisfaction.

With an agonizing slowness, he began to make tender stroking motions, moving his hips, dipping in and out of her meagerly at first, amazed that he could exert this much will over himself when what he longed for was a singular thrust hard enough to fill her completely.

He shook with the intensity of that desire.

He and this stranger had imprinted. And this sealed the deal. That's the way this went: eyes, thoughts, body, then soul. They had bonded, and all he knew about her was her name, and that she had pulled him up from unconsciousness, and how extremely hot she was.

Inside, she was tight and beautifully lush. He stroked her gently until that tightness began to relax and a rush of cream surrounded his erection. Even in man form, he nearly howled.

As he pressed himself farther inside her, Rosalind made more encouraging noises in her throat. When he stopped moving, she seemed to stop breathing altogether.

"I will find you," he said with a pledge that seemed to have been dragged from his heart.

Though she gasped, Rosalind didn't open her eyes.

"You understand what this means?" he asked gruffly, because her body, and what she was allowing him to do with it, had stolen his own breath away.

Her eyelids fluttered, the long, midnight-hued lashes dark against her flawless ivory skin. As he studied her face, her chin moved up and down once. She understood perfectly.

"All right," he whispered to her. "God. Okay."

His plunge into her rich depths brought another, louder, sound from her throat. It was a purr of encouragement. A nod to pleasure.

Colton withdrew, then sank his length into her again and again, building a rhythm that took him deeper and deeper, trying not to burst with the pleasure this gave him. He hung on to his sanity by a thread.

When waiting was no longer an option, he lowered himself to her body and drove himself into her with a force that rocked his body and hers.

Unparalleled gratification careened through him that was as violent as live wires crossing. And when Rosalind bent her knees, grabbed his buttocks with her hands and invited him to partake of the last remaining barrier, he felt the rise of an oncoming orgasm that would truly weld them together for life.

With his scent on her, and imbedded in her, no other Were could hope to gain her interest. That's also the way this worked. She would be his. *Forever. Until death do us part.*

And when she drove her hips against his, he tumbled over the rim of an abyss. One more move of his own hips, and he executed just one more powerful thrust; the exact one he had longed to make.

He reached the molten center of the female beneath him, not thinking of taking or claiming her now, but offering himself to her in a union that was tantamount to the binding of their souls.

"Rosalind."

The rumble started in his back, spread to his torso and careened between his legs. A similar rumble, like an approaching earthquake, tore through Rosalind, hitting and then overtaking them at the same time.

The room exploded with a light that seemed to carry in it all the emotion of the life Colton had lived so far. With their moist bodies pressed together in a rigid few seconds of suspended stillness, and their mouths locked together so that no sensation could go unresolved, the suddenness of the intensity of their mingled ecstasy ripped through them.

But so did something else.

One last peripheral sensation slid through Colton unexpectedly as he reached his peak.

In that moment of heightened awareness, as his body convulsed with pleasure, he was sure that Rosalind tasted not only like wulf, but of metal.

In her feverish mouth, and at her heated core, lay a hint of what he imagined silver to taste like. Silver, a concoction that was the bane of all Weres, purebred or otherwise.

Absurd.

He let the notion go as he rode the crest of a wave of ecstasy prolonged by each tremor that shook her.

And when the storm finally subsided and some time had passed without sound or motion, Colton was afraid to move. Afraid to believe. Opening his eyes, he again found Rosalind's eyes waiting.

Problem was those eyes were no longer green.

Liquid darkness swam in Rosalind's irises, drowning the color, turning them black. It was like watching a curtain drop over a verdant landscape. Like a dark veil descending suddenly to cloak something fine.

The sudden strangeness made Colton draw back. The skin on his neck prickled. His jaw tensed.

"What the—"

What had happened to Rosalind? Hell, had he just linked himself to a Were who might be something more than wulf?

He heard the word *special* in his mind, and knew it came from her thoughts. He didn't like the questions turning up.

Was the key to Rosalind's well-guarded seclusion the fact that she might not be just any *She* after all, but something else? Something far more dangerous?

Was that why she wasn't allowed out, when Lycan females were so scarce, and why she felt she was different?

Perhaps also sensing this, or seeing the concern in his expression, Rosalind opened her mouth to protest the look on his face. After a brief hesitation, she uttered a strangled cry.

Between her beautiful lips, so swollen and lush and pink, lay a pair of tiny needle-sharp incisors reminiscent of no wulf canines that Colton had ever seen. On her lower lip lay a fine sheen of pooled red droplets where she had bitten herself during their moments of shared passion.

Blood. On her mouth.

Dark blood, red as roses.

Before Colton caught a startled breath, his lover, his she-wulf, the female he had sealed himself to forever, moved from under him with an astonishing speed that was little more than a time-slip of barely disturbed air.

She leaped gracefully onto the sill of the tall, open window, where she paused in a crouch to draw her fingers across her mouth. Glancing at the smear of blood on them, her body visibly shook.

For a moment more she remained there, outlined by the night beyond, her silk shirt shining, her long, loose hair billowing in the breeze.

She looked at Colton with a shocked, pleading glint in her wild black gaze as she held up her hand to show him the red stain on her fingers. Then, uttering one more sound, a sob, Rosalind turned from him and jumped out.

Chapter 7

"What the hell are you?"

Colton swore to himself, shocked as he sat back on the bed where he had just made love to a…what? Certainly not the she-wulf he'd assumed her to be.

His heart was thundering. She'd looked like a vampire. Like one of the creatures that had killed his parents.

He felt weak, shaky, and not all from the surprise of having his new mate turn into a vampire-like creature before jumping from his window. Sex had taken effort he'd barely been able to muster before she had arrived. With Rosalind gone, and twisted by shock, he felt completely drained.

"Have to get up. Must find out what's going on."

Where was he? What was he to do now? Rosalind, God, whatever she turned out to be, had brought up the Landaus. Everyone in Miami would recognize that name. Prominent Judge Landau and his socially adept wife were Lycans from way back who obviously knew how to fit in with humans and had created a compound for their pack members.

He was in their house. Landau's house.

Colton got to his feet. Chills covered his body as he stumbled to the window. Rosalind had left a spot of blood on the sill. Seeing it, his stomach seized.

He looked out, seeing nothing below but the glow from windows that were lower to the ground than his. Backing toward what he assumed was a closet, he braced himself against the doorjamb as he opened it. After pulling on someone else's jeans that he'd discovered on a shelf inside, Colton limped out the hallway door and down a wide wooden staircase, the drag of one foot awkward beneath a numb left leg.

"If I have to crawl, I will find out what that was, and where she has gone."

This wasn't a choice. He had promised, if not verbally, then with his actions. He had fully imprinted with what he'd believed to be an eligible female Were; one who had the courage to follow him into a vampire ambush. Now, hell, she looked a bit like one of those same monsters. How was that possible?

He remembered the black pelt, and shuddered.

"She could have been injured in the bloodsuckers' attack, as I was," he said, needing to hear his thoughts. "If that were to be the case, and her fangs were the result, I am ultimately to blame."

She had seemed as shocked as he had been when she stared at the blood on her hand. He'd never forget the flatness of fear in those big eyes. He had hurt her with the shocked expression in his.

She hadn't known what would happen to her.

"Bloody frigging damn!" He staggered to a stop, catching sight of himself in a long mirror in the hallway. His legs threatened to give way as he stared at his image. It had to be someone else. Couldn't be him. A ghostly form looked back at him from that mirror, its colorless skin marred by red slashes, its long hair freakishly white.

"Christ, what happened to me out there!"

Rigid with the horror of that, Colton limped on, putting distance between himself and that image. He had to get outside, get air, find her. There was no time to ponder what he might have become. If he had hurt Rosalind, he had to put things right.

The Landaus had tended to him on the top floor of a three-story house. As he neared the bottom of the stairs, Colton pictured Rosalind jumping from such a great height. Did this mean she'd be dead, sprawled on the lawn? Weres were notoriously strong, and possessed the agility of big cats, but what would a dose of vampire do to that scenario?

His heart sputtered as if unable to rev properly. He wasn't sure he'd have the energy to make it to the front door, but he did. No one appeared to stop him from pushing through that door when he reached it.

The suddenness of leaving a closed space and stepping off the boards of a large covered veranda, into the night, offered up yet another surprise that stopped Colton in his tracks.

The night was composed of fragments of pure sensory bombardment that rushed at him from all directions at once—a barrage of sight, sound, scent, taste, arriving to flood and overwhelm his overworked, not yet up-to-par system.

This bombardment was like being caught in a whirlwind and felt like sharp knives were being worked into his eye sockets. It felt as though the mother of all migraines had rained down to provide a wallop, when the night and the moon riding high in it shouldn't have been anything other than normal fare for him.

Then again, he was no longer normal. He'd seen himself in the mirror and was pretty sure the world had made one too many wrong turns while he'd been asleep.

Sucking in a breath of sensory-filled air forced him down to one knee. What energy he had left seemed to have deserted him in a time of need, but he lifted his chin in stubborn defiance, determined to face this. He took in another breath that tasted strongly of wulf, and then he saw why.

Weres were waiting for him out here, as motionless and silent as a line of marble statues, on Judge Landau's front lawn.

Rosalind sped through the night, chased by fear, driven forward by a newly discovered, terrible speed that felt like flying.

She had landed on the grass outside of the house without injury. Springing to her feet, she had sailed over the wall before even making up her mind to do so, and was running to escape from herself. From what she had become.

It had to be part of that same thing her father had neglected to tell her about.

She'd had her first kiss, as well as so much more. And the experience had been beyond imagining. The sensations of their lovemaking remained. The spark her ghost wulf had ignited still flickered deep within her.

Though she kicked up her speed, there was no outrunning the fact that something had happened to both her and the brown Were in the park that had made their needs a priority. She didn't fully understand what that might be.

If she went back there, to the same spot under the trees where she had first laid eyes on the Were, maybe she'd find out what the key to their connection was. If she found more vampires, she'd wring the truth out of them. She had to try. Emotions were rife, and cresting.

The sickest question of all, one that followed her like a shadow, was about how many freaks the Were community might sustain in their midst.

Second in order of horrific fears was her new paranoia about being sealed off for good on her father's estate for having the wrong kind of fangs, never to set foot beyond its boundaries again.

The shocked look in the ghost wulf's eyes dogged her. That look had warned her about her changes. The blood on her fingers had confirmed it.

But she and the ghost wulf had fully mated. Their connection had been consummated. Two entities in transition, and who hadn't a clue as to what they were becoming, had kissed and then bedded. And despite the push to run away, Rosalind desperately wanted a rematch with him. Her body ached for another bed, or a stretch of green lawn…anywhere private enough to have the ghost wulf inside her.

"I have fangs. What does that make me?" she shouted into the quiet night.

Half-naked, she moved between the trees as if she'd

become a part of the breeze blowing through them. After her shout, she clamped her jaws and tried not to swallow the sickeningly sweet thickness of the blood filling her mouth.

Out here, unprotected by fathers and fences and a hundred acres of bayou swampland, she had to find answers or die trying. She was both herself, and not. A glob of darkness had partially taken her over, and if that darkness continued to spread in so swift a manner, there would be no gauging how long she had before being completely overcome by some new entity.

What would such a thing do to her mate? To their connection?

If she were no longer Lycan, would their imprinting fade?

If she were to become a vampire, they would be enemies.

The outline of the first large tree lay ahead, an old tree with scarred bark. Glancing up at it, Rosalind bent her knees and jumped, landing on the lowest branch perched on both feet, and with perfect balance.

She uttered a hoarse, muffled cry of terror at what she had just done. Kneeling now, she compressed herself into as small a mass as possible, with her arms wrapped around her knees. The vampires they had fought here had been hanging in these trees like bats, and she seemed precariously close to doing the same thing.

That seemed unthinkable, unreasonable. To the best of her knowledge, she hadn't been bitten or scratched when she'd joined the fight. Vampire blood and venom couldn't have reached her bloodstream, so there was no reason for vamp fangs to have appeared inside her mouth, and no explanation at all for being in a tree when werewolves were earthbound creatures.

She looked at the ground, thinking about how the bloodsuckers had stopped attacking her after she issued the howl that had summoned the other Weres. She was unable to see anything in it that would have caused the startling changes taking place.

So, why had the vampires backed off her before that fight had ended?

Why had she always been kept away from other Weres?

Did the answers to those questions go hand in hand?

Damn it, didn't her father understand that she, of all Weres, needed to know these things, and that it would be impossible to go on without knowing? Look what was happening to her now!

Blinking back tears of frustration served to clear her vision. Inhaling the night opened her senses enough to recognize the strong scent of humans strolling through the corners of the park, probably lacking the courage to trespass deeper into it.

She smelled their clothes, all the way down to the fabric and dye. She smelled their musky perfume.

"Nothing extraordinary," she whispered with relief. "Just more wulf senses."

Beneath her, the odor of vamp ash had gone. In the distance, behind Landau's protective walls, she sensed the ghost wulf moving.

"We're mated, and I don't really know you."

Rosalind hated the tears that ran down her cheeks.

Chapter 8

It took a full minute for Colton's eyes to adjust enough to pick the Weres out of the dark landscape, then he counted six large bodies in man-form before getting to his feet.

He glanced up at the sky to gauge the position of the moon, then focused on the Weres who weren't furred-up because the moon had passed her full phase.

"Landau's pack, I presume?" he said, feeling unnaturally winded and as if he might be sleepwalking. How long had he been here? he wondered.

"Did you see her?" he asked.

"Who?" one of them replied.

"Rosalind."

"Rosalind Kirk?" another Were queried.

This speaker was a big man. Tall, well built, fair-haired and recognizable as Miami's Deputy District

Attorney, Dylan Landau was Judge Landau's only son and pure Lycan through and through. Dressed casually in tan slacks and a soft blue shirt that spoke of wealth and privilege, and without one hint of the stink of the previous night's vampire attack on him, Dylan was a key figure in the fight against crime in this city, and lethal in his own right.

Beside Judge Landau's son stood another outstanding specimen of Werehood, slightly on the rougher side. Brown-haired, hard-featured, this guy's strong shoulders were shown off by a tight black T-shirt. His faded jeans were threaded with a belt that had a badge pinned to it. The golden shield of a detective.

This guy with the badge was Were, but not purebred Lycan. And since he was here with the Landaus, it had to either be Adam Scott or Matt Wilson that faced him, both of whom had been inducted into the Were clan after they'd been bitten while on the job. Both had helped to clean up a werewolf fighting ring last year run by a creep named Chavez. That feat alone could have earned either Scott or Wilson access to Landau's full-blooded pack. Among Weres, the Red Wolf and Wolf Trap cases were hailed as notorious.

He guessed the Were in the T-shirt was Wilson, without knowing why. Any other time, he would have been honored to meet the guy in person.

"Then you haven't see her," Colton said, straining to see beyond the line of formidable muscle barring his exit.

"No one has seen her," Dylan Landau said.

"She exited from that window." Colton pointed up at the house. Talking took a monumental effort. "I need to find her. You can help by pointing me in the right direction if your senses are working better than mine at the moment. I seem to be stuck in healing overload."

When Dylan Landau shook his head, the shoulder-length blond hair he was famous for spilled over his shoulders. "We're not supposed to follow her."

"Rosalind," Colton said. "Her name is Rosalind."

"Yes, I know," Dylan said.

"Then you do know about her."

"I know *of* her."

"What does that mean?"

"As I said, no one here has seen Rosalind. We've only heard rumors about her, and we've just returned to the compound several minutes ago."

"I'll be on my way, then," Colton said.

Landau and Wilson stepped forward at the same time to stop him. Colton nodded in understanding. "You're here to keep me from leaving?"

"Are you ready to leave?" Wilson asked.

"Don't I look like it?" Colton replied cynically.

He had avoided Miami's underworld of werewolves in order to better keep his own family's secrets, and regretted that decision now. Like him, these Weres used their special abilities to fight the bad guys, and wore their secrets well. They were distant cousins, of a sort. Comrades, if their packs were ever to socialize.

Yet he still felt coated in something heavy that dragged at the edges of his awareness. And the female he had bedded had sprouted fangs, jumped from a three-story window, and had gotten away with it.

"Actually, no," Wilson said. "You don't look like you're ready to go anywhere, especially if that means seeing people you know, or encountering the sort of creatures that seem to be making their home in the park."

Yes. The albino hair would be hard to explain, Colton admitted to himself. He'd have to shave it off before he showed up at his apartment. As for seeing others, these Weres were right, of course. He wasn't ready to go anywhere. He could barely handle being around those of his own kind. His senses were firing on too many cylinders. The night was filled with external chatter and the mingled smells of way too many things.

He felt sick. He felt different. And his face looked like a Frankenstein creation.

Worse than that, strange impulses flowed through him that he didn't dare to address, shouting at him with all the hype of his brain being hit repeatedly with a Taser. These Weres were kin, if not by line or by blood, then by species, and yet he wanted to kill them all for getting in his way. For stopping him from going after Rosalind.

But then Weres didn't kill other Weres, except out of dire necessity, when no other course of action was feasible and trouble rained down.

Colton had to pry his mouth open to speak, and fisted his hands to keep them still. "The question remaining on the table is whether you're the welcoming committee, or actually here to keep me from following Rosalind."

Dylan Landau spoke again, probably afforded that leeway because this was his family's house. "This isn't a prison, Colton. It's a place of healing. A safe haven. We know what those suckers did to your family. You are welcome here."

It had been a long time since anyone had called him by his first name, and Colton took another hit of regret.

He had to close his eyes briefly to sidestep a rise of emotion that caused a tug-of-war with his darker side.

Closing his eyes turned out to be a terrible idea, though. The night crowded in, clamoring with noise not unlike the static from his police radio, turned up to max. His ears rang. His head began to pound. He had no idea what frequency he was tuning in to, or what could be happening to him.

As his legs faltered, Colton caught himself before going down.

Landau had taken another step in his direction. As he did, Colton began to hear and comprehend that Were's thoughts, as well as the thoughts of the others. Those thoughts rushed in, overlapping, getting louder.

"What's going on?" he muttered, keeping his hands at his sides with a concerted effort.

The voices of the Weres across from him were like raised shouts.

Can we help him, after what's happened and what he has become? he heard one voice ask.

Ghost wulfs are creatures of legend. How can this be possible? said another.

He feels different, smells different.

Vampire scum did this. What can we do to help? There must be a way. He's one of us.

How could he have seen her, when no one else has?

Why is he asking for the freak?

Colton spoke to stop the deluge of what had to be a sudden arrival of a telepathic link to all of them. The chatter was driving him mad. He didn't like the word *freak.*

"I don't know what I am. I believe I might no longer be like you," he said, hanging on to his anger by the thinnest thread of self-control. "Something happened to me. I don't belong here."

"Let us help." That was Dylan.

"I need time to heal."

"You can do that here."

"I have to find Rosalind. If I'm like this, I have to know what has happened to her."

Dylan spoke again in a quieter tone. "I'll just ask you to think twice about disrespecting a father's wishes for his daughter's safety and well-being, whoever she is. We were warned against trying to see her."

"I have no intention of harming her." Colton cleared his throat, feeling as though something had gotten stuck in it.

"Then why the claws?" Wilson asked.

Colton looked down in surprised confusion. His claws had sprung, and were on full display. These Weres would be wondering how he managed that without a full moon.

He was equally as curious.

In the presence of a full moon, the others present would have to assume he was angry. Emotion tended to let transformations slip now and then. But here, now, their faces were dark with worry. None of them knew how adept he was at changing any time the mood struck him, rather than having to wait for the moon's permission. Only his family's line could do that, another reason for the Killion's remaining apart from the others. Nevertheless, the claws were a problem. He hadn't invited them into being, or even felt his hands change. One moment the claws weren't there, and the next moment they were, which meant that another potentially harmful secret had just escaped its net.

"I've been ill," he said, growing more and more anxious about the expressions on the faces in front of him. Inside him, his wulf gave a perfunctory whine.

"My beast takes advantage of the opportunity," he said, with no idea how or if these Weres would accept such an explanation. He'd never messed up like this before. It was as if his will were sliding back and forth between forms and he could no longer be entirely certain which shape was which, or who was in charge. It was as if the beast no longer lay curled up inside, awaiting its turn, but actually coated the surface of his skin.

He felt as though he had one foot trapped inside the tunnel of night that had swallowed him out there in the park, and like he had stumbled into a pit of quicksand.

Through it all, because of all that, a need unlike any he had ever experienced drove him, compelled him, toward what light he imagined remained open to him. He had to reach that light, find the one voice he craved above all others. He had to find Rosalind. Only then could he find himself.

Rosalind didn't care about the white hair. She'd seen the ghost, seen him. She had encouraged him to open his eyes, and then had opened her legs. And she had been right to warn him that being separated from her would hurt.

The desire for Rosalind was bigger than that, larger than the universe, and in this kind of need had to rest the answer to the riddle that had struck him in darkness.

Why had the vampires arrived here, now?

"Colton?"

Adam Wilson called him back to a reality that had him facing a wall of wary, sympathetic faces.

"I know a place where you can take all the time you

need to get better if you're worried about staying here," Wilson said.

"Speaking as a friend or the shrink you once were?" Colton asked.

Wilson smiled. "I wasn't aware that anyone knew of my former profession."

"Everyone at Metro knows. You're a hero there for what you did to help take the Chavez gang down."

"Okay. Then I suppose the next question is what you'll do when you find Rosalind?" Wilson said.

"You mean while I'm like this?" Colton ran a claw through his white hair.

"Yes," Wilson replied frankly. "If you don't know what's happening to you, how can you be sure Rosalind will be safe?"

"I gave her my promise not to worry about that."

Wilson nodded. "Then you have seen her, spoken to her."

"Were you thinking that I might have made her up?"

"Of course not. But other than a handful of elders, we just learned that no one here has known for sure of her existence before tonight. We only found out that she'd been here when we returned to find her scent in the air. Female Were, but nothing usual. Maybe you can tell us why the secrecy surrounding her is so great, and what the hell happened here while we were gone."

Again, Colton felt his human physical form begin to waver. His hands and face pulsed as if a full shift were imminent. He actually began to fear what that shape might be, since he felt so strange.

"Colton," Wilson said.

"Yes, I've seen her," Colton muttered. "She's beautiful."

When he looked at the faces staring back, it was to find that the Weres had stepped back and drawn together in an automatic pack response to sniffing out trouble.

Colton glanced down at himself to see patches of white fur covering his bare arms. He felt his body starting to strain against the tightness of the borrowed jeans.

"Well, well," Matt Wilson muttered with a sharp intake of breath. "What have we here?"

Chapter 9

Rosalind swiped at her tears.

Glancing down at herself, she saw that black fur covered her bare legs. Though the transition to wulf appeared to have stopped halfway up her shivering body, she sighed with relief, taking the fur as a good sign.

Her apprehension returned when she noticed that the overall scent of the park had changed. Its feel had changed.

She glanced toward the Landau compound with the certainty that her ghost wulf would soon come after her, and that she had no way to prevent it. She didn't want him to see her like this.

Another smell came to her unexpectedly, delaying her departure. People. Two of them. Male humans in pressed pants, wearing shoes with rubberized soles. She caught a whiff of leather, mixed with bits of metal and the dampness of perspiration.

Reflexively, she backed up on the branch, and pressed herself to the tree's resinous bark.

"No one has seen the bastard since the Tuesday night," a gritty voice remarked.

Rosalind recognized something familiar in the slightly nasal tone.

"He didn't show up for work. We learned that his family lives on the block where the other family was murdered. No one has heard from Killion's people, either. Neighbors say they're reclusive, travel often, and therefore might have been out of town when those killings went down."

"Lucky for them," the second voice chimed in.

"Yeah, so where is Killion? I saw him in the alley behind his family's house, then he disappeared."

"Maybe he knew those people and he needs time to mourn."

"He's a cop, Jack. We mourn with expressionless cop faces and then come back for more. You know that. He didn't call in, just up and disappeared. It's strange."

Rosalind placed the middle-aged voice and where she had heard it before. It was in the alley behind her brown Were's family's house. The brown wulf had talked to this man before hell had risen in the park.

Their scent filed into a reasonable order that began to make sense. These were cops. They were looking for the big Were, who'd gone MIA. She couldn't help with that unless he came now, hunting for her. If he did come, white and faded and ghostly, there would be trouble with these cops who were looking for him.

The strange thing was that trouble might have arrived already. Her jaws ached from the sound of these voices. Her body pulsed with the scent of blood. One of the men had cut himself, and the odor of crushed aluminum emanating from that tiny wound had the same effect on her as inhaling an oncoming storm system.

Her teeth began to chatter. Rosalind felt her lips curl away from her fangs, leaving them wickedly exposed. In horror, she realized that she had stood up, driven to her feet by a faint inner warning suggesting that she could easily hurt these men if she wanted to, and that if she did, no one else would find her mate.

The thrill of fighting the vampires returned to course through her. The fury of battle, the sound of slashing claws and gnashing fangs came back like distant echoes. So did an imagined sensation of biting into solid flesh, of sinking her teeth into a soft neck. Decent werewolves didn't bite innocent people. They weren't supposed to bite anything at all.

Her teeth were snapping. Her jaws were straining.

"No. Please, no," she whispered. "I'm not a monster."

In order to escape, she'd have to wait until the men moved off. She couldn't afford to let them see her. They were good guys, but they carried guns. Although she had been taught that a bullet, unless it was silver, wouldn't kill her, she'd also been taught that a bullet would hurt like hell and sorely slow her down.

Dizziness hit her, nearly knocking her sideways. The fur that had stopped halfway into its transition wavered as if a hand had run through it.

One of the men on the ground beneath her slapped a hand to his ear, glanced at his fingertips and looked up. There was a drop of blood on his hand.

God, had she shed some of the blood in her mouth without meaning to? Worse, had she bitten a cop without even realizing she had moved, her sinister action hidden in those seconds of brief dizziness?

"No!"

She had to take a chance and get away before anything else happened, and before these men found her. She had to get away before she hurt them, or herself, for real.

With a fluid leap that she hoped would be too fast for human eyes to capture, Rosalind landed soundlessly on the ground in the shadows. Whirling on her bare feet, she called up her wulf, hoping more than anything that the wulf would still listen.

"I think you should go back inside," Dylan Landau suggested with earnest concern. "It would help if we all knew what's going on."

Colton shook his head. "I told you I'm ill, and that this is the result. There's no time now for the explanations I need as much or more than you do. Rosalind is out there, alone."

"How do you know she's out there?" Wilson asked.

Colton patted his chest with a fist, an action reminding him of Tarzan. The pain she was experiencing centered in his chest as if it were his own. He shared that, as well as her anguish.

"It doesn't matter what we say?" Dylan queried.

"It can't matter. She's hurting. And I'm…this."

There wasn't going to be much more communication. Colton's face burned like a son of a gun, unlike the smoother morphing of his clawed hands and furry arms.

"What about you?" Wilson said. "Maybe there's a way to—"

"Reverse the damage?"

"Heal the worst parts of it," Wilson finished.

Colton stared down at himself. White fur now covered his chest, a discovery not all that comforting.

"You need to get out of my way," he warned in a deep, guttural tone.

"And you need to remember where you are, and who you are," a tense, authoritative voice said from behind Colton.

Colton spun with his claws raised. That fast, he had shifted and dropped to his haunches in a position of fighting readiness.

"We are not the enemy, my friend," a tall, thin man said from the porch steps. "Quite the contrary in fact, if you'll recall."

"Jared. Stay back," Dylan Landau cautioned.

Colton cocked his head at the sound of the newcomer's name. Jared. Jared Kirk. This was Rosalind's father. Rosalind had told him he'd need to know this name.

Ignoring Dylan's warning, the elder Were, dark-haired and dark-eyed, moved closer and spoke again to Colton. "Do you know where Rosalind has gone?"

Colton rose slowly, hearing the question echo hollowly inside his head.

"Can you lead me to her?" Jared Kirk asked. "She can't be loose in the city. It's imperative that we get her back, then return to our home. It's crucial. You must trust me on this."

By the time Colton stood, he was in man form and as close to being Colton Killion again as he was probably going to get.

"The questions can wait," he said gruffly, his vocal cords lagging behind in the latest shift.

"Yes," Jared Kirk said with a grateful nod of his head. "They can wait. Finding my daughter can't."

"We'll go," Dylan Landau said. "We'll search for her."

Ready to quelch that suggestion, Colton spun around. But Rosalind's father replied first to the crowd.

"I'm sorry I don't have the time to name you all, but please trust me when I say that I appreciate all of your offers of assistance. However, you're not fully equipped to take on my daughter at the moment. Only this Were can, I believe, if indeed it can be done at all."

Jared Kirk had alluded to Colton with a wave of his hand. Dylan fell silent, possibly due to the rebuff that Kirk hadn't in any way meant as a slight, and only a statement of fact, one that Colton had already started to realize.

Only this Were could find her, Rosalind's father had said. Meaning him. Another freak. A ghost. Rosalind's mate. He and Rosalind were different from the other Weres present and connected by an unbreakable link.

He scented Rosalind out there, not too far away. He knew she was thinking about him, and that she was scared. Inhaling her lingering fragrance amounted to a directional beacon guiding him to his unusual lover.

Colton turned his head. Dylan, Wilson and the other boys were staring at him, perhaps hoping to see what tricks he'd perform next. He tuned them out.

What is she? he wanted desperately to ask Rosalind's father, when he had just agreed to forgo the questions in lieu of finding the girl.

He nodded to Jared Kirk. Turning toward the eight-foot wall edging the lawn near the end of the driveway, and bypassing the astonished members of the Landaus' pack at a lope, Colton parlayed his limping pace into a run.

Chapter 10

Colton raced through the park with his hackles raised. Rosalind's scent had changed again, going from familiar to foreign and then back. She was melting back and forth between forms, just as he was.

He howled his displeasure over the situation, and the roar carried. No howl answered his.

Come back to me, my lover.

His head hurt. Sharp pains pierced his limbs as his injured body adapted to what he was putting it through. He hadn't healed completely, and the wulf internalized that pain.

Pure need drove him on.

Sensations of his own oddness tingled through him, but the act of running calmed his lust for the familiar. Most of the smells in the park were ones he recognized.

He had to keep focused. The sound of voices, some

of them in the distance and some inside his head, refused to allow him the moments of quiet he needed in order to get his thoughts together.

He let a second howl rip, and caught a whiff of flowers nearby.

She's here.

Colton slowed when he heard voices.

"Jesus! What the hell was that?" a man said with fearful agitation.

"I don't know. Probably a bird."

"Pterodactyls are extinct!"

"A neighboring dog, then, would be my second guess. What are you doing with your hand? Is that blood?"

"It isn't food coloring. Something bit me. And that sound was like no dog I've ever heard."

"Could have been a big bug that bit you. Who knows what's in these damn trees? But no dog I know of can fly high enough to nip at your ear, so chalk it up to really hungry mosquitoes. Man, though, this place is creepy. I'll give you that."

"We've probably seen enough of this cursed park to know there's no trace of Killion here. I'm heading back to the boulevard."

"You're not interested in finding out what made that growling noise?"

"Are you kidding?"

"Yeah, I guess so."

"You don't sound convincing."

"I like the guy, okay? Killion is one of us. I'd like to find him."

"He's not here, Davidson, so we can look someplace else."

"All right. Let's head back."

"Wait. What's that? Hell, I think that big dog is loose!"

"I'd hate to hurt a dog of any size, them being man's best friend and all."

"Even if it comes after you out here, like a four-legged maniac?"

"Is that it over there? Come on, I swear I just saw it."

"Hell with you, Davidson. I'm not going after that thing. I'm out of here."

Colton growled again as he crept toward the spot where his fellow cops had been standing, hearing them kick up dirt and grass as they trotted toward the street. There was no way he could call out to them. Though he wanted to do just that, and his heart hurt, he had to let them go.

Beneath the tree, he dropped to the ground, able to smell the blood crushed by the officers' boots.

Rosalind's blood. Fresh.

She had to have heard his call. To call again with the officers so close would be species suicide.

Colton raised his head, sniffed the air, then took off.

I might be hurting, he thought, *but my wulf knows what has to be done.*

Hearing the ghost wulf's roar, and feeling it rip through her, Rosalind's steps faltered on a cracked section of a concrete sidewalk. She had reached the street.

Moving cautiously, Rosalind noted the scent of a particular newcomer too late. Before she had made it to the nearby covered structure, a hand reached out to stop her.

"Do you really think that's a good idea?" a female asked, with a grip like a steel trap on Rosalind's right arm.

Rosalind turned. The newcomer's scent was Were, but not Lycan. Not from an ancient bloodline.

She withheld the desire to knock this wolf to the ground and be on her way. She had to be civil, and keep her damn fangs to herself.

"Where did you come from?" the woman asked. "Where are the rest of your clothes?"

Rosalind shivered. When had she again changed form? The full shift to her human shape must have been swift and automatic. It had to have occurred as she'd left the fringes of the park. Without fur-covered legs, she was half-naked, with only the hem of her shirt covering the tops of her thighs.

This had to be an odd sight. What should she do now?

The woman beside her was a dark-haired Were of about the same height as Rosalind, and young. She wore a uniform like the one the brown Were had worn until he'd been catapulted onto a divergent path. The name on her chest pocket said *Delmonico.*

Another cop.

Before Rosalind could summon the wits to reply to this female officer's question, another voice rang out from behind them.

"It's okay, Officer," said her lover, her mate, in a tone that set Rosalind's teeth on edge. "This is my problem, so I'll take it from here."

Rosalind and the woman holding on to her turned toward the speaker in unison. A ghostly figure stood beneath the branches of the last line of trees. His pale skin was shocking. Long strands of pure white hair fell across a portion of his handsome, hardened face.

He seemed twice as formidable as he had been before the vampire attack. The red welts crisscrossing his forehead and cheeks, when added to the light skin and dark-ringed eyes, would make him scary to onlookers of any species. The sight of him took Rosalind's breath away.

But whatever it was that she had become, the effects of their mating ritual hadn't been lost, or forgotten. Her cravings for this wulf hadn't diminished; had in fact grown stronger in her brief absence from him. Even the dark thing taking root inside her wanted to rut with him here, now, without a care for who might be looking.

She recognized the same cravings in him, and she stole a glance at the Were female cop whose grip hadn't lessened.

The cop blinked slowly and sniffed the air. "Don't know you," she said to the wulf in the distance.

"Came from the Landaus' place a few minutes ago," he said. "Chasing after an escapee."

"You know him?" the cop asked Rosalind.

"No," she said, struggling against the idea of shifting into the dark thing with needlelike fangs so that she would scare the hell out of this officer and be able to get away as planned. The emotions inside her were becoming oppressive. Every thought, action, desire, seemed larger than life and potentially overwhelming.

The Were cop sniffed at the air. "I can smell him on you," she said. "I also smell something else."

Facing the ghost, the officer named Delmonico added, "Different. Wounded. Lycan. Are you Killion, by any chance?"

Killion. The name brought on another flutter. Rosalind wrapped her tongue around the sound. It was his name. Had to be.

"I was the man you're asking about," her lover replied.

"Something happened to you after the deaths on Baker," Delmonico said. "This is the result?"

"Yes, but I can't speak of it."

"Everyone is looking for you. The force is exploring all avenues. Will you be coming back?"

"I don't think so. At least not for a while. Did they find…?"

"No. Not many know about your parents. We handled it. They've been taken away."

"We?"

"Adam Scott and myself."

"Thank you," he said sadly, soberly and with obvious relief.

The cop named Delmonico nodded and addressed them both. "It's safe to turn her over to you? You are all right, at least in part? Enough of a part?"

"No," Rosalind replied. "Not safe."

The emotional turmoil inside her was staging a comeback. She could hardly speak, was afraid to open her mouth and expose what lay inside.

"It's the only option," her ghostly mate named Killion said. "Her father is waiting. So is the Judge."

Delmonico nodded again. "Do you know who I am, Killion?"

"I do," he said.

"And why I'm concerned about wolves in this park, and about what I feared might have happened to you?"

"I know the details of what secret circles call the Red Wolf case, and about the rogue named Chavez. Adam Scott was your partner, and he was hurt. But this—" he alluded to the wounds on his face with a wave of his hand "—wasn't due to those things."

The cop let go of Rosalind's arm as if the white-haired Were had uttered a magical sequence of words that rendered him worthy of her trust. She spoke directly to Rosalind. "Best not to have anyone else see you like this. People here wear clothes. Will you go with Killion, or should I accompany you?"

"Can't." *Don't you see why? Can't you sense the changes?*

Before Rosalind had time to register the expression of surprise on Officer Delmonico's pert face, her ghost wulf had closed the distance and had swept Rosalind into his arms. With a respectful incline of his head to Officer Delmonico, he left the street behind, carrying Rosalind toward the shadowy spaces where the concept of normal in no way applied.

"You don't mean that, about not wanting to come with me," the ghost said. "I can read you like a book."

Carting her as if she weighed little, he ran like the wind in human form toward the Landaus' walls…where instead of returning her to her father, as promised, he shoved her up against a patched section of the stone barrier, lifted her legs and wrapped them around his waist.

He pinned her hands above her head with his large, shaky palms, and leaned in. The stone scraped at her flimsy silk shirt and dug grooves into her bare lower back and hips, but that was nothing. The eyes boring into hers weren't questioning or accusatory. They didn't seek the truth behind the fangs, or why she had left him so abruptly.

Killion's eyes, though pale, were bright with uncontrollable desire. He shook with the attempt to restrain that desire, just as she shook to restrain hers.

"You bite me," he whispered in warning with his face an inch from hers, "and I'll bite you back."

"Promise?"

With an exhaled breath and palpable anxiousness, he said, "Let me in, Rosalind. Now. Here. Take me in before I tear you apart."

Rosalind shut her eyes to manage the frightening, rising dark. With a rush of desire, she felt this ghost wulf's glorious cock sink into her womb possessively, aggressively, in response to the soft sigh of her breath in his mouth.

Chapter 11

The ecstasy of being inside Rosalind again was similar to the pain of being torn apart by enemies and then waking up alive, Colton thought.

Each thrust seemed an earth-shattering event. Every soft, very real sound of encouragement she made hurled him toward hot, sweet, ecstasy.

She was so very…fine.

This couldn't go on, of course, his mind warned. They couldn't continue like this because they wouldn't be allowed to. Rosalind's father waited on the other side of this same wall, and he was going to take her away.

Colton realized that the roughness he used to get at her was tearing Rosalind apart, and he couldn't help it. His mind was set on having her in every possible way, carnal and emotional. If she was to be taken away from him for any amount of time, he needed sustenance.

Rosalind accepted the roughness of this act as if she had been born to it. As if she had to have this as badly as he did, if only to put off and outrun her own demons.

She writhed against him, opened herself, rose to meet him. Her body took him in, massaging his hardness, accepting him with a passion that was ferocious and feral.

This wasn't merely good, it bordered on insane. And not once did she ask him to stop.

He had bites all over his mouth and cheek and neck from Rosalind losing herself in this mating. Colton smelled the blood that seemed to drive her further into a state of euphoria, and let that pass. He would confront that issue another time.

Touch, feel, taste and the sleek, silken sensation of being inside her rendered him worthless in curbing his need to possess her. Being embedded in her blistering heat was everything.

It was life itself.

It was as if he somehow temporarily shared hers.

When the crescendo inside him had built to an impossible level and screamed for release, he penetrated her just one more time with a deep, forceful thrust.

Rosalind moaned, then cried out again, vocalizing her gratification, forgetting where they were.

He came. With her. Simultaneously. The flood gates opened, and his soul's liquid ecstasy mingled with hers. Theirs was a unanimous gasp, a last reach for something beyond themselves that crowded out all other thought… for a while.

And though he wanted to stay buried inside Rosalind, their shouts had an unanticipated domino effect.

An instantaneous response came from beside them;

a gruff, angry stringing together of senseless words intended as a warning, and quite possibly as a threat.

In the time it took for Colton to zip up his jeans and turn Rosalind to face him, he found himself surrounded by Weres that had appeared from nowhere. All of them were elders, all of them were in human form, their auras saturated with hefty, polarized power.

With terrible timing, Jared Kirk had arrived with the big boys in tow.

But before any of them could offer up a protest or more harsh words on Kirk's behalf for Colton taking such liberties with the Were's daughter, a terrible new odor flooded the area on the south side of Landau's wall.

Everyone turned to face this new wave, including Colton.

"They have arrived," Rosalind's father grimly announced.

Vampires.

Above the loaded silence that followed Jared Kirk's remark, Colton heard Rosalind's soft growl of fear. His own fear took shape. He had faced these creatures before. He glanced nervously to each elder Were. As far as he knew, none of these Lycans could shift shape without a full moon. As men they were exceptionally strong, but against the supernatural flood of danger rushing in, they were much more vulnerable.

Taking a step back, Colton pressed Rosalind to the wall, placing himself protectively between her and whatever approached. His hunger for her was barely appeased, but Rosalind's father stood beside him, too close for comfort and reeking of anger. A tall, broad man with silver hair and a long face crowded him on his other side.

"Surely that's impossible," Colton said, his anxiousness escalating as the foul odor of sour earth wafted in. "Bloodsuckers don't dare to trespass here, so close to Were boundaries."

"Nothing about this is usual," Jared Kirk snapped, scanning the park where the trees were the densest.

"Luckily we're prepared," the silver-haired Were remarked in a voice backed by the steel of a practiced authority that made Colton sure this was the infamous Judge Landau himself.

"There may be no moon," said another of Landau's friends, as if he had read Colton's mind, "but since we have fingers and pockets, we have the next best thing."

The familiar smell of metal wafted to Colton, a smell he had lived with nearly every day on the job with the Miami PD. These Weres had weapons. They had guns.

"You don't imagine that will do the trick?" he protested impatiently.

"Special guns," one Were said. "Wooden bullets should do the trick."

Rosalind squirmed behind him, registering her tension with a sound that made the hair at the nape of Colton's neck stand up. She knew a fight was coming. Maybe out of all of them, and with her new fangs, she had the most to fear.

Her father stepped closer to her wearing an expression of wary concern. "We'll go now," he told her. "If it's not too late."

"We can hold them off," Judge Landau promised. "As soon as you go, I'll call the boys."

Kirk took his daughter by the hand. It could be that Rosalind's father realized what had happened to her the night Colton had become a ghost, after all. But maybe not. What was fair to assume, however, was that Kirk and the other elders had been expecting something like this and were ready to take on an influx of fanged parasites.

God help us all if there are hundreds.

"I'll help," Colton volunteered, looking around, sensing the vampires' closeness.

Turning to look at Rosalind, he saw that her eyes were downcast and cloaked by fluttering ebony lashes. She was fighting feelings that none of them really saw or recognized. He also noted that a single streak of white hair, two or three inches wide, ran from her forehead to the tips of her waist-long tresses. He had no idea what had caused this, or if he could simply have missed the discoloration before.

Now wasn't the time or place to address it.

"Rosalind," he whispered to her. "Tell me what this is. What comes here?"

"No," Kirk protested. "It's too late now. You've helped to cause this, and must help get my daughter to safety. Get her away from them. You must guard my daughter with your life."

All eyes turned to Colton, except for Rosalind's. She seemed to have retreated into herself. But her heartbeat had become his heartbeat, pounding, thundering in their arteries.

He wanted her all over again, here, now. He had to be inside her. Nothing else would do. No one else would do. Below his waist, he was still hard, still aching for Rosalind's molten sweet spot.

Yet the way the elders were staring at him put a quick end to his lust. Lycan anxiety filled the area with a palpable heaviness.

Colton didn't like how cold the night had grown in direct correlation with his thoughts about what hid in the park's shadows. And though he wasn't sure what the next vampire onslaught would entail, he sensed that Rosalind knew they were near, and that her current quiet exterior was misleading.

Jared Kirk seemed privy to this, as well. Rosalind's father knew the real answer as to why they all believed these vampires were coming for his daughter. Rosalind had confided to Colton that this council of elders kept secrets, and that she feared they had met to discuss her.

Without waiting to see what Landau and the others had in mind—besides wooden bullets—Colton, for the third time since he had met Rosalind, gathered her in his arms. Not because she was weak or helpless, but because of his intrinsic need to keep her close. Though her dark eyes glowed with rebellion, and her breath hissed out, she allowed his closeness, and seemed to understand how necessary it was.

Ignoring her father's expression of worried anger, Colton said, "Guard her with my life? Gladly. I probably owe her my life, or what's left of it. So, what are you waiting for? Lead the damn way."

He tossed Rosalind atop Landau's eight-foot stone wall with a seemingly effortless grace that left his weakened arms shaking, and left the others murmuring incomprehensible phrases behind him.

Chapter 12

Rosalind couldn't speak. But she did know that with one concerted physical protest, she could get away from all of them, and that if she did, the others here would be safe, at least for a while. Her white wulf, Killion, would be safe, too, except perhaps from his own demons.

Yet swell after swell of longing for him washed over her, as did the fear that if she left him now, he might never find her again. She might be alone forever after knowing the pleasures of bonding with this magnificent male.

Terror over that was like an added layer of pain.

If her father knew what they had done, and what their sex had accomplished, he made no mention of it. Things had too gone far. All was chaos, her father was thinking, and he was right. After planning to separate her from her white wulf, he had asked that same wulf to protect her.

On Landau's side of the wall, she allowed herself to be led away as if she were a senseless child. Her father's grip on her arm pulled her forward. His anger pushed her on.

She felt every step her ghost mate took. Each labored breath he took moved through her lungs as if it were her own. His pain was becoming her pain, as if such things were contagious. She still felt him between her legs…a ghostly leftover sensation of their lovemaking. She felt him sliding in and out of her, hard and dangerous and filling, with each pulse that struck her throat. Yet her father would see that it didn't happen again.

As they moved away from the park, Rosalind also knew that the effort to escape another vampire attack would be in vain. The Weres here would face them any minute now, and she would be gone.

Deep in her gut, she sensed that the fanged monsters would find her eventually, wherever she was, because of something she had done while in their presence that had exempted her from the fury of their fangs.

The call…

It had been that soulful howl she'd made out there that had slid her closer to the unforeseen abyss where vampires lived.

Making their way past the Landau house, where outside lights now blazed with the wattage of full daylight, Rosalind saw more Weres running for the wall. Young males turned to look at her only once before obeying the call to arms.

Landau's pack. They were all preternaturally beautiful, and terrible in their own right.

I have done this. Brought anger to them all.

One lapse in the rules, and the world had gone mad,

taking her with it. No matter how much she wanted or wished, it was too late to change anything.

Hunger. Hunt. Kill. Rosalind flinched as the remembrance of vampire hatred invaded her mind. The rancid emotion behind those words caused her to stumble, catching her father off guard. He dropped his hold on her wrist, and glanced behind them.

Rosalind spun toward the wall in the distance with a shriek of despair on her lips. She felt heavy, awkward now, as if the enemy's existence, so close, was causing her to drown. Unfamiliar fangs were extending, slicing through her gums, bringing hot jabs of discomfort. She could barely move her legs.

Her lover's arms encircled her waist. Killion. Cop. Were. Lycan. Ghost. "No, Rosalind," he said in her ear. "Whatever is happening, you can rise above. Bring up your wulf. Use your strength."

To her father, he said, "They're here now. We only have minutes."

"How do you know?" Jared Kirk demanded.

"Look at your daughter."

Her father, to his credit, showed no sign of panic as Rosalind's body transformed in her lover's arms, surrendering to the cult of the moon, and to his closeness. Only her white wulf's humanlike grunt of approval filled the silence for several seconds as his arms tightened around her.

For the briefest of moments, her eyes met with his. She saw herself in the brilliance of his gaze. Black wulf. Small, sleek, but with one noticeable difference: a vampire's fangs.

The white wulf wanted her desperately. She read that in him. He wanted to take her right there. Throw her down and impale her with the evidence of his glorious sexual vigor. A growl had stuck in his throat. Yet he was also afraid.

"The car is by the garage," her father barked.

There was a sudden rumble of a well-oiled machine. Someone had started the car's engine in anticipation of their departure. As they approached the vehicle, a dark-haired young woman stepped out of the SUV. Rosalind recognized the she-wolf. This close to Killion, she heard his thoughts.

Good cop, he thought. *Bless her, Delmonico is on our side.*

Though Rosalind growled, Officer Dana Delmonico, whom they'd met on the street, faced them as if they were old friends. And the white wulf's thoughts told her that Delmonico was soon going to be Dylan Landau's wife.

"Small world, after all," she heard Colton say as he opened the back door of the black SUV and waved Rosalind inside.

Her father nodded to Delmonico and jumped into the front, behind the wheel. He stomped on the gas pedal with a heavy foot. As the car screeched out onto the asphalt driveway, her mate's thoughts transmitted one more thing before the world went dark with images of bloodsuckers cutting through a line of Weres:

Delmonico and Landau. A pure Lycan and newly inducted Were have bonded together. Further proof that rules can be stretched or broken by a concept as simple as love.

They drove a long time, heading west from Miami and then south toward Florida's gulf.

Colton kept his eyes on Rosalind. One of the first things she had told him was that she came from the bayou country. This could have meant anywhere in several Southern states, but in Florida meant the Everglades. The last road sign Colton noted was of a place called Cape Sable before he finally succumbed to sleep without meaning to beside Rosalind, who had faded back into human shape once they'd left the Landau compound behind.

She hadn't said a word. Neither had her father.

When he woke, dazed, startled, the sun had risen, and he was alone in the car.

He sat up straighter, experiencing a rush of disorientation. His muscles were painfully bunched and aching.

How long have I been asleep?

Where the hell am I?

He felt sick, tired and apprehensive. The sunlight hurt his eyes. His joints were rigid.

"Rosalind?" he whispered, reaching for the door handle.

The clunk of the SUV's metal was the only sound in an otherwise silent clearing when he stepped out. Panic kicked at his stomach.

Colton waited, straining to hear any sound at all, and finally heard birds and the oddly foreign croak of frogs, signifying how close they were to water. There were no traffic noises. No planes passed overhead. There wasn't one sign of the everyday cacophony of people rushing around.

"Everglades," he muttered with distaste. "Jesus."

As a city boy, he felt adrift in unknown territory. He'd never even visited here. This was a foreign landscape, as different from his world as being dropped onto another planet. There wasn't even a sidewalk, or a streetlight. There was no movement at all, save for the quick rise and fall of his chest.

Colton glanced down, half expecting to find an alligator at his feet, and stubbed at the dirt with his foot. He expected to see something else in the lush jungle greenery surrounding him: vampires, hanging upside down from branches. But that was an impossibility, he realized with relief. Bloodsuckers were creatures of the night, and had to hide from the sun.

With a sweep of his gaze, he saw the house, or what posed as a house. He hadn't considered the sort of residence Rosalind and an elder Lycan like her father would call home, but this was a surprise.

The small, squat building was really a cabin built of rough-hewn timber log walls, with some sort of gray-green mortar packed in the cracks. It couldn't have contained more than a few rooms, beneath a green-hued pitched roof and a couple of chimneys made of river rock. A wide covered porch wrapped around the front and sides. The windows next to the front door had glass in them and the shades drawn, giving the place an abandoned look.

His cop background made him take a further survey of the site. Foliage, thick and riotous near the small garage, had been cleared fifty feet away from the cabin's foundations. The SUV was parked on a dirt road that wound in a curvy manner through the center of a particularly dense grove of unrecognizable trees.

Cop or not, Colton felt utterly alone as he stood there trying to get his bearings. Rustling sounds roused him. He braced himself, called out "Rosalind?"

The cabin's front door opened, but it wasn't Rosalind who stepped out.

"My daughter is resting," Jared Kirk said from the top of the steps.

Colton nodded without moving to meet him. He remained wary, and on guard. "Is she okay?"

"That's a matter of one's point of view, I suppose," Kirk replied frankly. "Sedation will become Rosalind's best friend in the days to come."

"Why? We're far from the vampires, aren't we?" Colton pressed.

"You don't understand what it is that you've vowed to protect, do you? What you've dared to love and befriend?"

Colton said, "A very hyped-up she-wulf, hyped because of reasons I can't yet fathom."

"Ah, then you have your eyes closed to the possibilities, my friend," Jared Kirk remarked.

The elder Were was being purposefully cryptic, and that was flat-out unacceptable after everything Colton had been through. Still, his training mandated that he remain calm and start the necessary interrogation.

"I've been hurt," Colton said. "My world is changing, as, it seems, are my alliances. I've just left everything I have always known and loved behind, most of it lost to me, so why don't you fill me in on a few things that might make this trip to the middle of nowhere make sense."

"Will details affect your willingness to protect my daughter?"

"Do you really expect me to answer that ridiculous question?"

Jared Kirk descended one step slowly, in the manner of a man who had been pushed to his limits. "You made a vow to guard Rosalind, and I will hold you to that vow."

"I've never broken a vow."

The elder Were's voice remained steady, in spite of how tired he looked. But Colton needed to know what was going on.

"Do you believe I'm responsible for what has happened to her?" he asked. "What *is* happening to her?"

"No. I'm not stupid or unreasonable. My daughter would have had problems with or without meeting you. Her acquaintance with you merely brought her to that end result quicker."

"You'd better explain that," Colton said.

"I'm not sure it's my place to try to dissect what no one truly understands."

"Try." Colton was adamant, his voice firm. Cop voice. Cop demand.

"Very well. I suppose you'll have to know some things if you're to comprehend what guarding her entails."

Kirk took another step with his hand on the carved porch railing before going on. "Rosalind is not like you."

"And?"

"She comes from Lycans, and our blood is in her veins. But she is also something else whose shape has been handed down from a distant side of her mother's family."

The rare black fur. Yes. She was different.

In the silence following Kirk's announcement, Colton got a question in. "How can Rosalind carry the scent of a full-blooded *She*, as well as the mark of the moon, if she is something else, as well?"

Jared Kirk managed to descend the last two steps. Facing Colton, he raised his hands and let them fall back to his sides in a gesture that suggested the futility of attempting to answer Colton's question correctly.

"Issues of the blood are tricky," he finally replied. "With those distant genes remaining dormant, my daughter had the potential to become so many things. We hoped she would be fully Lycan, and only that. Only time would tell us this."

Colton fisted his hands in frustration. The conversation wasn't moving fast enough. Nor were they getting to the heart of the matter in a clear enough fashion to satisfy the needs welling up inside him.

"I'm afraid I don't understand," he said. "You're either Lycan, or you're not. Half-breeds are another thing altogether. Bitees are still more distant."

"Are you prejudiced against diluted blood, Colton?"

"Certainly not."

"What if that diluted blood came from a vampire?"

"Can't happen. Our blood doesn't mix."

"Can't it? You were injured by vampires. The brutality of their attack and the venom in their fangs has changed you into what you are now. You're Lycan, but fully? Do you know that for sure?"

The allusion to his current condition was for Colton like a sudden slap in the face. He waited, speechless, for the elder to continue, considering the possible ramifications of what Kirk had said and feeling unsteady in his open-legged stance.

Kirk's hand again moved, reaching for the railing as if groping for support. He spoke in a lowered tone. "The medication the Landaus gave you will slowly leave your system. It has temporarily given you access to some of your former strength, but what is left after that's gone is anyone's guess."

Hell, this was ominous news that Colton didn't need or care to dwell upon at the moment, though he probably should have cared. He was tired, sure. Bone-weary. But his wulf was still there, coating his insides, waiting for a chance to be freed.

If they thought he might become something other than wulf without special medication, as Kirk had just suggested, then why would the Were entrust him with his daughter's welfare?

The last thought was accompanied by a tingling sensation that rivaled the moon's influence on his bones. Seconds of light-headedness came and passed that could have been an omen of the nebulous future Kirk had hinted at, if Colton believed in omens. As it was, he just took it for another symptom of fatigue.

Nevertheless, the situation here remained unclear. Shoving the hair back from his face and looking directly at the Were in front of him, Colton asked with trepidation, "Did the vampires bite her? Is that what you're alluding to?"

Kirk eyed him wearily before speaking in a voice hushed by sorrow. "They didn't need to bite her. In order to change my daughter, those creatures only had to get close to her. They only had to touch her, brush up against her, exhale their foul breath on her."

Colton observed Kirk closely, thinking his response ridiculous.

"This is why I've kept her from the world," Kirk explained, without having actually explained much at all. "I have sequestered her here for the same reason I would have kept her away from you and any other potential suitor. I had to explain to Landau and the other elders why Rosalind can't be in their gene pool. It's not your fault this has happened. It's mine, for taking the risk of having her with me at the Landaus'. I couldn't allow them to come here when this place has to remain secret, and I couldn't leave Rosalind here alone."

Colton's unease had grown by bounds. He felt extremely uncomfortable now. The tingling sensations on his face and hands had gotten strong enough to resemble a swarm of insects walking around. The muscles of his upper back twitched with the intensity of a recurring spasm.

He was shirtless, and shivered in spite of the muggy heat of the place. In his peripheral vision he watched strands of white hair blow in an unusual breeze that smelled sultry but brought on a chill. Those colorless strands in his face were locks of his own hair, longer than he remembered, thicker than before and peppered with Rosalind's floral scent.

With that scent, memories flashed.

A call in the park from a she-wulf.

A black whirlwind tearing into the vampires, fighting savagely by his side.

Rosalind in his arms, leaving bites on his mouth, face and neck.

Rosalind on the windowsill, holding up her shaky, blood-tinted hand.

The heat of Rosalind's insides as he thrust into her.

Her groans of pleasure. Her blackened eyes.

Her shock over discovering that her mouth was filled with something no other wulf had. Needle-sharp fangs.

Those fangs dragging across his skin when he had…

"It would seem," Jared Kirk said, "that Rosalind's

genes didn't remain dormant, and that they are showing up in full force. If she had been near to you first, Colton, she'd have been like you. Lycan, for all intents and purposes. But instead vampires overpowered her senses with their insatiable thirst and their craving for blood, and my daughter has taken on some of their characteristics."

Kirk's voice cracked with submerged emotion. After a long, deep breath, he went on. "If we hadn't gotten her away from them quickly, her adaptation likely would have been more complete than it is. From what I've seen, Rosalind is stuck midway through a transition between wulf and vampire that none of us recognizes. Maybe it's not too late for her to change back. Perhaps there's hope. I pray for that."

Colton stood there, feeling completely useless and only partly appeased. He supposed there was light at the end of this explanation, but he wasn't able to reach it. Though he opened his mouth to speak, no words came out for some time.

"That's why you have allowed me to come here with her, and to hold her," he finally managed to say. "You're hoping that between the two of us, between you and I, she will revert back to normal? To wulf?"

Jared Kirk shook his head and pointed at Colton. "Normal? You think you're normal? Look at you. No, my current fear is that if you get near her again, she may take on more of your ghostly attributes. That has already started. You've seen the white in her hair. But you were the second thing to change her, not the first. The result of being with you is more subtle. The vampire traits remain, though yours seem to have influenced Rosalind, as well."

Colton stared at Kirk.

"Hell," Kirk said. "My daughter is now part wulf, part vampire, and part whatever else that you are going to turn out to be, with the multitude of bites you received in that park."

"Yet I remain wulf," Colton said, "in spite of my injuries. Other than the color of my hair, I feel Lycan. A ghost of a wulf is better than a creature of the night."

"True," Jared Kirk agreed. His expression didn't soften. He didn't seem to realize what effect on Colton his words had; the suggestion that Colton might lose the wulf, and himself, in the end.

"So here we are," Kirk said. "You and me and whatever now swims in Rosalind's veins."

The sickness in Colton's stomach worsened, threatening to bring up bile. His legs had grown more and more restless. His mind warned that he should run now, get away from this crazy interlude...but he was still in the dark in more ways than one, and the Were across from him seemed to hold a handful of clues as to what that iffy, nebulous future hanging over him might bring.

What I might become if I don't fight for myself. And for her.

"I won't change," he said to Jared Kirk.

"Who can be sure?" Kirk tossed back.

"Yet you asked me to protect Rosalind."

Kirk nodded. "I don't know what else to do. You've bonded with her. Maybe you can influence Rosalind in ways no one else can. I will hold you to that promise, as I will hold you to a promise not to touch her again until we see what your changes might bring."

Colton shook his head. "How can I protect her if can't be near to her?"

"You must promise me, Colton, not to touch her."

"You know that we have imprinted."

"Yes. But I repeat that if you have a care for my daughter's safety and her future, you must comply. You must honor my request not to touch her again."

This was an utterly useless warning, Colton wanted to shout, and quite impossible. Even sick and shaky, he wanted Rosalind so badly, he had begun to taste her presence in that house. In his mind, he saw her outline. She was lying on a bed, with her long hair fanning over the edges of a pale pillow.

So very lovely, and so very silky, her midnight-black hair had spilled like that across his skin when he had taken her. When they had joined their bodies and their souls. He could taste her, feel the exquisite texture of her body, still.

He rolled his shoulders to stop the insanity.

"I'm not sure I can stay away," he earnestly confessed. "Not now. You don't understand."

Kirk held up a hand to stop Colton's protest. Colton ignored the Were's warning.

"I'm to stay here, be her guard dog, without getting close? How close is too close? How is that kind of relationship supposed to work? You have to see how absurd your requirement is. What about her? What she wants?"

"Her needs don't count. Cannot count."

"It's to be one freak protecting another, then?" Colton was angered into taking a step. "Is that it?"

"No. It's a male who has accepted a female, taking care of that female. Your police training will come in handy here," Kirk said. "I can't be sure they won't find her here. I can't be sure they won't try. If they don't, others will, now that she has come of age. Now that you've opened the door to her womanhood and dispersed the scent of her uniqueness into the world."

What Colton wanted to say in response to this absurd diatribe was *You are a crazy bastard.* The words he managed to get out were "What do you mean by *Others*? Others trying to get at her?"

He had heard and internalized the meaning of that special emphasis, the capital *O.* But it soon became clear that Jared Kirk had said all he was going to say.

Looking bone-tired and far older than his years, the Were's broad shoulders drooped. His face had taken on a gaunt, sunken appearance. Rosalind's father was worried. There was no doubt about that. Jared Kirk honestly feared for his daughter, and who might come after her.

Turning from Colton, Kirk said in a wavering rasp, "There's a place for you in the shed, and clothes and boots in the wardrobe. You must be hungry. I'll bring some food."

Then Rosalind's father was gone, closing the door on what Colton supposed had to be only the beginning of a brand-new nightmare.

Chapter 13

Rosalind stirred. Feeling a sensation of coolness on her cheek and a burning sensation below her right knee, she awakened fully, overcome with a sense of impending doom.

She wasn't drowning, running, howling, or pressed up against a stone wall by her lover. She was in her room, on her bed. Familiar scents were everywhere. Waning daylight seeped through the curtained window, casting long shadows along one wall.

Covering her eyes to close out the suddenness of the light, she waited for whatever would come next.

The room was quiet, undisturbed, but her heart drummed, its rhythm chaotically rising and falling without perceivable instigation or trigger. The nag of an awful pain below one knee demanded her immediate attention. Between her thighs, a flickering spark informed her that her lover was near.

She sat up and looked to the door expectantly.

"I'm here," her father said, dashing her hopes for the big ghost wulf as he appeared in the doorway too quickly to have been anywhere else. "You're safe."

The throb in her private places didn't lessen. Her wulf was near. It hadn't been a dream. None of this was her imagination. She could almost smell the magnificent Killion. Her body was telling her that she couldn't bear to be long without him in spite of recent events.

"Where is he?" she asked her father.

"Who?" he replied. But Rosalind read him easily enough, and in her new, even more impatient incarnation, despised the old games they played. She was no longer a child, nor childlike. In the past few days she had become someone else. *Something* else.

"I know he's here. I can sense him," she said.

"Colton is outside."

Colton. Hearing his full name brought her pleasure. Her lips parted as she sucked that pleasure in.

"Your protector is standing guard," her father explained, his voice backed by the strain of this announcement. He wasn't happy about having the ghost here.

Rosalind swung herself to the side of the bed in an attempt to get to her feet, and was yanked back before getting far. Tossing the blanket aside, she found the reason she couldn't budge, and the source of her leg's burn. She looked at her father questioningly.

"It's for your own good," he said, sadly.

"It's a chain."

"Yes. You might have chewed through a rope."

Automatically, Rosalind put a hand to her mouth.

"The fangs will probably appear as soon as the sun goes down," her father said. "Yet I'm hoping for progress since you're awake in the daylight and adjusting to the silver chain, when those things should have been problematic."

Waves of fear hit her and retreated, carrying flashes of memory and feelings of dread.

"What am I?" Rosalind demanded, tugging against the restraint, wanting to tear it off.

Her father crossed to the bed and sat down beside her. As his weight hit the mattress, Rosalind suddenly understood about the necessity of restraint. If she'd had fangs, she might have used them. The urge to do so, and to be free of the damn chain, was there, lurking in the darkness of her soul.

"I believe you're a mixture of vampire and Were at the moment, with the latter maintaining some hold," her father said.

"Secrets," Rosalind muttered, pointing to the chain. "Is this the result of withholding things from me?"

"I doubt that any explanation would have curbed your enthusiasm for ignoring rules, Rosalind. As parents, we can only do so much."

"Then the fangs are penance, payback, for desiring freedom? Could you possibly think that? How did this happen? I'm owed an explanation."

Her father patted her hand, allowing his fingers to rest on hers as he leaned in to place a kiss on her forehead. "I'm sorry," he said. "I prayed this wouldn't happen to the extent it has, but saw it coming long ago. I tried to keep you from it, and assumed that if you didn't know what resided within you, that thing would stand no chance of showing itself."

Another wave of darkness hit Rosalind. The shadows from the window had moved to the bed. The closer those shadows got, the more restless she became.

"How can I be part vampire?" Her tone was insistent. "And how could you have watched for it? That's insane."

"The Blackout," he whispered.

The sheer weight of her father's closeness and the kiss he'd placed on her forehead temporarily robbed her of the terrible, irrational urges to tug on the chain. His scent was familiar. His face was very dear to her. He was worried, and not bothering to hide it.

"It was different for you," he went on. "The Blackout phase came on earlier, and so very intense. As your body rewired to allow your wulf in, there were signs of other changes, as well. In your fever, your body mimicked other things, the likes of which I had never seen, as if those things had somehow gotten in through an open door."

Her father winced, remembering. "You shifted in and out of form relentlessly, fighting to be what you needed to be. You pulled through. Your abilities and powers grew, almost as if there weren't enough abilities to master, and then you furred-up into a rare, very beautiful, black-pelted wulf."

"Go on." She had to stop for a breath before finishing what she wanted to say. "Tell me more. Tell me everything."

Her father waited an unconscionably long time before obliging. Rosalind forcibly withheld her claws from springing. Already there were gouges on the walls of her room from the misplaced anger of her youth. Had this been part of the anomaly her father had seen in her early on?

"Your mother told me stories about an ancestor who

possessed abilities like yours. She told these stories to me so that I would watch for signs. Watch *you* for them, just as her mother had watched her," her father said. "I conferred with the elders at Landau's compound, fearing what your future might hold. They had to know about you, and why I hadn't presented you to one of their sons."

"So, what am I?" she demanded, dreading the answer to the question, and knowing she had to have it.

"Werewolf," he said. "But with something else at your core. Not just a she-wulf, Rosalind. Nor just showing vampire traits. I believe you are part something else, as well."

His expression had grown dull with sadness and regret. He spoke again before she could protest or argue.

"You have in you the traits of another supernatural creature, one that is noted for announcing oncoming death. Legends abound of this creature in other countries, but not so much here."

"What are you saying? What creature?"

"I fear that you are, deep inside, a hybrid. As far as I know, there has only been one such mixture, and that was your great-great-grandmother. The tale says she was a Lycan who was saved by the very Death-caller slated to announce her death. She lived, and went on to mate with another full-blooded Were. But there was a consequence for cheating Death. In being saved by a creature that was destined to cry of death, some of that spirit's traits passed into your relative. The offspring of her and her Lycan mate was unique. Special, with special skills like yours. She was called Night Wulf."

Rosalind scooted backward on the bed until she felt the hard support of the wall against her back. It seemed that her father would allow her no room for avoiding the secrets she had been asking for, but each one seemed like a blow.

"I guess," he said, "that those stories were true."

Rosalind wanted to shout for him to stop, and tell him she'd had enough. But she was riveted. She was starved for explanations for the turmoil that had always roiled inside her.

"Go on," she said.

Her father nodded. "From this incident, we must assume that your form can vary according to the species you focus on. You fought vampires, and so you became somewhat like them. You got their fangs."

He took a breath. "We must see if you'll change back to Lycan after leaving the bloodsuckers. I have no idea what to do if you don't. I doubt if anyone would know. The elders of the Landau pack saw you. They saw the fangs. I've promised to keep you away from the world until we do know what's to happen, for your protection and theirs."

Rosalind felt a howl rising that was frighteningly similar to the one she had issued in the park. She didn't dare allow it to escape. Her father's explanations had alleged that the other call had risen from unknown depths because she possessed depths she wasn't aware of. What was a Death-caller? What did that even mean?

He was also telling her that she had become stuck physically between Were and the vampires she been attempting to kill while aiding her big brown werewolf. And that her body also hid something else that labeled her a Night Wulf.

The title itself was ominous, and produced a shiver.

If that wasn't bad enough, her father truly believed

that she had become infused with the particles of a fanged, blood-drinking species that was her enemy. And it was true. Her Lycan teeth had molded to resemble those of another species.

"What's wrong with my pelt?" she managed to ask. "You say black as if that has meaning."

Her father got to his feet. He looked down at her with the same expression of frustration that he'd worn whenever she had ignored his counsel in the past. "There are no black-pelted werewolves, Rosalind. It was the first sign of something being amiss. An early warning."

Too stunned to speak, Rosalind watched her father head for the door. She felt sick. Her father hadn't wanted her to know any of this, but how could he have kept something so important from her? What had he been thinking?

She supposed he hadn't wanted her to feel different. Then again, maybe, just maybe, he'd had the protection of others foremost in his mind as he had harbored and basically held her captive all her life.

Black pelt, black heart?

Freak.

"I've protected you. I warned you about that excess energy," he said as the door began to close behind him. Before the metallic click of the lock, his voice took on a hint of her own level of despair. "God knows I tried."

Rosalind stared after him, hearing his words repeat over and over in her head. Inside her, alongside her wulf, lived some kind of Otherworldly chameleon that had to be chained now that it had shown up.

Could she be, in part, a creature that was a harbinger of doom, whose purpose was to announce the death of others, without knowing about it all this time? A creature able to absorb the traits of Others, and make them her own?

God…

Was that what a *Death-caller* was? Another word for Banshee?

Hadn't she heard in that disturbing howl in the park the unspoken message "Death comes"?

"Heaven help me."

All those secrets she had so desperately wanted to know about, all those whispers about being special, had turned out to be really bad news.

Chapter 14

Colton sat with his head in his hands on a cot in a room no bigger than eight square feet. The quarters were too small for pacing and too big for hiding from the current level of his pain, half of which he attributed to the surprise of so many recent discoveries.

Jared Kirk had told him that his pain might return, and the elder had no idea what that diagnosis meant. If the pain got any worse, he might lose his mind.

Nevertheless, he'd had to take the time to settle down and focus on the fact that rationalizations were the bane of his new existence.

He was becoming an entity that had no name other than ghost, and it was possible that term was indicative of the hazy area between being Lycan and some other nameless surprise.

There was also a fair chance that being a ghost meant

inhabiting the colorless, amorphous space between life and death in such a way that he might never get over it, or back to normal.

He had looked Death in the eye, he'd been told, but he didn't remember Death looking back. All that he knew for certain was that he had dreamed of a female's soft lips on his, of a hissed breath into his lungs, of consciousness slipping away…and that when he had awakened from the void, following his fight in the park, he had sealed himself to a female also in transition. His lover, in truth, had taken on aspects of the same monsters that had murdered his family.

"Vampire," he said with distaste.

In strange surroundings the word sounded even worse than usual.

If Rosalind evolved into being more like a vampire than she already was, what came next for her? A desire for blood?

Would their bond be broken by the same unseen force that had put them together, if that were the case? What if it wasn't? Would he eventually want to harm her for those new fangs or, God forbid, would she want to hurt him?

"Fine mess."

He wondered if vows had a pecking order that required the first one to take precedence. His allegiance to his family came first. It's what he had meant to take care of in that park.

Now, he had promised to watch over a female he was supposed to stay away from; one her father had insinuated might very well turn out to be a danger to others. This all seemed too much of a fantasy to be real…until he looked at his hands, which were ribbed with the evidence of wounds that a Lycan would be able to heal, if a Lycan were pure Lycan.

"Has all this come out of my wish for vengeance? In following my anger, have I somehow accidentally unleashed dark forces that are beyond my comprehension?"

His question fell flat in the wood-paneled room. Colton glanced to the window, high above the cot, for enlightenment, needing to feel the sun on his face, wanting a reminder of the touch of Rosalind's healing heat. Wanting her lips, her eyes and her luscious body.

Was Rosalind's current transition his fault, since she had been helping him when it occurred?

Each pulse that thrummed against his neck brought with it a ribbon of pain, and at the same time, an unquenchable carnal craving for Rosalind. The image of the savagery of his parents' deaths had dimmed for the moment, overtaken by a new threshold of lust for Rosalind, whatever the hell she was to become.

And whatever the hell was to become of him.

What if he proved to be the last of his clan, and this imprinting had gone astray?

Conversely, even if he had let his parents down by not being able to protect them from all existing evils, couldn't he make amends by saving Rosalind from a similar fate?

Jared Kirk had said that vampires might come after her here. Not only vampires, but other things, as well. Colton had no idea what that meant. Police training was so far from the parameters of this world, it did him no good at all. Otherwise, he might question why the Landaus, who had brought him back from the brink of death, couldn't have helped Rosalind in some way.

"Well," he whispered, watching dust motes dance as his palm hit the surface of the cot, "I suppose we didn't give them the chance."

It was a moot point now. They were tucked away in the Everglades. He truly was out of his element in this balmy jungle. What help he could offer here might turn out to be minuscule at best.

Another ribbon of pain struck somewhere behind his rib cage. He wondered if it might just be his heart, aching.

"Rosalind," he whispered, needing to say her name. Needing to see his body's reaction to the thought of her, and if that reaction had dimmed with the meager attempt at reasoning.

Nope. He wanted to see her right now. He was tired of waiting this out.

"Rosalind," he repeated, louder.

The effect she had on him hadn't been lessened by the shed's thick wooden walls. If he turned his head, he knew he would see her. If he stopped the tumultuous thoughts from whirling, he'd hear her calls.

Thinking that, Colton's heart gave one hardy kick, as if starting back up after a stall. That kick was for Rosalind, the woman he wanted so completely. Her heat beat at him in waves, and as though she was there, by his side. Her voice was in his ears, her own need reflected in the eyes he couldn't actually see.

"Sweet wulf."

My lover. For better or worse, my mate.

Frustration ripped through him as Colton got to his feet.

"Who else will come for you?" he remarked as the idea of Others arriving weighed heavily in his mind.

Jared Kirk obviously feared who and what those Others might be. The elder Were did have his daughter's safety at heart, and that was why he seemed like her jailer.

"A freak to protect a freak," Colton whispered.

Kirk knew how hard his request would be, to protect Rosalind without touching her. Colton wasn't sure he could honor that request, despite its significance. Rosalind was like catnip to his wulf, and she called out to him now, in his mind, in a voice like fire.

Or was that fire merely another stab of pain related to his injuries?

No matter which thing it turned out to be, and hoping to keep his sanity intact for a while longer, Colton covered his ears.

Evening arrived. Before checking the clock on the table, Rosalind knew when she woke up that the sun sat lower in the sky. She'd grown colder and more restless. She hadn't meant to sleep, dreading the coming of night, but had been so tired.

The ache of the chain around her ankle had doubled. As if the links had been dipped in flames, they now robbed her of breath each time she moved. But her jaws were taut in a way that wasn't normal, and had to be indicative of the awful changes in her mouth that her father had been waiting for.

Hell, she really was a mixture of Lycan and monster. More than just a freak, she was an abomination. And yet it was curious how much she felt like herself, in spite of all that.

Tugging again at the chain, Rosalind glanced to the locked door, then to the window. She had always been strong, and felt a surge of strength now. She had never craved freedom more than she did at that moment. Freedom, and a big brown werewolf's overheated loins.

Bracing herself on the edge of the mattress with both hands on the chain, she yanked as hard as she could. The chain stretched by inches. The wall behind the bed groaned. Crawling on hands and knees, Rosalind found an iron ring embedded into the wall's support beam. That beam had cracked slightly.

Riding out a wave of dizziness, she stared at the heavy metal piece that had to have always been there, hidden, for such a time as this. For a time when her father's long-anticipated fears might come true, and an abomination would need restraint.

Her father had planned for this. He had been prepared.

"Damn him. Damn everything."

Her body tightened by anger, Rosalind tugged again at the chain, utilizing the power of her bunched muscles. She heard a crack, and fell back as the ring came free.

Quickly, she got to her feet.

Dragging the short length of metal links, Rosalind crossed the room. The chain clanked on the floorboards as she opened the window, and again when she climbed onto the sill and was met by a dark, damp, slightly sinister Everglades breeze.

"Haven't you heard of doors?" someone asked as her two bare feet hit the ground outside.

Rosalind stayed in a crouched position, ready to spring away.

"It's not safe for you to be out here," Colton Killion said. "Not tonight, or any night in the near future, I imagine."

Rosalind straightened slowly and narrowed her gaze on the space beneath the grove of trees bordering the driveway. A lightness shone there that wasn't affiliated with the moon. It was her ghost wulf's paleness.

Her heart dialed into the rapid rhythm of his, finding it familiar, liking the sensation of two hearts beating as one. She easily scented the passion he withheld, and headed toward him, drawn by the pheromones in the air.

"Wait," he cautioned in a tone tinged with uncertainty. "Don't come closer. You can't get closer."

She paused to absorb what he had said. The warning hurt more than the fangs stretching her mouth out of shape.

"So," she said, searching for control that was already slipping. "You believe my father."

"Don't you?"

"I have fangs, so what's not to believe?"

"Do you have them now?" he asked tentatively.

"Yes."

To his credit, Colton didn't wince or drop his gaze to her mouth.

"Your father says that touching you will make things worse," he said.

"I wonder if anything could be worse."

"It's torture," he confessed in a voice hushed by strain. "You warned that it would hurt if we were separated. Being here and unable to touch you trumps that."

Rosalind was afraid to shut her eyes or ignore his warning. What if the things they had been told were true, and instead of him changing her, she'd hurt him instead? His musky, masculine presence hadn't been dulled by his circumstances. He seemed to fill her vision, larger than life, every bit as sexy as he had been.

Her longing for him threatened to outweigh any scrap of common sense she tried to drum up, when she had never been particularly good at common sense in the first place.

"My father didn't tell me enough. I don't think he knows what to do," she said, lowering her gaze.

"Neither do I," he confessed.

"Did he tell you what to expect? Why I'm chained?"

"Chained?" her ghostly lover repeated, as though his throat had gone dry.

She moved her foot. The chain made a dull thudding sound in the dirt.

"Hell. I had no idea," he said.

"Now that you do?"

"I'm staying. I'll try my best to keep them from you if your father is telling the truth. But who, I wonder, will be able to keep me from you?"

Rosalind hated common sense almost more than anything, but couldn't give in this time. Not yet. The male across from her had been hurt enough already, some of it at her expense.

"Who does he believe will be coming?" she asked. "He failed to mention that to me."

"He's guessing that vampires may have your scent, and now that you're more like them it will be easier for the vipers to find you."

"Why would they want to find me?"

Hearing his short bark of frustrated laughter, Rosalind looked up.

"I suppose," he suggested, "that they might want what I want, if they had any normal body parts left."

The laughter hadn't reached his eyes.

"But the thought of anyone else getting near you for

any reason whatsoever is not only unacceptable, it's outright disgusting."

He paused to draw in a breath. Rosalind did the same, as if their lungs were united in the search for air.

"If they arrive, I'll fight them. This I swear," her ghostly protector said.

"And if they don't come? If no one arrives and this is nothing more than supposition and my father's personal fear?"

He touched his mouth, his gesture alluding to her fangs. "Don't those make your father's fear reasonable?"

"Yes." Her voice was faint.

"Vampires are the children of the night, Rosalind. Perhaps we only need to worry about that."

"Night has always been our time, too. Wolf time. Are we to ignore what we are?"

"For a while, we'll have to fight our nature. In the meantime, it isn't a good idea for you to be out here after sundown."

"But I have only just found you," she said, taking one more step toward him and changing the subject completely. Or maybe just bringing their attention back to it. "And you're to stay away from me."

"I'm here," he reiterated, his expression highlighting the dark circles under his eyes. "I'm here for you. Trust me on this."

"Maybe never to touch me again?"

When he didn't reply to that terrible question, Rosalind shook her head. "Guarding me won't be an easy job. I'd rather face what's coming now than let this draw out."

"Please, Rosalind. Listen to reason." His hands were

raised, as though he had already forgotten that he wasn't to touch her.

She held up a hand. "Your wulf calls to me, and I have to refuse that call. The night also calls to me. If I can't have one of those two things, I'll take the other, or go mad."

Her anger faded when sadness replaced all other emotion on her ghostly lover's face. That sadness overwhelmed her, though there was nothing she could do to stop it.

"You are Lycan," he said. "As am I. We can withstand this. We face what life brings, and land on our feet."

Rosalind looked at him with pangs of regret so deep-seated, it felt to her that her soul was aching. This brave Were had been wounded while trying to avenge his family, and might never be the same. There was no greater show of respect for his family than that kind of sacrifice. And he'd do it again, for her.

She had tried to help him, and honor his fight. The result had joined them together, and at the same time brought them more pain.

She could not remain apart from him, and feared to try. Colton was the epitome of what every Were should be. Still, she so very badly wanted him to forget about honor and promises, and pretend they were back at the Landau's wall, in each other's passionate embrace.

The remembered heat of that meeting made her thighs quiver. The ridiculous idea that vampires could possibly experience emotions like regret and sorrow made her feel slightly less frightened as she stared at Colton. And because she felt those emotions, and so much more, she supposed that she couldn't really be like the creatures her father feared would find her. Her mind was her own. Her lust for Colton was the desire for mating with a Were, wulf to wulf, not for biting him with another species' teeth.

Her body thrummed and twitched for the kind of mating that had sealed them together in the first place. She wanted him, now; everything he had to offer. She wanted to kiss him, straddle him, take him into her body and make him howl with delight. She wanted to tell him this.

If he'd believe in her, she could confess such a thing. If he would meet her halfway, anything was possible.

Please take that step, she sent silently to him.

I need you. Can't you see?

"Rosalind," he whispered, as if her name were some kind of magical talisman for retaining his wits. In his voice lay traces of the dilemma he faced with her father's mandate. This magnificent male was choosing to do the right thing.

Rosalind backed up, fighting a lump in her throat, sure she'd choke if she spoke again.

"What is it?" he asked, concerned, striding forward to stand in all his white glory near the base of the steps. Tall, proud, Were, in spite of the visible remnants of his injuries and the draining away of a golden future, the sight of Colton Killion hurt her. They both wanted the same thing. Yet he was unable to throw her to the ground and do to her what they both craved because…

"You made a promise to the wrong Kirk," she said to him.

His interrupted breath moved her lungs. Her pulse matched his, beat for beat. And she couldn't have him because they were both something other than what they were supposed to be.

"It's too much," she added.

Cursing the initial rise of rebellion that had gotten her to this point in time, she whispered, "If you can't touch me, then you can't stop me."

Spinning as if the links attached to her ankle were no more than a nuisance, Rosalind took off at a dead run in the opposite direction, refusing to allow her tears to fall.

"Shit!" Colton shouted. "Are you insane?"

His words hung in the air, useless. The fanged, feisty Rosalind had already disappeared into the tangle of trees.

He took off after her. What he would do when he caught up with her was anyone's guess. If he didn't touch her, he'd have no way to bring her back. Reasoning hadn't done the trick.

Where the hell was her father, anyway?

The house was dark. No lights lit the porch or yard; just the faint glow of a partial moon behind the trees. Didn't Kirk believe in electricity? Without lights, anything could hide in the dark.

His heart rate peaked as he stretched his stride. Rosalind's special scent saturated the air, and in that scent, he could perceive the state of her emotions. She was angry, nervous and sad. A terrible mix for running through a night that might be populated with monsters.

He glanced at the trees as he raced by, thinking how bloodless Rosalind's beautiful face had been, and of the wildness in her eyes.

"Rosalind! Stop!"

He was feeling at odds with the world around him.

Dismissing the pain shooting through his torso, and on legs as heavy as lead, Colton ran. He hoped Rosalind wasn't actually as nuts as this action made her seem, and prayed that the bloodsuckers actually had no way of tracking what their now doubly dead pals had witnessed in that park.

It took exactly twenty more big strides for him to find out that his wishes weren't worth much.

Chapter 15

What lay hidden in the dark made the rest of the already strange night seem tame by comparison.

Colton stumbled to a sudden halt. Hate twisted his gut. The vampires had arrived like a plague of bloodthirsty locusts. A series of eerie, high-pitched signals arising from corpse-like throats rent the croaking, frog-infested night. And then the frog sounds ceased.

There was no more pain in him, only cold. It felt to Colton as though his life was slipping away from him one chilled inch at a time as he waited for whatever would happen next.

"You can't have her. I'll die first," he shouted as the weight of the vampires' presence added to the thickness of the dark's unsettled atmosphere.

He cast glances in all directions, whipping his head from side to side, seeing nothing, but sensing the dead gathering someplace not too far away from where he stood.

Without stopping to wonder why he sensed this connection to them, Colton strode forward, heading for the trees. He knew better than to shout for Rosalind because if she answered and the vamps hadn't already found her, they certainly would after that.

Heaven and hell were here, on both sides of him. A succulent lover vied for his attention, as did the plague of blood-drinking creeps.

"I suppose I've already cheated Death once," he muttered. "Maybe I owe him one."

Rolling his shoulders, he moved on, determined to see this through. Damn if he didn't hear Rosalind's voice before the protective thoughts had dissipated, though.

Her voice was raised. She was egging the bloodsuckers on, taunting the monsters, inviting them to find her.

A horrible thought entered his head that caused him to stagger. What if Rosalind was hoping to die, and in that way set both herself and him free from this ongoing nightmare?

The thought was so dreadful that Colton shook off his hesitation and sprinted toward the echo of her voice.

The brush he fought his way through was thick, damp and clingy. His borrowed boots sank into a half inch of mud that slowed him down by tugging at his steps like quicksand would have in some other godforsaken place.

Pushing through the foliage fiercely, he managed to find a path fragrant with Rosalind's scent. Out of necessity, he ventured a whisper.

A reply came in the form of a startled roar of protest.

Not Rosalind. Someone else. Not vampire, but Were.

Colton spun in place, sniffing the air. Detecting a Lycan presence behind him, he leaped to one side of the path and vaulted over a fallen tree as the newcomer's presence grew stronger. No full moon rode the sky tonight, which meant that this Lycan walked in man form. Since this place was so remote, there was only one Were this could be.

Jared Kirk appeared on the path, wearing dark clothes that blended with the surroundings. A dangerous expression hung on his features. Grasped in his hands was a strange instrument Colton had seen in history books that had been modified with a futuristic flare into a lethal-looking crossbow.

"I asked you not to touch her," Kirk said as he approached. "In light of that, I figured you can't fight this one alone."

Colton nodded, relieved.

"How many monsters are there?" Kirk asked.

"More than one. Do you have any idea where Rosalind would have gone?"

"I think I do. How close are they?"

"Their foul stink is all around us, but they must have gone ahead, after her, alerted by her voice."

Kirk nodded. "She wasn't always so foolish. Not until this."

"She's leading them away from the house," Colton said, only then realizing that this was true, and that something in her scent had communicated her intentions to him. "Leading them away from you, is my guess, and away from me."

Kirk seemed to momentarily slump before regaining

height aided by a rigid spine. "All this sacrifice non-sense is for the birds. I don't want to lose her."

"Neither do I," Colton confessed.

Their gazes met.

"So be it," Kirk concluded with a wave of his hand. "Do you have any more secrets that might help, other than having already survived a vampire attack, and having some inner connection to my daughter?"

"As a matter of fact, I do," Colton said. "Small help as it may prove."

Calling up his anger, letting the night breeze waft over his tingling skin, Colton tore off his shirt, unbuttoned his pants and kicked off the cumbersome borrowed boots. With a glance to a sky mostly hidden by the tall trees, he envisioned the moon shining there, and opened his eyes wide to let that light in.

An incendiary heat began to churn in his muscles as he began his transformation. In the blink of an eye, he was a werewolf…big, strapping, white-furred, with an insatiable appetite for kicking vampires back to the hell they had arisen from.

Facing Jared Kirk with trepidation over what this new kind of confession might bring, and with his razor claws raised, Colton let out an ear-piercing howl.

"Dear God," Kirk whispered, letting the oath fade as Colton turned toward the rose scent that he knew would lead him to Rosalind.

The monsters had heard her call, Rosalind thought.

She should have been scared out of her wits. Instead, her rage for all the changes these creatures had brought to her life gave her the fuel she needed to fight them now.

The first gaunt, white-skinned spirit appeared as if it had risen from a bog. The second one dropped from a tree in the same way its malevolent brothers had fallen on Colton that other night.

They didn't immediately attack; just stood there looking at her as if they were waiting for something or someone else. Rosalind gritted her pointed teeth.

"I'd rather be truly and completely dead than be like you," she said when neither of the monsters moved.

The creatures didn't respond. When one of them cocked its bony head with a stiff movement more reminiscent of a robot than anything that had once been human, Rosalind remembered how she'd used her claws to tear through the necks of their brothers, and how simple that had seemed at the time.

"You're not welcome here," she said.

The cold brush of a third vampire came in from her right side. Rosalind ventured a glance. This one was by itself, and had stopped several feet away from where she stood.

It resembled the other two. Nothing she noticed made this sucker seem different. Yet the way the two vampires on her opposite side focused intently on the newcomer suggested some sort of vampire pecking order.

"Go away." She directed this warning to the tall, sinewy creature with frozen, emotionless features. "This is wolf ground and you are trespassing."

"Wolf?" the vampire repeated in a dry, mocking voice.

"I'm still one of them in spite of some recent additions," Rosalind warned. "Don't be fooled. I'm more wulf than not."

The other two vampires made stunted, grating

sounds as if tendons had to move in order for them to use their voice boxes. The ugly noises matched their grim exteriors.

Rosalind's claws burst through her fingertips. She hid her hands behind her back. Simultaneously, or at least in rapid succession, her incisors began to lengthen. She didn't dare cry out against this, sensing that any move, even the slightest visible flutter, would set these creatures off. She had to stand her ground, hide her fear and catch them off guard, if that was at all possible.

One of the monsters inched forward.

Rosalind screamed inside at the intrusion. The back of her neck chilled up.

As if it had heard her feral protest, the vampire who had spoken to her grinned. There was no mistaking this show of exaggerated fangs for anything other than scare factor. Between pasty lips were two sharp, yellow teeth that were much longer than her own.

"We came for you," the vampire announced, the weakness of its voice yet another example of deception, and of an untapped hidden agenda.

"Go back to wherever you came from while you're still able to," she shouted.

"We came for you," one of the others echoed, confirming for Rosalind that vampire thoughts ran along one thread.

"Tough luck," she snapped. "I'm happy where I am. If you get any closer, I'll show you just how happy being a werewolf makes me, and how good at it I am."

A silent alarm went off inside Rosalind seconds before two of the monsters lunged. Chattering fangs came at her as she ducked sideways and raised her claws.

The first swift strike hit one vampire in the chest and

sent it staggering backward with its sorry excuse for flesh torn down to its ribs. Thin blood, black in color with a putrid odor, gushed from the wound.

Rosalind didn't have time to see if that freak was out of commission. Another vampire was at her throat, tearing at her shirt as the third bloodsucker looked on. She fought the attack off with a grunt of disgust and a rising rage, moving fast, striking hard.

The ferocity of her hatred for these creatures caused a dramatic internal burn. Her throat heated up. That heat quickly spread to her shoulders, arms and finally to her chest, where it called up a glimpse of unfamiliar power, a power out of focus and comprised of sizzling crimson sparks.

When she shoved the monster off her, it flew through the air. Unfazed, it leaped back to its feet and came at her again. Before it reached her, though, the toothy vampire she thought of as the leader of this group had her by the throat in a tight grip. So fast, she hadn't seen this coming.

Its bleached, awful, angular face came close. "Not wolf," it said with a jaw-shattering snap of fangs. "Not anymore."

Vampires flowed through the trees as though the night itself had become liquid. Shades of dark on dark. Stealthily creeping shadows.

Colton jerked to a stop with Kirk at his back. His lure had worked, at least in part. The howl had brought some of the monsters to him, and every one of them attending this little hunting party would be one less to reach Rosalind, wherever she was.

He sensed five bloodsuckers and smelled another

three in the distance. The odor of those distant three had mingled with Rosalind's scent, which meant that if they hadn't yet found her, they were close.

He roared with fury.

Kirk had the crossbow in position, sited on the path. The elder Were gave an angry grunt as the vampires came on, temporarily setting aside his innate fear about what Colton had turned out to be. Colton matched that grunt with a growl that rolled threateningly through the tangle of trees.

A pair of vampires materialized together. Eyeing him with red-rimmed eyes as if unsure of how to proceed against some new thing that reeked of power and death, their uneasiness rumbled through them in discordant hisses and squeaks.

Perhaps they recognized the results of their damage to his face. Maybe they smelled the strangeness in his blood, there because he had survived an attack from their own kind.

Their hesitation worked to Colton's advantage. Kirk's bow sang with a high note, striking one monster in the chest and passing all the way through. The silver-tipped wooden arrow had staked the creature's withered heart, and shattered the viper into a shower of dust. But such a weapon also had in its makeup the promise of a dual purpose. Its silver tip could just as easily bring down a werewolf, or the ghost of one.

Had Kirk been late to this gathering because he was adding the silver coating to the arrows, thus hedging his bets?

There was no time to consider that. More vampires dropped in, their ranks totaling four. This might not have been a problem, once upon a time, but with one

Were in man form, and one still wobbly on his legs, it posed a threat.

The four vamps charged as a team. Colton's claws, like moving gears of revolving steel, cut cleanly through the first. A second arrow from the crossbow took down another. As Kirk reloaded, Colton felt the Were hesitate for a moment before shooting wild, missing an oncoming bloodsucker by a hair.

"On your right!" he shouted to Colton, and Colton whirled in time to fell a vampire with a staggering blow of one swinging arm. Seconds later, he was on the creature, straddling the downed freak so that he could get a better look at it.

Black eyes, intently focused and devoid of emotion, stared back as the creature writhed on the ground. It moved like a rabid dog, its fangs snapping in an attempt to get at Colton.

Colton's growl, as he tore the creature's head off with both of his hands, avowed: *She is not like you, and never will be.*

Bouncing back to his feet to grab hold of the bloodsucker that had leaped onto Kirk's back, he added: *Neither am I.*

Kirk wheeled and ducked, dislodging the attacker. With surprising dexterity, the Were was up again. His next arrow slashed through the bloodsucker at close range, and the fanged viper exploded in Colton's face.

Where is she? Colton silently demanded as the ashes rained down. Brushing the gray dust from his face, he turned toward the scent in the distance. Kirk followed his gaze.

"Go," Kirk said. "Save her."

Needing no such permission, Colton took off, utilizing every bit of speed he possessed even as he started to feel his energy drain away. It was too soon for a battle like this. He'd faced Death not that many days before, and hadn't finished healing. Although rage drove what strength he did possess, he wasn't right inside. He knew this. So did Rosalind's father.

The situation was extremely precarious, and the silver tips on Kirk's arrows were meaningful. Maybe Kirk knew something Colton didn't about what being a ghost meant, and that bit of unshared knowledge was what hung like a barrier between them.

Rosalind.

Chanting her name made Colton feel closer to her as he chased after the fragrance of roses, sensing that trouble wasn't far ahead.

Chapter 16

Rosalind stared into the eyes of pure evil, meeting the gaze of the monster holding her with a black gaze of her own.

Likely she didn't fear this as much as she should have because her wulf waited, held back for now, but clawing at her insides, ready for action. It was possible these monsters didn't know about her ability to shift with or without the moon's permission. It was also possible that the vamps wouldn't know what to do with a Night Wulf, if the darkness she had hidden inside her were to suddenly unfurl.

"What do you want?" she demanded, her breath nearly completely cut off by the vampire's grip on her throat.

Her demand was met by silence. She considered whether these monsters had limited resources for speech, and if this one had used up all of his. Its eyes glowed like polished stone.

She sensed something else. There was mist on her skin, and then a sudden temperature drop in the small clearing where she and two of the attackers stood.

The vampire holding her lifted its head. Its comrade uttered a whine. And before Rosalind could allow her senses to form an image of what was about to happen, a white beast, huge, muscled and angry, shot forward with the speed of a bullet, and she was knocked to the ground.

The werewolf was lethal in the cold swiftness of his strike. It was also a sight she would never forget. This wulf was much fiercer, much more dangerous than she remembered. Dark stains ringed his muzzle, matching the circles beneath his eyes. His chest was as broad as a lion's. His teeth were bared.

It was her lover.

The sudden silence in the clearing was alarming. As one vampire went down beneath the ghost wulf's hurtling bulk, the remaining vampire with a hold on Rosalind began to drag her toward the trees. But its grip on her neck had slackened when she fell.

Wresting herself free, Rosalind jumped to her feet. Lunging at the creature, she shifted shape. With the power of her wulf flowing through her, she drove the monster back with black-as-midnight furred arms and a vampire's lethal incisors.

She pinned the monster to a tree before it had time to register what had gone wrong. And as she stared at what she held, her vision went red, as though the night itself had changed in color and texture.

Rosalind blinked, listened. There was silence in the empty chest of the monster. There was no breath.

Not like you.

Her head bent forward. Her fangs grazed the monster's neck as she sniffed out the perfect place for a final kill. But she was torn from her attacker by the muscular power of a larger beast, and flung to the side. Leaping back, Rosalind fixed her gaze on the frozen face of the surprised vampire who dared to trespass on private property this night, as the white ghost of a once golden-brown Lycanthrope dealt that monster its fatal blow in her place.

Ashes swirled in the energy-enhanced space with the fervor of a small tornado. The night turned from red to gray. And then her white wulf turned to her, covered in ash.

He reached out to her with his arms open, wulf calling to wulf, and it seemed to Rosalind that those arms were all that mattered in the world.

She went to him, and felt his arms close around her. Enfolded inside his revved-up heat, she experienced a moment of pure bliss, and a sensation of security that she'd never felt before. That moment, however, was followed by a jolt of unexpected pain that shook her head to foot.

Alerted by the sound she made, the white wulf let her go.

Not me, she sent to him.

She wasn't hurting. It was his pain she was feeling; pain that continued to rip through her even though they no longer touched. Jolt after jolt of physical agony blasted her. Swaying, she closed her eyes.

A growl brought her back. Colton's growl.

She could hardly tune in with her attention. He was trying to tell her something. Confused, racked with the knowledge of how Colton was really feeling, though he managed to appear in control of his injuries for the most part, Rosalind glanced down.

She was still furred-up. Her muscles were tense and corded with strain. But her pelt was no longer a pure, midnight black. Fine streaks of white, like a manifestation of the streaks of Colton's pain, ran through her fur, a matrix of ghostly lacings that altered her appearance completely.

Dazed, Rosalind looked to the ghost wulf that now stood a few feet away. He met her gaze knowingly, his wolfish face registering an emotion much deeper than either surprise or fear.

Her father might have had been right, and Colton had finally realized this. By falling into his arms, she had taken on some of the outward aspects of yet another entity. A ghost wulf's characteristics. If she had stayed there, in his embrace, what would have happened? Did any of them know?

She ran her tongue over her fangs. Still there.

Looking up at the sky, Rosalind opened her mouth. Her howl, which seemed to go on endlessly, rang out with a disturbing blend of anger, frustration and utter despair.

Colton melted back into human form. Somehow, he had to reassure Rosalind, comfort her when neither of them knew what was going to happen next.

"It's all right," he said. "It has to be all right."

She had again closed the eyes he desperately wanted to see return to their former emerald green.

"Change back," he said. "Change now."

Rosalind did as he asked. In a swift download of human traits, she lost the wulf parts and stood there facing him, the defiance in her expression gone, her hair tousled and half in her face.

Her sleek, bare skin glowed with a faint sheen of moisture. Her long hair covered her breasts. Her legs were unsteady.

Attached to her slim ankle was the short length of chain that her father had tried to bind her with. Its cuff had branded her flesh with a reddish ring that resembled a burn.

Colton studied her naked loveliness. In human form, the only sign of her body having adapted to anything ghostlike were the number of white streaks riddling her hair, and the fact that she had gone pale, to the point of being as white as a sheet.

He exhaled, restraining himself from grabbing her. Maybe the white hair and paler skin wasn't too significant, but what the hell did he know? Each time he touched her, would she change more? Because of her nature, and what lay in her bloodstream, would she beat him to what he was going to become?

The effort of restraint cost him. His energy had diminished. He had so little of it left.

"Don't presume to know what's best for me," he gently chastised, with his theory on her having run away to save him from vampires in mind. "Because anything having to do with you getting hurt would be the end of me."

She remained motionless. Not even a hand moved.

"What's to become of me, Colton?" she asked. "If I'm not to be Lycan, then what I am is anyone's guess.

I swear I didn't know this when I came to you. When we..."

"Bonded."

"Yes," she whispered.

"It doesn't matter," he said. "I was attracted to the Lycan in you, and I see it in you still. You're beautiful, Rosalind. You're my wulf, and it's too late to take back anything we've done. Nor would I want to."

After a beat of silence had passed, she said, "He will keep me here forever. You know that."

"Surely that's important, at least for the time being. You do see this?"

Her gaze slid past him. "How many more of them will come?" She then repeated a question from their earlier conversation, as if it had more meaning for her now. "Why do they want me?"

"We'll have to find out. It will be our goal."

"I want to touch you."

"I'd like nothing more."

"I want more than that."

"So do I."

"How can anyone like us be isolated without going mad?" she asked.

"You're not alone. I'm here."

Rosalind raised her chin, and turned her head. "I won't be chained," she said to her father as he approached. "I may be an abomination, but I still have my mind."

Kirk set down his crossbow, and removed his shirt. Careful not to move too quickly, he draped the shirt around Rosalind's thin, shaking shoulders.

"All right," Kirk said, his voice low, almost ragged. "No restraints."

And then, unexpectedly, Rosalind's father slid soundlessly to the ground.

Colton could now see that the shirt covering Rosalind was stained with blood. He smelled the iron in the air.

The vamp that had jumped on the elder Lycan's back had to have dealt Kirk a blow that Colton had missed at the time. Blood ran from the wound and dripped down his left arm, but Kirk's neck was clean. The blood drinker hadn't taken a bite out of the elder, and for that, Rosalind's father was extremely lucky.

Rosalind fell to her knees beside her father before Colton had drawn a full breath. She didn't need to address the blood pooling on the ground beside him. Demonstrating the truth in her statement about retaining her wits, she said, "The wound is deep, but not from teeth."

Colton nodded. "If there are more bloodsuckers around, they'll be on us like flies."

Gesturing for Rosalind to step aside, he picked up her father and slung the big man over his shoulder. He wasn't going to mention how much this hurt, or how very weary he was.

"Do you know where we are now, and how to get back?" he asked Rosalind.

"I know exactly where we are," Rosalind said with a sweeping glance that covered the area. "This place is sacred. It's where my mother was killed."

Colton took seconds to confront that news and the pain Rosalind had to be feeling on top of all the other things going on. But there was no time to spare for condolences, and no time to think about his parents.

"Let's get your father home," he said through gritted teeth, fearing that calling up his wulf again so soon after losing his strength wasn't in the cards. He'd have to carry Rosalind's father the old-fashioned way and hope the cabin wasn't far. He had to make sure nothing further happened to Rosalind on the way.

Cop and Were, he thought. He'd never needed the strength of being either of those things as much as he did right that minute.

"Lead the way," he said to Rosalind. "Be on guard."

"I swear to you that they will never sneak up on me again," she promised.

And he believed her.

Chapter 17

No vampires appeared or attacked on the way back to the cabin. Nor did Colton smell their nasty presence.

Rosalind had adopted a pace that was sensitive to his burden. Jared Kirk was a large man and a wulf. The combined weight of both proved formidable for the ghost of Colton's former self.

However, having Kirk injured meant the Were couldn't take care of his daughter for a while. In his favor, as an elder, Kirk would be able to heal quickly enough and be back on his feet soon. In the meantime, without Kirk acting as guardian, would their deal of keeping his hands off of Rosalind be honored, or broken?

Colton's sable-haired lover seemed to walk a fine line between fragility and a noticeable toughness of spirit. It had to feel to her like she had a split personality; a tug-of-war between the wulf and the darker forces trying to get at her.

Seen from behind, in human form, partially naked, and moving gracefully through the brush, Rosalind looked much the same as she had before this latest fight. She smelled the same, and that fragrance continued to affect him in ways too personal to acknowledge.

Still, he'd seen something in her eyes, and had heard a chilling note in her voice when she had promised him that vampires wouldn't be able to sneak up on her again. Because of what swam in her blood besides wulf, she had the ability to hide things from him that otherwise would have been in the open between an imprinted pair.

Rosalind seemed to glow in the night, her skin lit from within. Every move of her shoulders, legs, head, brought home the fact that he had only held her for seconds, and she was already showing changes. She moved like an animal.

He now understood the danger of Rosalind being close to others, but had yet to notice how the vampire attack tonight might have altered her further. He hated himself for watching her so closely, searching for a glimpse of evidence that she had slipped a notch further away from wulf.

The path widened at last. They had reached the clearing and the cabin. Rosalind spoke over her shoulder as if reading his mind. "I can do this."

"I know you can," he agreed.

"But you're worried."

"I've been worried since I woke up in a Landau bedroom."

"About me?"

"And about me."

"Well, at least you're honest." She waved a hand at the house. "Can you bring him inside?"

"Yes." He had just about enough strength left to get up the stairs. After that…

"It's probably best if you stay here until I get him there," he suggested.

Rosalind's slender fingers raked through her streaked hair. She stared at the tangle of black strands laced with white and said as he moved up the steps, "Why were you a cop?"

"To take care of people, and out of an earnest desire to see the little guy kept safe from the big bad predators of the world."

"You didn't have to put yourself out there for anyone," she said.

"Didn't I?"

"So now you'll take care of me."

He nodded, and shifted Kirk's weight. "Maybe I can redeem myself in some way."

"For what?"

"Not protecting my family when it was needed most."

Rosalind fell silent, probably hearing his unspoken amendment. He would have added, if he had both time and more breath, that if he couldn't do this one task, he wasn't worth the space he took up on the planet's surface. And that the goal of protecting her might in fact be the only thing keeping him on his feet at the moment, as well as keeping him from going stark raving mad over the injustices in the world.

"Meet me here after I put him down," he said. "We should talk about what to do. Together, we can reason things out."

Rosalind's eyes were hooded by rich, lush lashes that Colton wanted to feel feather over his skin. No matter how tired he felt, his feelings for her remained savage in intensity.

He swallowed back the urge to take her now, here, and shout to hell with all the rest.

Damn that vow. Damn your father for making me agree to such a promise.

Rosalind, in all her Lycan glory, with no hint of vampire fangs showing at the moment and the percentage of white in her hair gaining on the black, said, "The first room on the left is my father's."

Colton trudged slowly up the steps. He needed rest, sleep and the food Kirk had neglected to bring. More than any of those things, though, he needed to stay awake and keep Rosalind in sight. For now, anyway, and until he was relatively sure she was okay, he had to remain vigilant.

He also had to make sure that holding her for a few precious seconds hadn't done more damage to her continually rearranging system than what immediately met the eye.

As for himself, he was going to be cursed if he did or didn't do what he wanted to do…*Throw you on these steps and take all the pleasure from this union that we can get. Forget the consequences. Give in to our spirits.*

The thought had merit. Fighting it took all of his willpower. The idea of never being able to touch her or get close to Rosalind made the world and his place in it unthinkable. But the ridiculous idea that they would be compatible if she were to also become a so-called ghost was nothing more than a nagging suggestion.

Colton kept walking.

The house lay cloaked in a darkness he'd grown sick of. He crossed the floorboards to a back room, and laid Kirk on a quilt-covered bed. He then headed outside where the breeze, though humid and filled with strange swampy odors, made him breathe easier.

Rosalind was waiting for him, and so damn beautiful he fielded a spasm of pain separate from what he had so far been tolerating.

His arms were covered in her father's blood. He looked from her to those slashes of red. "What about the…"

"Blood?" Rosalind finished for him.

She was gazing into the distance, possibly gathering information he couldn't process.

"There's hardly a moment that doesn't include thirst," she confessed. "I'm not sure if it's theirs or mine. It comes and goes, but I don't think the thirst is for blood. Not for me, anyway. It's more like an urge for something I haven't yet figured out."

"What could that be?"

She cocked her head in thought. "This feels a little like lust. And like hate. The feeling contains all of the characteristics of a rising addiction that can't be escaped no matter how hard I might wish to be free of it."

She left him with that, floating up the steps effortlessly with her long hair flowing behind her.

He almost caught her hair in his hands to tug her back to him. Watching her go, though it was only into the house, was torture.

Not knowing what else to do, Colton sat on the steps with his head in his hands. He felt ill; worse now that he'd heard Rosalind's confession. He was confused, but it was imperative that he go over the options for guarding the area, as if he actually had some. This wasn't Miami. Every direction looked alike. The isolation of the Kirks' property could either be a boon or one hell of a continuous problem.

He had no inkling of how much time passed, other than noticing how the moon's path across the sky had progressed. When the smell of food reached him, his stomach roared to life. He got up on shaky legs as the door behind him opened.

"I heard your stomach growling from in there," Rosalind said, holding a plate in one hand and a glass in the other.

"What?" she added. "Preparing food isn't a talent you'd expect from a black-pelted vampire-wulf hybrid?"

Colton eyed her curiously in the faint light from the lantern she had looped over one elbow. In spite of the situation, he smiled at her remark. Funny, he thought, how normal some moments could be in the midst of chaos.

In the flickering light, he searched Rosalind's face for evidence of the black tornado he had once seen. The fighter. The empathizer. The hybrid. All he found were those large eyes looking back at him. Eyes that made his wulf stir restlessly.

"I'll be back after I finish bandaging my father," she said.

"Will he be okay?"

The conversation was stilted. Their mouths wanted to be used in other ways that involved a meeting of their lips, hot, moist tongues dancing in tandem, and drowning deep kisses.

"He'll live, just like we all seem to," Rosalind said.

Colton stared at her, not with the gaze of a protector,

but with the focus of a predator. Although he had Rosalind's father's blood on his arms, her addictive scent masked it; that dark floral mixture that was almost feline, highly sexual and impossible to resist.

He finally looked down at the plate in his hand. Temptation, he'd learned the hard way, was one hell of a beast.

Chapter 18

The chain attached to her ankle had become a pain in the ass, but Rosalind no longer felt the burn of the metal. She moved her foot impatiently, and strained to hear the night sounds. All she came up with was Colton's quiet breathing, coming from outside, and the slow thump of his heart. He hadn't moved. He was waiting for her.

Her desire to go to him burned in her like a wind-whipped fire, but she was scared, and didn't dare act on her urges. She sensed that something darker than her fears was approaching, out there beyond Colton's heady presence. The oily feel of this encroachment slithered across her skin, dirty, evil, foreign.

The monsters had found her again, and she was on her own. Colton could barely move. Her father was flat on his back. It wasn't right to involve them, see them hurt again, when this was her fight and her strange destiny.

She'd have to face this alone.

She bit her lip hard, tasting blood, regretting the secrets she hadn't shared with her lover, and wondering if omissions counted as lies.

She'd told Colton that the sight and scent of her father's blood didn't affect her, when it did. She had wanted to rub her face in the bloody rags at first. In the swamp, she'd fought the impulse to suck her father dry for keeping important information from her.

"What if you knew that, my lovely ghost?" she whispered. "And that the growing darkness inside me is like the creep of filthy fingertips up my spine. Insane, and quite inhumane."

She blinked slowly against the intensity of her regrets.

"When you opened your arms to me, I began to slip away, as if slowly losing my grip on reality."

She had assumed for a brief time that she might become one of the same shadows she had always despised. Worse yet, something her father feared.

"What would be left of me if I were to give in to that darkness? If I were to fade away, allowing others to dictate my future and how my life would or wouldn't go after this?"

Blinded by the terror of those thoughts, Rosalind looked to the window. She could use it to sidestep Colton's watchful gaze. She could go out there and meet her future face-to-face.

Get it over with.

Which choice would hurt her lover the least?

"I wish you could help me," she whispered to him.

And as fast as that, Colton was in the doorway. She wasn't really surprised. She should have realized he could hear her whispers, and possibly some of her thoughts.

His troubled eyes met hers. His heart was racing. But he would not touch her again, she heard him thinking, hating that reminder. He didn't dare hold her, because if he did, some new hell might carry her away.

Always, his thoughts were to protect her.

"I feel the same," she said, and felt her face drain of all remaining color. Though Colton's closeness brought a much-needed heat, the disturbance in the distance had grown icy.

"You're not alone in this," Colton said.

"Are you afraid of me?" she countered, searching his face.

"No. Other things, but not you."

"What other things?"

"The silly ones you're about to embrace."

Rosalind's hands fluttered by her sides. The pull in the distance dragged at her soul.

"Tell me what's out there," he said.

"Monsters."

He nodded.

"You're in pain," she said.

"Aren't you?"

"This close to you, I share yours."

"Then it seems true that your changes might have to do with emotion and feeling. A saturation of empathy."

"And the vampires? Did I empathize with them?" she said.

"What did you feel out there, the night you followed me and helped me in the park?"

"Hatred."

"Why hatred?" he asked.

"For what the blood drinkers did to your family. For what they had done to you."

"You didn't know me."

"I wanted to."

He took a moment to think about that, then said, "What did you feel, Rosalind? Exactly. Can you describe it?"

"I was angry. You had spurned me. That's why I followed you."

"When did that change?"

"After going inside your house. Hearing your howl of grief."

Colton nodded again, as if this had started to make sense to him. Excitement pitched his voice. "You helped me fight them. You sympathized with what had happened, and fought the bloodsuckers, by my side. You transferred your anger to them."

"You think that's why I became like them? Anger did this?"

"Emotion could have done it," he said. "Maybe hatred was necessary for you to access the strength to fight, but it also allowed whatever is in your blood to manifest against the creatures you fought."

Rosalind saw how serious he was. "Are you suggesting that I might take on the aspects of the creature producing in me the strongest emotion at any given time?"

"It's an idea worth considering, isn't it? Better than nothing? A starting point?"

Rosalind touched her hair. Several streaked strands slid through her fingers. "My feelings for you make me more like you? I transferred my emotion back to you after the attack tonight, and that could have saved me from adopting further vampire traits?"

"And caused the white in your hair," Colton said. "But I'm still wulf. I truly believe that. I will heal completely. And if I'm right, this could be the reason you remain wulf after we touch."

Rosalind tuned in to his excitement in the same way she adapted to the way his heart was beating.

"Come here," he said. "Closer."

She balked at his invitation. Both of her hands clutched tightly to the windowsill beside her.

"What if," he began, "you only have so much space in you for changes? What if most of that space is filled with something other than vampire?"

She read his thoughts. He couldn't remember much about the laws of physics or mathematical averages, but the suggestion about space had a certain rightness to it that spurred him on.

"Who's to say that if you felt strongly about something other than vampires, you couldn't lose the fangs and replace them with something else? Something better?"

Rosalind turned. "My father must know about this." She thought of the metal ring in the wall that had awaited the possibility of a chain attached to her ankle, and the reasons for remaining secluded from other Weres. "He's the only one who might."

"Then he will have to enlighten us. In the meantime, we can hope I'm right, can't we?" Colton said.

She took a second wary step toward him, hungry for his enthusiasm, compelled by their imprinting to further the bond.

"You want to test this theory out on our own?" she asked.

"Don't you?"

"No."

"Why?"

"Because if I become more like you, and we're not sure about what that is, what could be waiting for me, for us, might not be the better thing. If you're wrong about this theory, and even about feeling like a wulf, it could turn out bad." She took a breath and added, "I could turn out bad."

She watched Colton raise his hands as if he couldn't stop himself from comforting her. Although Rosalind wished he would actually cross that line, she couldn't let him know that. Her bed was in the corner, just four feet away. Her thighs were quaking for a stroke of his bare hands on her naked flesh. She desired real closeness and a respite from thought. She wanted him inside her, filling her, his actions erasing all the doubts.

But her assessment about his condition had been correct. He was in pain and barely managing to control it. Instead of healing completely right away, as he should have been able to do after his injuries, the visible evidence of how close he had come to death had stayed with him, lingering like a layer of fog.

How much of that pain was due to the injuries he had sustained? Did his theory about Others cover him and his condition, as well? Was he becoming something other than Lycan, with ongoing pain as the symptom of that eventual change? Part of that change? The catalyst for it? What was a ghost, if not merely an awkward color discrepancy?

She was visibly trembling now, and desperate for comfort. Yet she had every right to be afraid. They could not connect without the possibility of further consequences.

Although her lover was hurting, he was hard, swollen with the anticipation of sharing her breath. Again he was reading her thoughts. *Just a hand on hers. His mouth on her mouth.*

It was at that moment Rosalind felt herself again start to fade. Her spirit flickered in and out of the present as if losing its form.

She dropped to the floor, sat down hard and lifted her face to her lover. Her lips parted. "More of them are on their way."

He turned to look behind him, then crossed to the window. When he pivoted back, she found herself standing by his side without knowing how she had gotten there.

They were inches apart. The souls of their wulfs were mingling.

"How do you know?" Colton asked, his face tense, his shoulder muscles bunched. "I can't smell them."

When she offered him a sad, mirthless smile, he said nothing about the evidence of the sudden enlightenment that protruded from between what she knew were two bloodless lips: fangs. Longer than before. Sharper than ever. A telling sign about exactly who was coming for a rematch.

She watched a thought about the kind of shape he was in at the moment flit across Colton's features. She felt his heart sink into an uneven rhythm.

"Where are they?" he asked. "How far away?"

She gazed beyond him. "Not far."

Her white wulf swore under his breath. She thought his face shifted slightly to the vague outline of his wulf. "How many are there? Can you tell?"

"Let me go to them," she said.

When her eyes met his, her stomach clenched. Colton's wulf was burning hotter than ever, and a kind of sweet oblivion rested in the acknowledgment.

"And do what?" he demanded, his eyes not leaving hers. "Surrender? Give in to them? We don't know what they want with you, or what might happen. We can't know that without some guidance."

The spike in his pulse spiked hers. He'd wanted to bed her, protect her, be her mate, and all those needs were becoming tangled, mired in mystery.

"I can find out what they want," she said. Her voice quavered.

"At the risk of placing your life in peril? Forget it, Rosalind. Whatever they want, they want badly enough to come here in waves. I don't like the notion of that, and what it might mean. Master plans, as part of a vampire's vocabulary? Strategy? It's unheard-of."

Rosalind made herself turn to the window. If she maintained eye contact, her heart would break. No matter how determined Colton was, if she closed the distance, he would cave to his beast's superior urges.

"I don't see that we have another choice," she objected. "I started this. Me. I won't see you or my father harmed any more than you've been harmed already."

"Then it's a good thing you have no say in the matter."

Though they had bonded, he wasn't her captor or keeper. He was older, and maybe wiser in the ways the world worked, but she also was fluent in wulf. She knew these woods. This was her playground. And out there, tonight, she hadn't even begun to fight.

"We have to bring your father back to consciousness," he said. "He'll have to provide some answers, quickly. Can we wake him up? Do we have time?"

"Not much time."

Again, she watched Colton search the night beyond the glass. Though his skin was feverish, he was riddled with chills. Still, at that moment, when confronted with an immediate problem, Colton Killion looked every bit of the strong, virile Were she had first seen.

His head was lifted. His eyes were wide. She took a step that brought her closer to him, fighting the instinct to rest a hand on his rigid back.

"Do it," he said with the gravel of pain in his voice. "Wake your father now. Wait this out. Give me more time."

It took a gigantic effort to back away from him and turn for the door. Only then, when an unuttered sob of distress closed her throat, did Rosalind realize how long she had been holding her breath, and that the monsters in the trees had stolen it.

Chapter 19

"Kirk," Colton said to the Were on the bed in a tiny room no larger than Colton's room in the shed.

Green eyes met his.

"The vampires are staging a comeback."

Kirk's eyes closed.

Colton spoke again. "You told me Rosalind will attract others now that she's reached a certain age. Why vampires? What others, and why? How would anyone know about her, so far out here?"

"She's more than Lycan," Kirk said softly. Speaking was obviously difficult for him.

"Yes, you mentioned that. I've seen her change, and I think those changes might be due to a state of heightened emotion. Am I right?"

Jared Kirk turned his head and opened his eyes. "What did you say?"

"Emotion. Rosalind may be reacting to emotion, to strong feelings in others and in herself."

"That isn't what a Banshee does," Kirk said.

Banshee? Colton was blown backward by the term. He found himself on his feet, with his jaw tight, sure he'd heard that term somewhere.

"Explain," he said, not sure Kirk would be able to utter ten more words in his present state. "Quickly."

"A Banshee is a feminine spirit." Kirk's voice was faint, but accommodating.

Colton leaned closer to the bed. "And?"

"Said to be an omen of impending death, or doom."

"What?"

"They are spirits often associated with families and bloodlines. Rosalind's mother's family had one, though that kind of spirit had never come to rest in the blood of the family it had attached itself to until..."

"Until what?" Colton asked impatiently.

"Until one did."

Colton felt like a Were with a one-word vocabulary. Harsher this time, he said, "Explain."

Kirk gasped to draw in more air. "The MacAirlie clan's Banshee, what they called a Death-caller, was to warn of the death of one of them, but had grown too close to the woman she was to have given over to Death. Maybe that Death-caller craved the kind of life others around her had. No one knows for sure. That Lycan female lived to mate with the Were who found her alive at Death's door."

"Yes." Colton's skin had grown colder. "Go on."

"The result of this Lycan union was a Night Wulf. A black Were that carried the moon mark on her arm, but had other abilities, as well."

Night Wulf. This was the source of Rosalind's unique black fur. She carried something else in her blood that came from long ago. Could this be true?

"Who was that child the Banshee saved?" he asked.

"Rosalind's great-great-grandmother."

Colton had to take a minute to process that information. He wished he could calm down. "Does this explanation imply that a Banshee's spirit might have become housed in the Lycan she saved? That's how the unusual characteristics and black pelt come in? It reflects the Death-caller's presence? Jesus. How does something that happened so long ago affect Rosalind now?"

"I don't know. Maybe part of that Banshee's spirit has been handed down to Rosalind, and she's showing herself. Maybe, as you say, emotion calls that spirit closer to the surface. Possibly, a threat of imminent death is what a Death-caller would recognize. God knows what resides inside Rosalind. I prayed that nothing would show up at all."

The expression on Kirk's face made Colton's throat seize. He barely got the next question out. "But you know about it. About that spirit. How do you know? Has it shown up before this?"

Kirk turned his head on the pillow and said with a reluctant sincerity, "I'm afraid I've seen it before."

"When?" Colton's cop voice had taken over. He was the interrogator who demanded answers.

Kirk's voice sputtered, as if the words were painful. "In Rosalind's mother."

Colton didn't remember getting to his feet or placing his hands on the mattress. His face was close to the elder Were's when he spoke again. "Her mother was a Night Wulf?"

Kirk tried to nod his head. "Rosalind doesn't know. I didn't tell her. I was sure it couldn't happen again, so close in time. After her Blackout phase had passed, I saw that it could."

Colton pushed off to pace the room, again thinking about Rosalind's shiny black pelt, and recalling Lycan legend about how impossible a pure black pelt was supposed to be.

"Bullshit," he said, glancing at Kirk. "Right? Are you putting me on, hoping to chase me away?"

He'd mated with a creature that also had the ability to herald death? Could that be true?

Another memory returned, throwing him back in time to the night in the park when he'd heard Rosalind's howl—the sound that had started all of this by alerting him to the presence of a she-wulf.

"Hell," he whispered. "Had she been calling me or keening for the death of other Lycans?" Which turned out to be the slaughter of his family.

Had the events that transpired that night been enough to have kicked a latent spirit into action?

Or…God, had a wulf with a Banshee inside her been howling for *his* death?

Impossible.

This wasn't Ireland or Scotland, for Christ's sake. It was Florida. He was alive. Changed, but breathing. So, what did any of it mean?

Unless…some of her spirit had been passed to him that night, so that he would survive.

Colton considered that possibility now. Had Rosalind saved him in order to become his mate, just as the other spirit had done one hell of a long time ago? Could a dormant spirit in her blood have manifested that night in the park?

It was crazy. Far-fetched.

"Okay," he said, out of shocked frustration. "Tell me how we help her."

"Keep her safe."

"Surely," Colton said, "you knew better than to think she would remain here forever, or even be willing to?"

"Here, she was Lycan, like me."

"It was an artificial life, Kirk. A kind of forced stasis. She wasn't who she was destined to be. If what you say is true, part of her soul was sleeping."

"Yet she remained Lycan. The longer she did, the better."

"Yes, and look at her now." Colton leaned down again. "You do know how to help her in some way, if you were with her mother?"

"It was her mother's wish to live here and to segregate ourselves from the others. My mate never set foot outside of these grounds. She never went through this. I came here by invitation from my wife's father, and I stayed."

"Knowing what she was, you stayed?"

"Yes." Sadness lowered Kirk's voice. "And I never regretted it. Not for one single second."

"Yet you would scorn me for wanting the same thing?"

"I would have saved you, or any other suitor, from the isolation that both I and my daughter have endured."

Colton put a hand to his forehead, then ran his fingers through his hair. "Well, it's too late to worry about that. I'm bound to Rosalind, as she is to me. I want to help her, now more than ever, and I'd like you to tell me how to do that." He faced the closed window. "Emotion has to be the key to her unwilling transformations. She loved you and was therefore like you all this time. She wanted me, and…" The white in her hair. The lightened skin.

He returned to Kirk's bed. "None of that explains why vampires might want her. Why would they come here? Bloodsuckers are already dead. How could a Death-caller be of use to them?"

"I don't know." Kirk cleared his throat, and grimaced at the effort it took. "Vampires could be attracted to the dark spirit in her. They might sense the likeness of a Death-caller. On the one hand, she would know how to find death because she feels it approach. With that ability, she could easily alert them to the location of their next meal."

"And on the other hand?" Colton pressed.

"She can alert mortals, or any other species, to the approach of monsters."

Kirk tried to sit up, and made it to his elbows. It sounded to Colton as if the Were said, "There's more." But when he looked, Kirk had fallen back, his energy spent.

"One thing is for certain. It's no longer safe for her here," Colton mused. "Vampires know where she is, and want something. The bastards have arrived."

"Then we must take her away," Kirk said.

"Where? To a more populated place where there are far more emotions running rampant than in these woods?"

The question hung in the air as another sound reached Colton, drifting in through the windowpanes.

Rather, the lack of sound is what caught his attention. Outside, at that moment, there was no noise at all.

"As I said, it's too damn late now," he said regretfully, heading for the door.

Rosalind dropped to a crouch on the porch. She snapped her head from side to side, searching the night.

A wave of palpable tension ran through the trees, leaves shuddering in its wake. The air felt dense. In the distance, she perceived the stench of death and destruction.

Without turning to look, she was aware of Colton's approach. She didn't acknowledge him, unable to speak and afraid to try.

He came close, but she was beyond fear and running on instinct. Straightening, she backed up and away. "Can't touch," she said. "Not now. Not yet."

She tried to make some sense out of it for him, perceiving his distress. "If I'm like them, I can feel them. It's best that I do feel them because I'll know where they are."

"Do you know a way around this next confrontation?" he asked.

"There's no way around it."

"What are you feeling when you say you can sense them?"

"A rising blackness, bleak and dreadful, unfurls inside me, almost as if they're pulling that darkness to the surface."

"God, Rosalind, I—"

By the time Colton had stopped whatever he had been about to say, she was already at the bottom of the steps, facing the trees on the south side of the house and the path leading to the swamp.

"There are five." She glanced at Colton over her shoulder.

"Is that all?" he said drily, following her gaze.

Her big Were didn't look frightened, though Rosalind observed how his body had stiffened with this news. His anxiety had mostly manifested in his rigid arms and back. He rolled his shoulders and clenched his hands.

"Please don't imagine that I'll allow you to run off by yourself in order to meet them face-to-face, because that's not happening," he said. "There's a chance you can control what happens to you."

She swayed slightly. "How?"

"I have no idea, really, but what if it's like controlling your wulf? You learn to stifle the urges and tuck them inside. You start to appreciate the changes and what they mean."

Rosalind studied him, reading the truth of this statement in his face, and sensing that he believed it.

When she turned her head, he jumped down to meet her.

"What? What is it?"

"They're moving," she said. "Heading toward the place where my mother was killed."

"Tell me how you know this."

"The ripples in the night are the wake of their movement. See it in the trees? Vampires run like a dark wind, like nothing else on earth that I've seen. It's as if they don't possess bodies at all, and are some kind of misty substance that can defy the laws of nature."

She added, "Scratch that last part. We already have seen evidence of lapsed laws of nature, haven't we?"

Colton said nothing. She heard his heart thundering.

"Also, it's like I have a homing beacon inside me," she went on. "My inner darkness is attracted to their darkness, like mercury coagulating or drops of liquid merging with a larger pool. I see them clearly in my mind. I can nearly make out every detail."

This statement was met by more silence. She guessed he didn't even know where to start in tackling that.

"I have to go there, Colton. They're defiling my mother's memory. They won't stop harassing me unless I do something to make them stop."

"Maybe that's their point," he said. "They zero in on that particular spot because it has the most emotional ties for you, hoping to lure you to them. Otherwise, why wouldn't they just come here?"

She met Colton's gaze and could tell he was assessing the situation, determining what to do. In a gleam of moonlight, she saw his claws spring forth.

"It's me they want," she said.

"Over my dead body."

Oh, yes. God, how she loved him, right then, right there. She loved this ghost with all of her tormented, black-tainted heart. Colton Killion was willing to lay down his life for her. She had observed the signs of this kind of selflessness in him before.

Were. Cop. Gentleman. Lover. Fighter. Protector. He was all of those things, rolled into one…

And that was the reason she couldn't allow him to fight her battle. The world couldn't afford to lose him. Lovers didn't lead their soul mates to their deaths.

That thought brought her out of a trancelike state. Excitement began to simmer in her nerves. She looked at Colton and almost smiled because she didn't see his death here. She didn't sense it. Didn't feel it. If she housed a creature that announced death, as her father had inadvertently told her, through Colton, then surely Colton was not going to die tonight. She was closer to him than to anyone. She would know this.

In a flash, she was off and running. For the first time in a while she felt ready for whatever these monsters were going to dish out. If instinct was all she had, it was conceivable that she and Colton would come out of this alive.

Black fur, soft and familiar, sprang from her pores to cover her legs. Her arms looked thin, pale and human before they began to shift shape. She ran her tongue over her slowly descending fangs and howled passionately with a Lycan call that sounded like the cry of an exotic bird.

Death to them all. Save my own.

There was a scrambling noise behind her, and nothing she could do about it. "If you're determined to follow," she shouted to Colton before her wulf completed the takeover, "you'll have to keep up."

Chapter 20

Rosalind's life passed before her eyes as she ran. The stink of vampires wound itself around those memories, becoming more intense with every stride.

Not long now, and I will find you.

Back again into the past she went, sliding down memory's tunnel with the hope of discovery.

Her Blackout phase, her father had told her tonight, had been the start of his recognition that she was different. But she didn't remember much about it. She'd heard that few females survived the process of the human body rewiring itself to become Were. Yet she had embraced that new life with her arms open, relishing her wulf's powers and constantly gaining more.

Her early rebelliousness now seemed to have been a selfish, frivolous trait, and highly dangerous. Then again, what was the point of lingering on that time when she'd moved so far past it?

Besides, that same stubborn streak is what had brought her to Colton. In no way could she ever regret that. The ghost behind her understood that she was different, and still wanted in.

She wished she had known her mother. There had been no women or she-wulfs in her life. She had always felt empty, despite her raw strength. And all that time, the empty space inside her had been nothing more than a sleeping Death-caller waiting for a chance to awaken and declare itself.

Yes, she wanted to shout back to Colton, she had heard every word her father had told him.

A branch hit her in the face. Rosalind growled, and heard that same branch hit Colton. Her lover was here. He was close.

It took real effort not to turn around and jump into his arms. She knew that once she was in his embrace she would feel only Colton's love, both physical and spiritual, pouring in.

Her mother had had her father to care for her, until Analise MacAirlie Kirk had been cut down by hunters who had either been after the pelts of mammals or out to bag a gator.

Had her father tried hard to protect his wife? She had no doubt about that. The question was how a bunch of bloodsucking fiends from hell knew about the sacred location of her mother's grave.

Along the lines of Colton's theory, could vampires also read and crave the highs of emotion?

Another growl bubbled up from her throat.

"Rosalind." Colton's voice was gruff, but he hadn't shifted.

Of course he read her. Their souls were entwined.

I have done this to you, she longed to say to him, knowing he wouldn't turn back no matter what excuses she flung his way.

I'm not worthy of your love.

She dared a glance behind her.

Colton's chiseled angles produced their own shadows. He wore her father's blood on his left shoulder, and on both arms. The welts of his wounds were now a pinkish-white, crossing his cheeks in raised parallel lines of scar tissue. More lines encircled his neck, at the base of his throat, looking like a necklace of lace.

He had meant to say something else. Speak meaningful words that would equal a different kind of sentence, trapping her in a world that wouldn't allow for the smallest, slightest touch between lovers.

How much more distance could she stand? A lifetime's worth? Sixty seconds?

She wished for just one more kiss.

Yet if his lips were to feather over hers, it wouldn't be enough. There would be no holding back the advancing degree of her needs. Even in her wulf's shape, her arms tingled and twitched. Her breasts strained with the memory of his hands on her. Phantom fingers seemed to cup the private place between her churning thighs, calling up the fires she had to tamp down.

Her fur was mottled now. Black and white. The ghost's spirit was spreading through her as she moved on, ignoring the impulse to turn back and face Colton instead of the vampires.

Please. Save yourself from what hides in the night, my love.

Wishful thinking was bad, and a distraction. The place was crawling with vampires, and all she wanted was to end this and have Colton for herself.

She was brought to a staggering halt by his hand on her arm. Guilt flowed through her. Had she driven him mad by telegraphing her own desires?

A snap of his arm turned her around. "Shift," he said in a voice as ragged as she felt.

She looked into his eyes.

"Shift back," he repeated. "Please, Rosalind."

It took her seconds to comply, despite the danger around them.

"This is what we have to look forward to," he said. "This is what's in store for us. Danger and mystery and monsters. But let's not lose sight of the end result, whatever turns up between now and then."

"Promise," she said. "Promise me that will be true."

The lips she had stared at, wishing they would meet hers, did just that. Colton's mouth closed over hers savagely, as if he needed to prove something to her. As if he would be the only one to devour her.

He didn't touch her in any other way. His body remained apart from hers. Just lips on lips. His mouth on hers. And the fire that raged in that kiss seared the air between them, turning the chill of a monstrous night to a molten red-hot.

Colton's mouth was reaffirming his promise as the ground rippled beneath their feet. The earth seemed to be warning them of supernatural trespassers getting closer and closer, of other beasts in the landscape rushing in.

For a few seconds, though, stolen from time and backed by the exquisite seduction of her lover's mouth, Rosalind began to believe they could do this, that somehow, it would work out.

In Colton, there was hope.

The second his mouth left hers, blackness descended.

Blinded by the shock of losing what she held so dear, Rosalind tore herself from her lover and spun around to confront whatever was out there preventing this future.

To confront the advance of five fanged blood seekers that would mess with her for reasons of their own.

Vampire stink flashed like a yellow beacon in the dark.

Colton watched Rosalind twist away from him, her body already half covered in fur and strung tight with tension. She tore through the brush, toward the awful odor, leaving him standing there, staring. Then, as though he'd been infused with a shot of liquid adrenaline, he called up his wulf.

His beast came on like thunder rolling down a runway, hard and fast, in a transformation that left him panting. Sinew snapped. Tiny bones broke and realigned as his flesh expanded. His blood began to boil, as if he had swallowed a furnace.

The whole wulf universe rushed forward to banish what was left of the human. For an indeterminate amount of time, there was nothing but the sound of his pulse accelerating, and then something inside him screamed for him to take a breath.

An awareness of the position of the moon came to him, as did the direction of the wind that ruffled his white fur. Animal smells crashed in, and the foul odor of evil at its basest.

The beast's heat took the edge off his pain. Power replaced it. On legs like steel, he took off after his mate, angry, hungry, with the beast's undivided attention locked on the path the she-wulf had taken.

He was fast and incredibly fleet, and caught sight of Rosalind before a full minute had passed. She made audible sounds that reached him like tortured syllables, but if Rosalind was speaking, he didn't understand the language. The possibility of this being some sort of vamp communication made him angrier.

There came an answering cry to her jabber. More of a shriek, really. Rosalind had lunged upward on her Night Wulf's powerful hind legs to dislodge a vampire from a stunted tree, and had the pathetic bag of bones on the ground before he reached her.

Clawlike hands tore at her. Bottomless black eyes refused to close as she straddled the creature, roaring her displeasure.

And then another vampire hit the dirt on Colton's right, followed by a third.

They were lightning fast. Like wind, Rosalind had told him, but they were more like a blur of dark on dark than a streak of displaced air. The blurs danced and swirled, taunting him, never in one place long enough for him to land a swing. The monsters seemed to suck all the air out of the area, though vampires didn't breathe.

He caught one by spinning on one heel, and with a well-placed canine of his own, tore through the skinless flesh. Black blood dribbled down his chin to dampen and discolor his snowy-white fur. A little jolt went through him, as if he had bitten through an electrical cord.

The wulf knew what to do, and the man inside it went along for the ride with his human thoughts intact. *Help Rosalind. Keep my promise.*

Given that, and the powers he and the Night Wulf beside him were seemingly able to access once their bodies were in sync, this attack should have been laughable. Only five vampires, total, against two furred-up creatures that only existed in legends?

Yet Colton's attention was divided by the demand to see to Rosalind and the need to watch her back. So when the vamp in his hands exploded into a storm of putrid gray ash, he jumped onto the chest of the freak she had on the ground, tore at the branch above his head and, with the jagged edge of his makeshift stake, went for the spot that would effectively terminate that monster's useless, lifeless life.

Rosalind was already on the third. Colton grabbed the fourth, wondering briefly about the location of the other remaining bloodsucker.

But there was no stopping these wulfs.

With uncanny speed and a raw, unleashed fury, Rosalind exploded the flailing vampire in her grip. Colton took care of his. When the dust had settled, they stood with their backs pressed together in the small, muddy clearing.

A slight smoky smell reached them. Colton glanced around, preparing for the next onslaught. But no other vampire arrived to try its hand at boxing with a ghost and a wulf-Banshee-vampire hybrid. In fact, no further sound reached them at all.

Colton looked to Rosalind.

Her dark eyes looked back.

In the distance, a low rumble started up. Quickly, the noise got closer, louder, becoming mixed with the silky sound of brush being trampled.

Rosalind bolted—not away from the oncoming rumble, but toward it.

Here we go again, Colton thought, tearing through every curse his Miami PD partners had taught him.

When he rounded a grove of trees, he saw a dark SUV skidding to a stop. At the same moment Rosalind landed on its roof with a metal-denting clank of her ankle chain.

"Get in," Jared Kirk shouted from the driver's seat. "It's not what you think. The vampires weren't alone. There are others here."

Colton knocked Rosalind off the roof with a swipe of his left arm. As she dropped to the ground, they both shifted shape. He wrenched the door open. In a chilling replay of their escape from the Landau compound, Rosalind preceded him into the backseat, and then her father, grimacing with pain as his hands yanked at the steering wheel, stepped on the gas.

Chapter 21

The SUV swerved on a soggy section of the path, then righted its direction, heading, Colton guessed, back toward the house. Kirk was hunched over the steering wheel. His back was heavily bandaged. His knuckles were white.

"Others?" Colton demanded. "What the hell do you mean?"

Before Kirk could answer, Rosalind made a soft sound beneath her breath, as though she had an idea about what her father had meant.

Her face, colorless before, had gone translucent. Her skin seemed thinner in the light of the dashboard, showing every one of her fine lavender veins. Eyes, dark just moments before, flashed with a hint of their former emerald green.

"Others?" Colton repeated more forcefully without

taking his eyes from her. "Rosalind said there were five vampires. We're missing one of them. Is that what you mean?"

"Not vampires," was Kirk's slurred reply.

"Not werewolves, either," Colton snarled in frustration. "There's no moon. So what does that leave?"

"Demons," Kirk answered in a whisper that no one other than a Were could have heard.

Colton's insides churned as if his beast had grabbed hold of him. His claws, an automatic result of that strain, punctured the leather seat.

"You're kidding," he managed to say.

"You'll just have to take my word, wulf."

Rosalind's avoided his eyes. Her features were benign, showing no emotion at all. They could have been taking a ride for the enjoyment of taking a ride, for all that look told him.

"What does everyone bloody-well know that I don't?" he shouted, so very tired of being the last one to the party. "Demons? What makes you believe that?"

Kirk didn't have time to answer. As they spun wheels past the garage, the acrid smell of smoke grew stronger. Something was on fire. It was the house. The roof was blazing with flames, and had partially caved in. The porch was an inferno.

Beside him, Rosalind made a small sound of regret deep in her chest. Both that sound and her skin's translucency made her seem terribly vulnerable, young and small.

He wanted to hold her, now more than ever. For all her former fierceness, his lover's sudden sadness was like a strike to his own heart.

"To hell with this," he said.

"Don't," her father warned. "Colton, listen to me. Do not touch her. Please. For her sake. For yours."

The idea that he should listen to her father and go against everything he felt at the moment made him take another swipe at the seat. As the leather tore, Rosalind's eyes met his.

She was trembling, and chilled to the bone without her fur. Her slender hands covered part of her face.

He just could not take much more of this, because he knew that she couldn't take much more. He didn't see how things could possibly get worse.

"Demons did that? Started the fire?" He felt uncommonly winded with the return of the pain that had been pardoned by his wulf.

Jared Kirk had gone silent, the last of his energy all used up. Nevertheless, the Were had found enough energy to try to remove Rosalind from this new mess.

Kirk had loved Rosalind's mother and had guarded her from this sort of thing for years. No doubt he saw reflections of Rosalind's mother in Rosalind; maybe even in this current replay of events. Hunters after pelts and gators, Rosalind had told him in regard to her mother's death. But odds were that wasn't true.

The stiffness of Kirk's neck told Colton that the elder Were had been through all of this before.

Colton faced Rosalind helplessly, hurting for her, for himself and for her father. He pondered where they might go if hell's doors had been opened for some reason, and why vampires and demons were prolonging this mess.

His heart shattered into pieces too fine to easily reunite when Rosalind's hands fell from her face and he saw a tear slide down her frozen, expressionless cheek.

"I'm sorry. You'll have to drive," Kirk suddenly announced. Pulling the car to the side of the road, he slumped forward. "I'm not quite myself."

Colton was beside him in a flash. Warning Rosalind to stay back with a guarded glance, he felt for the Were's pulse. "Weak, but there."

After lifting the big Were and placing him in the back of the SUV, Colton got behind the wheel. He allowed himself one comment on the issue facing them all.

"Damn it to hell and back, where was he taking us?"

"Back to the Landaus'," Rosalind replied, keeping vigil over her father. "Who else might know what to do with creatures like us?"

There was, Colton thought, just no arguing with that.

The lack of scraping sounds meant that Colton was keeping his claws to himself. Rosalind sensed his anger and his frustration.

Her suggestion to go Judge Landau's had been met with a grunt of disapproval, though Colton was already driving at breakneck speed in that direction.

They had gone a good distance before he spoke again. "Why demons, Rosalind? Do you know anything about this?"

"Sorry," she said.

Another span of silence followed that she was afraid to break.

"I'm not sure Landau will want us," Colton finally said. "Let alone know what to do about recent circumstances. We will have to tell him everything. You know that."

His eyes were bright in the rearview mirror.

"The judge can call the elders back if they've gone," she said. "One of them has to know what this means."

"Demons, Rosalind?"

"It isn't your fault. None of it is. If I had an entity inside me all along, it would have eventually come out anyway, in one circumstance or another."

"But it was me you followed that night."

"Yes. So what if I was supposed to follow you, and there is something at work here other than chance?"

She could see him thinking about that.

"I'm changing," he said. "Without the wulf's power, I'm barely hanging on. It's as though I'm growing thinner, losing substance. Strange, isn't it, when you're gaining substance? I'd almost tend to think you were finding mine."

"I'd release you if I knew how," she told him, her stomach in knots at the thought of that. "I'd break the bond. You don't deserve this."

"Your father didn't ask to be released," he said. "Do you imagine I would want to?"

"Fathers have to love their daughters, even if they're different."

"He must have loved your mother tremendously."

Rosalind considered his remark.

"Like me," she said. "My mother was like me. That's what he told you."

The tension in Colton's tone had been negligible, and meant that he was withholding something. A thought, or another theory?

"I'm sorry," Colton repeated.

She climbed to the seat beside him. The leather felt cold on her bare legs. "What are you thinking?"

He gave her a sideways glance. “You’re not the only one.”

She let that settle. “Night Wulf,” she said. “My mother was one.”

“You did hear what your father told me?”

She nodded.

“Then you know there was no way you could have avoided what’s inside you,” he said. “Yet you are blaming yourself.”

Each time Colton pointed the car in a new direction, Rosalind groped for new meaning. Her mother had been a Death-caller. She was like her mother. In a strange, roundabout way, this brought some comfort. A little, anyway.

She moved her foot. The chain attached to it jangled against the floorboards. “Just in case, my father said. I suppose he meant to keep me from going after the vampires like the rebellious idiot I have always been, but I took this chain to mean that he thought I was the monster who needed to be shackled.”

“God, Rosalind…” her white wulf said, without being able to finish the sentiment.

“Here’s what else he said, at the Landaus’. ‘I conferred with the elders, fearing what your future might hold. They had to know about you, and why I hadn’t presented you to one of their sons.’”

Banshee. Death-caller. Night Wulf. Shape-shifter. She was all of those things, and had to be watched for the signs of something odd making an unscheduled appearance, in the way her mother probably had to be watched.

“I am like my mother,” she said, solemnly, swiveling on the seat to get a better view of Colton’s silhouette.

"Maybe my mother wasn't killed by random hunters or by accident."

With utter and complete sadness, her lover, her protector, her mate, said, "Maybe not."

"Not that it makes me feel a whole lot better," she remarked, waiting anxiously to see the lights of Miami that would eventually appear in the distance, and hoping demons were really a myth.

Chapter 22

By the time they reached Miami, silence had fallen between them. Colton headed for the Landau estate less eagerly than he would have imagined under the circumstances. He had no idea how this freakish little party of tired, filthy, undressed beings would be received by another wulf's pack. For the Landau family and their elegant associates, the hasty return of a ghost and a Night Wulf might come as a shock.

Hell, he already owed them more than he could ever pay back.

When Rosalind finally spoke from the rear of the car, where she again sat with her prone father, he guessed it was because she had seen and recognized the pillars of stone marking the Landau gates.

"Will you stay near me?" she asked.

"I won't let you out of my sight," he replied. "For any reason short of…"

"Death?"

"Yes."

The tall iron gates were closed to intruders. As the SUV pulled up to them a siren went off in a single burst of sound, and more lights came on. Immediately, two men flanked the vehicle, appearing from nowhere and looking as dangerous as the rest of Landau's Weres had been when in man form.

Colton wasn't sure what he'd say or how he would explain his presence here. However, instead of engaging Colton in conversation or asking for identification of any kind—which would have been impossible for Colton to produce anyway—the Were nearest the driver's-side window nodded his head, said, "Killion, right?" and stepped aside.

As the massive gates swung open, the overhead lights dimmed back to a wattage more reminiscent of starlight than a prison yard. Reluctantly, Colton pressed on at the slowest pace possible, in the SUV's lowest gear. With that kind of introduction—the siren and the lights—Judge Landau and everyone else here were sure to know they were coming. It was also obvious that Landau felt he needed this kind of beefed-up protection.

Colton dreaded this visit. Yet Rosalind's safety, as well as her father's, had to outweigh his own discomfort.

Tonight, after hand-to-hand combat with vampires, finding out that the she-wulf he'd mated with was actually some sort of throwback to a Celtic death spirit, and that a bunch of demons, unseen but felt, had burned Rosalind's house down…facing the Landau pack in a prettily decorated living room with explanations about their arrival had to circle the bottom of his all-time worst wish list.

Landau had been left with rabid vampires on the rampage the last time they had met. The guards and the lights were a symptom of Landau's estimation of more trouble brewing. *Smart man, Judge Landau.*

"We're back," Colton announced.

Two more Weres awaited them halfway up the mile-long driveway, wearing dark clothes and carrying weapons. Colton was surprised to see that those weapons were crossbows similar in design to the one Rosalind's father had carried.

Vampire trouble, then.

The Weres didn't stop him, nodding as he passed them by, but Colton wanted to speak to these guys. Landau's personal guard force, members of the Landau werewolf pack who were more like himself in his Miami PD gig, were doing their bit to keep the peace in a city that had no idea there were werewolves in their midst. Or vampires.

For the first time, Colton wasn't sure how well the simple rules for being a protector that he had lived by would apply in the future. He'd be facing other Lycans of equal status who would expect him to come clean about everything. To top it off, he looked like an albino. Would anyone here take him seriously?

Colton blinked slowly as the house came into view. It was a formidable place modeled after a plantation mansion. Three stories tall, with a facade of brick, its main feature was wraparound porch. Tall pillars supported the roof of the wide veranda. It seemed that all sorts of things with calm, genteel exteriors could be deceiving.

As Colton braked by the front steps, he counted three

more Weres waiting for him. Two men, and a woman. It wasn't difficult to recognize Judge Landau, with his silver-gray hair. Beside him was Landau's son, Dylan. He guessed the third had to be the Judge's wife, the healer who had tended to him during his first visit. If it had been any other time or circumstance, he would have brought her flowers. Maybe even kissed her cheek.

He cut the engine and got out of the car as quickly as he was able to, given his disintegrated levels of strength. He was hanging on by a thread, but he had to see this through.

"Killion," Judge Landau said in greeting.

Colton heard no irony or sarcasm or hidden meaning in the welcome, and experienced the first bump in his resolve to remain as distant as possible. In that greeting lay no hint of an acknowledgment of Colton's white hair and skin being anything other than normal. He found no inkling whatsoever of the dislike of having to face a freak.

"Hello," he returned. "Sorry to trespass on your hospitality again so soon. Jared Kirk has been hurt and his daughter is in the car with him."

Landau passed his son a look, and Dylan turned to go into the house. Rosalind was likely the cause of Dylan's hasty retreat. The judge was taking no chances with a strange, death-related entity, even after more or less accepting the presence of a ghost among his brood.

"We'll see to Jared at once," Mrs. Landau said, moving toward the car. Speaking directly to Colton, she added, "Perhaps we can see to Rosalind's comfort before we do that?"

Landau joined his wife. To Colton he said, "Rosalind

can have the same room she had when last here. She might feel better in familiar surroundings."

"Would that room include a bolted door and bars on the windows?" Colton asked before thinking about how rude that might sound. "She already has a chain on her ankle. A gift from her father before he was hurt."

Mrs. Landau looked earnestly stricken.

"Actually," Landau said, nudging his wife toward the SUV's rear door, "the room has a pretty view of the backyard, as well as new curtains made by my wife."

Colton wanted to hide from Mrs. Landau's lingering gaze, but the stronger motivation was to protect Rosalind, and in doing so, honor the promises he had made.

"She'll probably like that," he said. "And maybe we can think of a way to remove the chain before too long? It's done real damage to her ankles and shins."

Colton was close enough to the elder Were to see Landau's eyes shut briefly, as if word of that chain had somehow tortured him. "I'll get the tools," he said, "and come right up."

Colton's tension eased a bit more at the sight of the Landaus' concern for Rosalind. He inclined his head to them. He had to trust these Weres because no other option remained.

"Rosalind," he said gently as the rear door opened. "It's safe to come out."

Jared Kirk moaned as the car's interior light hit him, and tried unsuccessfully to open his eyes.

Rosalind, on the other hand, was nowhere to be seen.

"Need I ask if this isn't a good development?" Judge Landau observed, taking in Colton's surprise.

Colton didn't answer. The way his stomach had begun to knot seemed answer enough.

Landau gestured with a hand, and out of the dark two Weres responded. The big Weres with arms like professional wrestlers. Carefully, they lifted Kirk up and carted him away, under the judge's wife's supervision.

"You look beat," Landau said to Colton.

"Beat doesn't even begin to cover it. But I'll find Rosalind. She can't have gotten far."

Landau came closer. "I don't usually man the place like this. It's highly unusual. That last vampire sighting, when you were here, led us to believe that the imbeciles have become more aggressive. And now, for a while at least, we have to be overcautious about safeguarding our own."

"They didn't actually come here?" Colton asked.

"We didn't let them get this far."

"How did that turn out?"

"It was nothing we couldn't handle. Nevertheless, that made two attacks on Weres in a few days, and they were too damn close to these walls. I'm sorry about your parents, Colton. I didn't have the chance to tell you so before all of this. It couldn't have been a random targeting. I fear that kind of horror might be the start of a vengeful retaliation against those of us keeping watch over our more vulnerable human neighbors."

Colton nodded. "Has there been anything with the vampires since then?"

"Not even a fang," Landau said.

"I'd stay prepared, then. According to her father, they're likely to know Rosalind has returned."

"Then it isn't safe to go out there alone," Landau advised.

"Thanks, but I'll manage."

Colton hoped to God he'd be able to find the strength

to go after her, and prayed that no one else, fanged or otherwise, would find her first.

"Wait," Landau called after him. "I can't let you go alone. You'll need help. Give me a minute."

"Who would you send to accompany me when I'm hunting for a Night Wulf, Judge? You've kept Dylan and the others from knowing about her for quite a while."

Landau's jaw tightened, probably due to the name Colton had given Rosalind. Yet Landau had been in on some part of this revelation for a few days now, and couldn't pretend otherwise.

"I was volunteering myself," Landau said. "A minute more, while I pick up a weapon or two, won't get her into more trouble."

"So you might think," Colton whispered as Landau sprinted up the front steps. "If you didn't know her as well as I do."

Since the Landau estate was now overrun with Weres, Rosalind could only ponder the chances that the folks inside those gates didn't know what she was by now. What were the odds they'd allow her any freedom or shelter when she was a monster magnet, and there might be demons on the loose?

Her legs weakened at the thought of what a creature with that kind of moniker might be like, but she kept walking, directionless.

She didn't know anything about Miami or cities; hadn't a clue where to go now that she had run away from Colton. Her father would be in good hands, though. She'd seen what the judge's wife had done for Colton, and the care they had taken to be kind to another Lycan line.

Colton had told her he felt like he was growing misty inside and less like his old self. Though he wasn't sure what that meant, Rosalind wondered if that felt anything like her new sensations. Her heart went out to him. Her body wanted to go back to him.

She felt him thinking about her. He was worried, and struggling to come to terms with her vanishing act. Her pulse erupted to match his, so far from his. His lure remained strong and nearly all-consuming.

She felt sick.

Glancing over her shoulder at the Landaus' walls, she fielded a tinge of regret that came with a renewed swell of fear. Going back would place all those Weres in danger. She had caused enough trouble already, had brought enough pain to her father and the others. No way could she hit them with the possibility of yet another breed of monster.

"Going back is an impossibility," she said aloud. "What do I do next?" Would demons come this far to find her, and skip the compound if she distanced herself from it?

She had no money and no clothes. Without a doubt, she looked like the monster she was, and was still dragging the damn chain around.

She didn't get far before her legs finally gave out. She sat on the grass, surrounded by the foreign smells of a foreign city.

If she was so special, then she had to dig into that specialness and come up with a way to combat what was happening to her while keeping everyone else safe. She had to at least try.

Determined, and with the help of a tree, she got to her feet. With her hands hanging limply at her sides, she struggled to formulate a plan that didn't involve being scared out of her wits.

First, she had to find clothes. Then she had to find a way to remove the chain.

"How do I accomplish that?"

Frantically, she tuned into her surroundings, scenting humans in the distance and also…someone walking atop Landau's stone wall.

Not Colton. Female. Recognizing this particular smell, Rosalind stood tall, with the hair at the nape of her neck bristling.

The female walking along the top of the wall had the grace and flexibility of a cat. Slim, and not too tall, she wore her dark brown hair at shoulder length, and out of her uniform, in jeans and a sweatshirt, looked just as formidable as she had the last time Rosalind had seen her.

"Delmonico," Rosalind muttered, recalling the name that had been engraved on the officer's name tag.

It didn't take Delmonico long to sense Rosalind watching her. "Who's there?" she called out softly. "Show yourself."

Rosalind nervously stepped out of the shadows.

"You again," Delmonico said, widening her dark eyes.

"Naked this time," Rosalind returned.

"Why is that, exactly?"

"I'm on the run, and didn't have time to address wardrobe malfunctions. Plus, my house was burned down tonight."

"There's blood on your legs."

"Some of it is my father's blood. He's inside your walls now."

"Jared Kirk."

"Yes."

"You haven't run very far, then. He has been taken inside. Why are you out here?"

"No one would or should willingly accept an abomination into their homes. That warning should be cross-stitched, framed and hung above every front door."

Delmonico blew out a breath. "I see."

"I'm pretty sure you don't."

"Then why don't you enlighten me?"

"I'm afraid of people running away if I do."

"Has anyone run away from you?"

"Very few know about me, to date. That doesn't mean they have to accept what baggage I bring with me when they do know."

"Is that why we weren't asked to go after you?" Delmonico asked.

"Neither Colton nor Judge Landau would allow contact, I'm sure."

"Then you must be pretty lonely."

For the second time that night, tears gathered in Rosalind's eyes. She tried desperately not to let them fall. All she had to do was jump over the wall Delmonico crouched upon, and her mate would be there. She wasn't sure how she could want him so much, and miss him so ferociously. Every cell in her body called out to him.

"Heck, I don't see anything wrong with you, except for the lack of clothes," Delmonico observed. "And the blood. Come with me and I'll outfit you."

"No. But thanks."

Delmonico looked into the distance. "They're coming after you now."

"I know."

"Can't I help?"

"Would you help, against their wishes?"

"They are my pack, and my family. They'll be yours if you'll give them a chance."

"I'm a different kind of wulf. Beyond that, I harbor a darkness that draws darkness to me. My father called me a Death-caller. I'm probably not safe to be around, and won't see anyone else harmed."

She had no idea why she was telling this to a stranger, and a member of Landau's pack. Maybe it was because she'd never been around another female.

Delmonico had a pretty, wise, intelligent face, and wore a calm expression. As a police officer, she'd be used to freaks…that's what Colton had thought when the three of them had last met on the city street.

"That's an altruistic plan," Delmonico said. "And complete hogwash, just so you know. More than a few of us also possess an intrinsic need to help, and to protect. If we tempered that need to only include the morally pure or the physically weak, what kind of world would this be?"

"Mine," Rosalind replied.

"I think you'll find that isn't true. I'm willing to help you." Delmonico pulled her sweatshirt over her head. Shaking her hair free of the collar, she tossed the shirt to Rosalind, then straightened up and reached for her zipper. "I don't keep many clothes here. I'm a guest, but Dylan can spare me something."

Climbing out of the jeans, and dropping them to the ground, she added, "I'll come with you, wherever it is you're going, if you'd like me to. However, I strongly recommend that you either let the white wulf catch up with you, or that you get behind these walls. The night has a strange thickness to it that I don't like."

"Colton, the cop you knew of, the white wulf, is what he is because of a vampire attack. He went after the bloodsuckers that killed his parents, and was hurt."

"I know about his family. I also know that there's nothing wrong with being different," Delmonico said, standing on the wall half-naked in some sort of flimsy undershirt and a pair of black lace underwear. "Wouldn't most people be surprised to find out what we are?"

Rosalind stared at the jeans before picking them up. They smelled like worn denim and the perfume Delmonico probably wore when around humans for any length of time.

"Your mate is lucky," Rosalind said to the off-duty cop, meaning it. She liked Delmonico. "And I appreciate the offer."

"But no thanks?"

"I'm poison. I have to go before that poison chokes you."

"Suit yourself," Delmonico said. "You know where to find me."

Rosalind nodded, and with Delmonico's gracious gift of a sweatshirt and jeans in her hands, and Colton's scent and mystical allure getting stronger by the second, she turned back to the park to find a hiding place.

Chapter 23

"It's odd," Judge Landau said as they scrambled over the wall, "how I can't find her scent."

Colton scented Rosalind easily, and could also make out her aloneness and her fear. "She smells like night, and like wind in the leaves."

"You have her scent in you, Colton?"

"It has become a part of me."

"Then you actually have—"

"Yes. We have mated."

They leaped to the ground on the far side of the wall and stopped short. Landau turned his head. "Dana?"

"I'm here," a soft voice returned, after which Officer Delmonico, minus her clothes, landed soundlessly beside them on bare feet.

Colton sucked in a breath. The last time they'd spoken, Delmonico had been in uniform, with a grip on

Rosalind's shoulder. Up close, and out of those unisex clothes, Dylan Landau's she-wolf looked beautiful. Her fighting-fit body showed sculpted, long, lean muscle. She had long brown slightly curly hair, an oval face and large eyes, dark in color, that were fixed on him.

"Sorry if this embarrasses you, Killion," she said. "As it happens, I gave my clothes away not more than five minutes ago to someone who needed them more than I did."

"Rosalind." He reacted with the familiar nerve burn when he said her name.

"Actually, the name she gave herself was Night Wulf," Delmonico said.

Landau interrupted. "Did you see where she went?"

"Yep," Delmonico said. "She headed west. I've never come across anyone like her. Her shape seemed to fuzz at the edges when she spoke to me, as if she wasn't quite solid. I thought to myself that she may be tough, but she's also scared. She wouldn't come with me when I asked her to, which doesn't say much for my powers of persuasion. Sorry." She patted her bare thighs. "I didn't have my cuffs with me."

"She's hurting," Colton said, gazing at the park, thinking he could almost see Rosalind there, and that her presence was, for him, like a strong radio signal.

"She had a chain wrapped around her ankle," Delmonico said. "That has to hurt."

Colton hadn't forgotten about the chain. Thinking he could hear its echo rattling as Rosalind ran, he set off after her, rudely leaving Landau and Delmonico behind.

Rosalind, he silently called. *It's all right. I'm here.*

Her fear breezed over his skin like a layer of ice over heat. The taste in his mouth as he took in air was again like crushed aluminum. Rosalind would be in human shape and wary of another change. Yet outside Landau's compound lay a strange human world unfamiliar to her.

Landau caught up, forcing Colton's attention to split. "She's not the only one out here," Landau said. "This time, it's humans, up ahead."

Colton smelled those humans who had a preference for artificial fragrances like aftershave, scented soaps and shampoos—things most Weres shunned in light of their heightened sense of smell. Another odor emanated from the park, as well. Metal. This new flavor of a scent kindled a memory he didn't have time to explore.

He and Landau jogged toward the center of the park, where Rosalind's trail guided him. Having Landau beside him felt curiously similar to running with his father. Some of his sense of loneliness faded to a dim, dull throb as he locked the memory of his father away with others that were too painful to confront.

"She's weaving through them," he explained. "No trouble this time. Nothing she isn't capable of handling, I hope."

Landau grunted in reply, perhaps not wanting to waste his breath as they picked up their pace.

It wasn't long before they saw the men they had scented. Aware of Landau's hesitation, Colton slowed. As soon as he saw who strolled in this park, he slipped behind a tree, leaving Landau to face them. For their sake, not his.

"Judge Landau?" Officer Julias Davidson, of all the rotten luck, said in a surprised tone. "What are you doing out here at this time of night? You do realize how dangerous this place is?"

"Out for a run," Landau replied, faking a shortness

of breath. "My son is out here somewhere, so much faster than his old man that he'll beat me to the street."

"Mind if we accompany you to that street?" Davidson asked in that way cops had of giving people the feeling they were going to do what they wanted, no matter the response.

"Not necessary," Landau protested.

"I'd feel better about it," Davidson said stubbornly, and also a bit reverently…perhaps out of respect for the elder man, Colton guessed, and possibly also to score some future points in court.

Landau had the sensitivity not to look where Colton had hidden himself. "Well," he said to Davidson, "I've probably lost the bet already, anyway. I'm not as young as I used to be, you know. Dylan will win this race, hands down."

"How about if we pretend I didn't hear anything about a federal judge's personal gambling habits," Davidson joked. "If you want to jog ahead, we'll follow. Doesn't running without shoes hurt your feet, though?"

It's useless, Colton sent silently to the Were. Davidson, attitude aside, also wore the badge of a protector, and most of the time he took that job seriously. *Change of plans.* Landau had to lead the cops to the street. The judge, for all his Lycan power and strengths, had an image to maintain. That image, and the shape that went with it, were human.

His own forced companionship with Landau had been terminated. Colton felt sorry about that.

Raising his chin, he sniffed the air. The really disturbing thing about this encounter was that the officers' weapons hadn't been what saturated the area with the odor of metal. Nor had anything the judge might have been carrying in his waistband and pockets triggered the smell. Something else was causing it. Colton glanced across the grass in time to see a flash of what looked to him like the backside of a man's naked body, streaking through the trees.

His heart gave a thump of disapproval.

His beast growled a warning.

The bad wolf criminal element had been wiped from this park a while ago, and cops had been on patrol tonight. So whatever was here had eluded the park's human guardians.

His claws sprang through his skin in reaction to whatever his beast had sensed, and the familiar undulations began in his shoulders as his ligaments began to stretch.

This naked streaker had been no vampire, so what did that leave?

Colton's chest heaved. His ribs cracked, with his spine following suit. He tore his borrowed shirt open and unbuttoned his pants without too much thought about how many times he had stripped lately, and how outrageous the events of the past forty-eight hours had been.

"There is no earthly way a demon could have found us so quickly," he protested as his wulf unfurled. But then demons, by their very definition, weren't earthly.

Once his shift was complete, Colton ran so fast that he virtually skimmed the ground. If it had been a demon he'd seen, and if it had been hunting for Rosalind, he had to be there when the cursed thing found her. He had to hope to God that a demon wouldn't touch her.

As if Rosalind had left a trail of breadcrumbs, her lightly floral scent beckoned to him. She hadn't lost that fragrance or left it behind in favor of others crowding her system. That one thing alone gave him hope. Amid all the changes, Rosalind's she-wulf maintained a firm enough hold on her to overpower the rest.

That she-wulf was what he wanted to find, coax forth, capture, bed and love. They'd had sex in human form, and it had been good. Many more experiences like that, and their wulf sides would want in on the deal. He couldn't imagine how that would go down. Wulf to wulf…

Another flash of white downgraded his speed to a lope. Keyed up, his fur rippled with tension. This wasn't a damn demon though. The bright spot of light turned out to be a lamp post marking a driveway, the first of many driveways bordering the neighborhoods surrounding the park.

Rosalind had gone into public territory, for who knew what reason, with what might or might not have been a demon trailing behind. Being anywhere near to a human neighborhood like this one amounted to a dangerous setback.

Growls rattled in his throat.

He bared his teeth.

Damn it, he had to lose the fur. Things were bad enough without giving the people here a reason to call the cops.

How strong were demons? How crafty, fast?

This didn't have to be a demon.

Jogging, naked, Colton veered off the sidewalk, aiming for an alley behind the closest row of homes and praying that in one of those backyards he'd find some clothes to borrow, hanging on an old-fashioned line. And that the presence of a Night Wulf would scare barking dogs indoors.

Chapter 24

Rosalind had known the exact moment something new began following her, and tried to process the symptoms of this acknowledgment.

Whatever the creature was, its presence made her head hurt. The vicious pounding behind her eyes caused the landscape to swim by in a blur of movement. The lights she passed beneath were like streaks of pain. Her mouth hurt from clenching her teeth hard enough and long enough to fracture a jaw bone. Her wulf exhibited signs of a rare distress that had made her muscled hindquarters quiver.

Her heightened senses didn't like this new thing shadowing her.

Outlines of fences, formerly solid, melted into wavering liquid forms. Buildings became fluid, their edges filmy and undefined. The pavement she raced across buckled in her peripheral vision, though it seemed okay when she glanced at her feet. Either the world was actually losing its shape, or she was losing her mind.

The only thing completely in focus now was the feel of the entity behind her. Awareness of it had become a distress.

Not human, not vampire, not Were. *Demon? Really?*

Afraid to face such an entity in the open, in the darkness from which both it and she had been born, she had instead brought it to civilization. Still, the artificial lights people needed to make them feel safe did nothing to lessen her fear, and streets of houses filled with sleeping humans seemed utterly alien.

Why had she come this way?

Realization struck when she found herself in a corner yard. Familiar smells stopped her cold. This was where she had heard her lover's wail of grief, and where she had viewed the cause of his despair. On this street sat the house where Colton's parents had lived and died; now a place where no one would want to willingly return to.

Over the fence in a bound, Rosalind fled to the alley where she had once watched Colton shift shape. In her mind's eye she saw him there, golden, angry and hurt. That image bolstered her courage somewhat. They had both been Lycans then, at least on the surface, and ignorant of what lay ahead. She had been young in spirit and very naive.

She found the house that still reeked of Lycan death. In the yard behind it, she pulled up to make her stand.

"Come and get it, you bastards," she said.

Dread set in the minute Colton's feet hit the pavement. Rosalind had made a beeline for his parents' house, forcing him to confront his compartmentalized feelings about the terrible events that had taken place there.

He hadn't lived on this street with his parents for years, but had spent a lot of time with them. For that time, he'd forever be thankful. Again, though, why would Rosalind come here?

Vaulting over the fence and landing in the alley, Colton paused to listen for whatever a demon might sound like, not expecting crackling hellfire and devilish laughter. An atmospheric heaviness covered the entire area, as if something not of this world had punched its way through.

He heard nothing at all for the span of several shallow breaths, and then perked up. A growl.

His body lurched into action. Hopping one more fence, he sighted Rosalind crouched on his parents' back step.

Glorious, rare black fur covered her legs and arms, and her claws were raised and gleaming. At her feet lay a pile of clothes that didn't smell anything like her, and probably would have confused any creatures coming her way.

Although she might have been scared, Rosalind was magnificent in the fierceness of her pose. Her she-wulf had taken over, leaving no room for debate about the mastery of her Lycan bloodlines. Even in the face of danger, she radiated with the scent and strength of a pure, dangerous wulf.

She made no gesture of acknowledgment. Her eyes were trained on a darker area near the garage. When she growled again, he turned in what felt like slow motion.

He didn't see a damn thing, though the mere thought of a demon in this yard was viscerally disturbing. Adding a menacing growl to the echo of Rosalind's, Colton stayed frozen in place in case the thing by the garage advanced, feeling sick over the fact that the yard still smelled like blood.

Rosalind balanced on her haunches over the exact spot where his mother's headless body had lain.

Narrowing his concentration, Colton awaited what would come next, afraid that if he moved he would spark an unconscionable reaction in one of hell's denizens.

He felt Rosalind shift position and reluctantly looked to her. When her dark eyes darted to meet his, his heart began to hammer. She was gearing up for a strike, no longer content to play the waiting game.

The air tensed around him. An ungodly, otherworldly shriek that completely stole his breath tore through the quiet. High-pitched and ear-piercing, it shattered the windows beside where Rosalind crouched. A rain of broken glass showered everything, looking like a typhoon of confetti.

In motion, Colton's first thought was for Rosalind's safety, and to hell with the demon. But she jumped to her feet and met him on the walkway before he had registered her astonishing move.

Something else met them in the center of the yard: a glistening, hard-bodied entity with a humanlike shape and no eyes in its twisted face. This thing rammed into Colton so hard, he stumbled sideways. After quickly regaining his balance, and with the sound of his own blood rushing in his ears, Colton stopped, stunned.

In the seconds he had taken to right himself, Rosalind had fallen to the ground, and the demon was leaning over her.

Raging, Colton lunged and knocked the demon away.

Whirling, he showed his teeth, ready to take on this thing. But the demon seemed to have vanished, taking its filthy intentions with it.

Colton fell to his knees bedside his mate, who had shifted back to human form. Without giving a damn about what damage further closeness to her might do, he gathered her to him, cradling her body, rocking her gently and growling her name.

At first glance, he saw no evidence of serious injury. Her fur had protected her from most of the glass. Splinters of it sparkled in her hair like pieces of fallen stars. Only one jagged shard angled through the smooth, flushed skin of her right cheek.

Instincts screamed for him to go after the demon that had hurt her and tear out its throat with his bare hands. A wildness flowed through him that he had only experienced once before, on the night his parents had died.

Sanity seemed to be slipping away from him by degrees.

When Rosalind's eyes opened, she gazed up at him calmly. Raising a hand to touch his white muzzle, she said, "Stay with me, wulf. No one dies tonight."

He had to honor her request. He had to let the demon go. She needed him.

He saw no sign of demon in Rosalind. This monster hadn't touched her. But he had.

With a swift reverse shift in shape, Colton watched the last of the white fur disappear from his arms. He waited for whatever Rosalind's reaction would be. The answer came as he looked into her eyes, which were not black or green, but gray, and continuing to fade.

"Are you all right?" he demanded, wary of that

change being related to him, and unable to do anything about it. Unable to let her go.

"Hold still," he crooned, fingering the piece of glass imbedded in her cheek. With a gentle tug, and not so much as a grimace from Rosalind, the glass came free. Colton tossed it away and pressed a finger to the wound to stop the trickle of blood seeping from the cut. Then he bent down to kiss the spot, startling them both.

The moment stretched in complete silence, broken only when he asked, "Has it gone?"

"Yes."

"It didn't reach you."

"You didn't give it time."

"I'd have killed it if it had."

"I could feel it," she said. "I could feel the soulless being's spirit trying to get inside me."

"Did you tell it there's no more room?"

When she shook her head, glass scattered, making tiny tinkling noises as the pieces hit the concrete.

"I want so badly to go on holding you," he confessed.

"I want that, too. I feel your pain, way down deep, Colton. How can you stand it? How can you stand up and face that kind of pain?"

"Job to do," he said tenderly. "Though you're making that as difficult as possible."

She smiled, and the wound on her cheek oozed more blood. But that smile was worth everything to him. It was the first one he had seen in a while, and was as dazzling as it was brief.

"I tried to get away from you and the others," she explained.

"Yes, and how well did that work?"

When she smiled again, dusted with glass and as white as a sheet, Colton was sure his heart would break.

He uttered his vow…to her. To the night. To the moon, and whoever else might be listening. "I will do anything and everything in my power, forever, to protect you, and keep you selfishly for myself."

Her hair, as white as it was black, her gray eyes, her light skin… Was a ghost so bad? Two ghosts?

He lightly kissed the lips that had temporarily upturned. He kissed her forehead, her injured cheek, her hair, her long, graceful neck. His free hand moved over her, exploring, seeking anything unfamiliar that he'd have to deal with. That *they* would have to deal with.

If Rosalind could become what others around her were, she would remain Lycan. *I'll see to it.*

His mouth came back to hers. He deepened the kiss, separating her lips with his, daring her tongue to dance with his. Her breath was shallow, though her heart raced. Though he felt her energy charging upward to engulf him, she didn't wrap her arms around him, afraid of what else she might do.

He was nearly blinded by his desire for her—for possessing her in every possible way. He had never been so hungry, so demented by the emotions flooding his body and his mind.

Reason, like a blinking light way off in the distance, warned that he couldn't devour her now, here, in this place. It wasn't right. There wasn't time. And yet with one more stroke of his lips across hers, and upon hearing her gasp of reciprocated longing, some of the horror of what had taken place in his parents' house began to fade.

He wasn't alone. He and Rosalind, whatever incarnations they ended up in, would be a family.

As if his life's blood had begun to return, one precious drop at a time, Colton's pulse steadied. Utilizing what was left of his willpower, he drew back just far enough to speak.

"Rosalind, what did the demon want?"

"It wanted you," she replied.

Chapter 25

The meaning of those words eluded Colton at first. Maybe, he thought, he hadn't heard her correctly.

"Me?" he said, his mouth still hovering over hers.

She couldn't have meant that the demon had been waiting for him, as in him personally? Nevertheless, the remark had a haunting vibration that sped through his mind like the tail of a comet.

"Is somebody in there?"

An unfamiliar voice broke through Colton's mental jumble with the force of an unexpected electrical discharge.

"Who's there?" a second voice demanded with stern authority. "We heard noises. Stay where you are. We're coming into the yard."

It was the police. Colton smelled them.

Obeying that command, of course, was utterly impossible. Colton shot to his feet. The uniforms couldn't find him like this, and see what had become of him. Not only did he have no badge or ID, both he and Rosalind were stark naked, breathless, rather scary-looking and sprinkled with broken window glass. To an observer it might look as though they'd tried to break into the house.

He turned his head. Dana Delmonico had told him that the terrible event on this premises had been taken care of, no doubt by Weres on the force who found it in their best interest to help cover this particular murder up. If that cover-up hadn't been accomplished correctly or had been done too hastily, the current window breakage would result in further investigation.

These cops weren't Were.

"We've got to get away," he said, tugging Rosalind to her feet.

She was light. Her thinness had been further accentuated since he'd first seen her. Her ribs were countable. Her arms seemed frail.

She stood proudly before his scrutiny, comfortable with her nakedness, as all Weres were, but trembling from the circumstances they found themselves in. Rosalind didn't fear vampires, and maybe not even demons, but she wanted nothing to do with the Miami PD.

Colton wanted to feed her, fatten her up, pacify her fears. He wanted to keep her within the circle of his arms and assure her that nothing outside their relationship mattered. But he saw, as she moved with the grace of a panther beside him, that her waist-length hair, salt-and-pepper-colored moments before, was now completely white. No black remained, and therefore no evidence of the Night Wulf.

This was the result of a kiss, and of holding her in his arms so briefly.

"Ghost," he said softly, tenderly, as the uniforms on the other side of the fence fumbled with the lock in the gate.

"Landau's is the safest place now. Are you good with that? Will you trust me?" he said to Rosalind. "They will help. I'll be there with you, and it will be all right."

She nodded.

"Promise you'll follow me there," Colton said. "Promise now."

"I promise," Rosalind said, reaching for the pile of clothes on the steps.

Having gained that assurance, Colton leaped through the open window of his parents' house with Rosalind in his wake just as the backyard gate finally swung open behind them.

"Wait. Stop!" both officers directed.

"Sorry, boys," Colton tossed back.

Seconds later he and Rosalind were out the front door and sprinting with a speed that matched the sound of the wind in Colton's ears.

They moved in tandem, side by side, in a rhythm that made Rosalind's heart pound. They were leaving the human neighborhood behind, but the imprint of the demon's silent message stayed with her.

It hadn't wanted her.

It wanted Colton.

She was afraid to slow down, afraid the demon's evil intentions would make her turn around and hunt for it, so that she could wring answers from its scrawny neck.

The hellish monster hadn't had a mouth, or eyes. It

was composed of mounds of tight skin stretched over an otherwise humanlike form, with exceptionally long arms. It had communicated through vibrations in its body, by rubbing bone against bone.

It had followed her, but didn't intend to harm her.

It had wanted Colton, but hadn't stuck around.

The thought made her ill and threatened to topple every theory they had pieced together so far. Things were quite the opposite, in fact. For whatever reason, that demon had used her to get to her mate. She had led it to him.

Her thoughts reformed as she ran beside Colton, with terrible results.

If that monster hadn't wanted her, was there a chance the vampires hadn't wanted her, either? Could they also have been after her lover? But…why?

There had to be more to this story than met the eye. The pairing between Colton, specifically, and herself was what her father had actually been afraid to let happen.

She and Colton. Two entities able to shift shape at will, unlike other Weres. Special beings. Wulf. Now, one of them was a night creature and the other an entity out of Were legend.

She didn't like this terrible line of thought. Now that the floodgates of thought had opened, though, her ideas took on a life of their own. What-ifs became directions.

If a demon wanted to find Colton, and that applied also to the vampires, there might be a possibility that the bloodsuckers that had murdered Colton's family had done so in order to call *him* out, knowing he would follow them with a Were's need for vengeance. They hadn't gone away, but had been waiting in the park.

"Colton!" she exclaimed between breaths, her body again filled with dread. "Colton. No!"

If any of those thoughts proved true, Colton was in the dark about what was happening, and was in real danger. He was the one who had to be careful. She had a Death-caller inside her, and yet her lover might be the entity in trouble.

"Colton," she said again, softer this time, almost pleading.

How had all this started, she wanted to ask him, if not by her coming to his aid in the park? If not imprinting with him immediately, with the first glance in his direction, before fighting off the vampires?

What had made her want to belong to him, and him to her, in a relationship with a supersonic ascent?

His wail of agony.

Not hers.

Rosalind focused on that memory and dug in with her razor-sharp claws.

The sound Colton had made, exemplifying his grief, and in this very neighborhood, is what had chased away her anger over his early rejection. His wail of unimaginable pain had to have been what succeeded in sealing her soul to his.

His wail. *His* call. The pain and death in that heart-rending sound he had made after finding the remains of his loved ones was the language that a Banshee, whose deal was to announce those same things, would recognize and identify with.

She had been drawn to his pain. It had been love at first sight. Like calling to like. She had accepted this, confronted it, reveled in it. Did that make her a cohort of the monsters in the area? Had her need kept Colton from seeing the possibility of his own peril?

She, usually so fleet on her feet, stumbled.

The data seemed flawed, the gaps insurmountable. Colton had been right. Judge Landau and the elders were their only option for finding the truth.

Perhaps sensing her distress, Colton slowed. In the heat of the balmy night, chills covered his naked body, mimicking hers. Having told him something of the demon's desire, his mind would be as active as hers in attempting to process that information. There was so much going on in her mind, she couldn't enter his.

Rosalind shook her head hard to clear it.

There was someone up ahead.

A silver-haired man was headed their way beneath the lights of the tall Landau gates. Backed by the two big Weres that had stood guard at the gate, the silver-haired Lycan tossed some clothes to Colton and gestured for the gates to be closed after them.

Colton's sigh of relief when the sound of iron hitting iron resonated in the night moved through Rosalind as if she'd made it.

Chapter 26

There were more Weres on the front lawn than Colton had ever seen. Young Weres and old. Landau, his wife, his son Dylan and Dana Delmonico were the recognizable few. Beyond their somber presence stood the rest of the Weres Colton had met in this same area the last time he'd faced a welcoming party.

Had that only been two nights ago?

The difference was that he felt almost glad to see them this time.

"I'm truly sorry about that," the judge said as the gates closed. "I couldn't get rid of those officers in the park. They wanted to drive me home. Then they waited here for a while. Is everything all right?"

"Not unless you can discount the presence of a demon in Miami," Colton replied.

"A—"

"Demon," Colton repeated. "An eyeless, mouthless bastard that Rosalind says was looking for me."

He turned to Rosalind, who was inches from him and staring nervously at the reception line. "Do you want to go inside? Your father is probably waiting to see you."

When she shook her white-haired head, a rustle of murmurs went through the gathered crowd. Colton had forgotten how her appearance had to have surprised them. The younger Weres, Dylan and his pack, had never seen Rosalind. They hadn't been allowed to see her.

Here she stood. A creature possessed by a spirit that none of them understood, although it would have been easy for them, as Weres, to pick up on the subtle Otherworldly aspect of her aura. It was all there in her scent, along with that seductive fragrance of flowers.

Rosalind, just inside the walls, had donned a blue long-sleeved sweatshirt and a pair of jeans. Her feet were bare. Her hair was tangled and she was covered in blood. Looking battle-scarred, she faced them all defiantly. Truly special. One of a kind.

He knew she was shaking inside.

Colton stepped in front of her possessively to ward off the stares. To the judge, he said, "Do you have any idea why a demon might want to find a wulf?"

Landau frowned. "I've never heard of a demon actually existing, not to mention showing itself in public."

"I have," a woman said, stepping forward and into the light of the porch.

All eyes turned to the auburn-haired beauty who was flanked by Matt Wilson, the Were detective Colton had met the other night.

"I run a facility not far out of the city center," she

said. "A psychiatric hospital. A few days ago I felt a presence hanging around outside and went out for a look. I saw what I now presume might have been your demon skirting the perimeter of the fence. When I turned on the lights, it slunk away."

"Then there's a chance it wasn't after me," Colton said, turning to Rosalind. "I've never seen that place."

"It was looking for you," Rosalind confirmed.

"Why?"

"Black heart," a deep voice said from behind them, and everyone in that yard spun to find Jared Kirk, standing in the house's open doorway.

"What's that?" Judge Landau barked.

To the judge Rosalind's father asked, "Do we want to talk about this here or in private?"

"I think it's gone too far to be considered private," Colton replied in Landau's place.

Judge Landau glanced to his son, and to his pack of gathered Weres. Dylan spoke up. "I think we need to know what's going on. We're the peacekeepers here. How can we do our jobs if there are secrets we aren't privy to, or if some of this missing information can put not only innocent bystanders, but those we love in jeopardy?"

Kirk stiffly took a seat on a bench. He gathered his thoughts before speaking again.

"My daughter," he said, "is not just Lycan. She is part Death-caller, a Celtic spirit who deals with death. Not handing it out, not walking hand in hand with Death. A Banshee, as some call them, merely acknowledges the coming of Death, and warns humans of its approach."

His voice had dulled, but he continued. "The spirit in Rosalind is a messenger from the Otherworld, and something we know little about. Hence the need for protection and seclusion."

"That doesn't mean she's a danger to others," Colton said, realizing how rude it was for them to be speaking of Rosalind's secrets, and about her, as if she wasn't there.

"I believe that she's no danger if the spirit is contained," Kirk said.

Colton was of a mind to pick Rosalind up and take her away from this. But she needed these explanations as much as any of them did. Probably so much more.

"I didn't guard her for other people's safety, really. I guarded her for her own welfare," Kirk said. "Telling myself otherwise, and allowing myself to believe it was for the sake of others that she had to be hidden away, was perhaps my best way, my only way, of finding justice in keeping her apart from all of you."

Dylan Landau spoke up. "You said black heart as if that's something significant. What does it mean?"

More murmurings went through the crowd.

"Rosalind will become something else if she…"

"What will she become?" the judge asked when Kirk let the explanation die.

"Night Wulf."

Colton heard Rosalind's soft, lamenting whine before her father's explanation had concluded. It drove him forward so fast, he shocked Jared Kirk into silence when he faced the elder Were from a closeness of less than three feet.

"Maybe I spoke too soon and she has heard enough for now," he said.

"Yes." Kirk nodded sympathetically. "But this affects you, Colton, if you're the demon's target."

Colton nodded for him to go on.

"I had to accept that you had mated, and along with that the possibility, the hope that you would adhere to my request never to touch her again until we knew what the situation was. In ignoring my request, you've placed her and yourself in danger. The others who come after her will want to be rid of you. You now stand in their way. As her mate, they need your removal in order to make Rosalind realize her full potential."

Light-headed from the strain of standing up to this after all that had gone on before, Colton raised a hand to stop the Were. Rosalind had other ideas. She appeared beside him to stare at her father.

"Black heart," she said. "What is that?"

Kirk looked pained by the smooth deception of his daughter's calm expression. Though his reluctance showed, he met her gaze.

"A Night Wulf is created if you, Rosalind, were to mate with a species in whose chest rests a black heart. An evil heart. Rogue vampires, demons and fallen angels will all fight for the right to turn you, to possess you, in order to bring this thing into being."

"I thought that's what I am already," Rosalind said weakly.

"No. Not yet. Not ever, hopefully. Because that creature would, I believe, have the potential to rule any species she chose."

Colton put his arm around Rosalind's waist, able to feel her tremors roll through him.

Her father spoke again. "Keeping you from actualizing such an inheritance has always been my goal. Keeping you hidden from those kinds of beasts was all I ever wanted."

Colton staggered forward. "You thought I'd have such a heart? Because I'm what you've called a ghost?"

Kirk's patience was worn, his face haggard. "I didn't know what the vampires had done to you. I thought you might be the key to a Night Wulf's conception. I was wrong."

"Who killed my mother?" Rosalind asked. Colton thought her voice sounded sad.

"Something other than demon. Something worse." Kirk's wide shoulders sagged. "They all came eventually, after so much time without a sighting or hint of their presence. And they came at once. I didn't know until it was too late. Your mother slipped out to meet them without my knowledge, and while you and I slept. She sacrificed herself for you and for me, knowing we would go through it all again when you were old enough, but wanting to give us some time."

There were tears on Rosalind's face when Colton pulled her closer. The tears streamed down. With gentle fingers he stroked her face, wiping away the dampness. "You are blameless, innocent and vulnerable," he said to her. "I don't care who is after you or me. We can beat this and find the truth."

She looked up at him with pale gray eyes. "They nearly killed you the first time I followed you. Your parents dying was bad enough, but that didn't have to be connected to me, to what I am."

Then she stiffened and looked to her father. "I didn't know Colton until the night the vampires attacked his family. Those monsters couldn't have been trying to take him from me."

Leaning over, she spoke to her father clearly. "Secrets. There are more. I can taste them."

Kirk shook his head as if some parts of this mystery were too hard to comprehend.

"The ridiculous part of all this," Judge Landau chimed in, "is how they can think they can tackle a werewolf pack to get what they want, when what they want is for the most part Lycan."

The judge approached Rosalind cautiously, not afraid, Colton sensed, but taking care not to alarm her. "What else can you tell us about this, Rosalind? You must know something."

"Colton and I were meant to be mated," she replied without hesitation. "I don't see how vampires could have predicted that ahead of time and gone after his family."

Landau appeared to consider her statement. His gaze fixed thoughtfully on Jared Kirk.

"Do you understand that, and what might cause her to believe she's right?" he asked.

In the lull of silence following Landau's inquiry, Rosalind repeated her tiny sound of distress. Whether or not her father fully comprehended what was going on, Rosalind had forged some sort of link to the truth, and knew it.

"What is it?" Colton asked her.

She turned her luminous eyes to him. "Memories."

"Tell me about them."

"I have to speak with my father alone first."

"Use the house," Landau said.

Reluctantly, Colton stood aside so that Rosalind could see the doorway. "I'll hate every minute you're in there, and out of my sight," he confessed. "I won't leave the porch until you come out, or call."

Kirk looked pretty much like a doomed man, Colton

thought, as the elder Were, with hunched shoulders and a solemn expression, followed his daughter inside.

Colton placed his back to the doorjamb and stared out at the gathering of Weres. "Any problems with this?" he asked them. "Or with hosting us here until we figure out what to do next? Because if there are, we'll honor that, and go."

"No problems," Judge Landau replied, as spokesman and Alpha of his pack. "None whatsoever."

The rest of Landau's pack hadn't moved a muscle.

Chapter 27

Rosalind preceded her father into the Landaus' living room, feeling trapped there. Feeling wild, and way too feral to make use of a chair.

She began to pace.

"The last time I was here," she said, "I eagerly waited for Colton to heal, naively believing that everything might be okay once he did. It was you who frightened me with hints of the secrets you were keeping. Maybe things would have been easier if you had shared those secrets with me."

"You have matured," her father said in response. "Quickly. I'm not sure you would have listened or understood just days ago."

She retraced her steps. "'This male is not for you' is what you told me. And that Colton wouldn't have been compatible before the fight, and certainly not after it.

Also, you said that I'd have no idea what would happen if..." She let that empty sentence linger a while. Her father didn't break the silence.

"You said that I couldn't help him, that I couldn't remain near him. It was imperative, you told me, that Colton and I were separated, the sooner the better."

She hesitated, and looked her father in the face. "But the thing I remember best of all was that you said two extremes were never destined to meet."

Rosalind walked toward the window, able to feel Colton out there. Allowing his presence to calm her, warm her.

"Two such extremes, Father. A Lycan with an unusual spirit inside her, and a Lycan warrior who had nearly lost his life and retained it as a ghost of his former self."

She was again standing above him. "How did you know what to expect? Because it's quite obvious to me now that you did."

Her father's Lycan-green eyes were bright in the indoor light. "I didn't know anything for sure," he finally said. "Until I heard this ghost's name."

"Killion."

"Yes. Once I'd been made aware of that, I realized that it was probably already too late for the both of you."

Rosalind put her hands on the arm of his chair. "Too late for what?"

"To reverse or withhold your bond. It was, you see, more than a case of like meeting like, and after all this time..."

Circles. They were going in circles, when all her father had to do was tell her the truth.

"I don't think anyone comprehends what this bond

means," her father continued. "How could they? I'm not sure I believe it."

"They? Who do you mean? What do you mean?" Rosalind demanded.

"The monsters."

"What wouldn't they believe?"

He looked directly into her waiting eyes at last, and she saw the resolution on his face. "That you, of all Weres, could have met up with the heritage of that damned Banshee who started all this," he said.

She waited for that to make sense, but it was gibberish he'd fed her. Not the truth at all.

"Heritage?" she echoed.

Her father waved a hand at the door. "Colton Killion comes from an old line. One in particular that was distressing to me. Colton is from the same lineage as the Were who mated with your great-great-grandmother, Rosalind. He's from the same family. How's that for the long-range designs of fate? After generations, by jumping a wall in a city where you were only visiting for a couple of days and supposedly behaving yourself, you met up with someone out of your rising spirit's goddamn past."

He shook his hand, still raised, as if cursing the fate he'd just spoken about. "It was fantastical. Far-fetched. Who could have believed it? How could I have trusted my instincts on the matter? I knew only that you had locked onto this Were with an uncanny adherence that seemed absurd, given that you hadn't even really met him. You'd only seen him once, out there, beyond these walls. Isn't that the truth?"

Rosalind frowned, not really understanding this at

all. “Yes,” she said. “That’s true. I saw him for the first time in the park.”

“It likely was the spirit in you that recognized him, and it didn’t take much. I don’t begin to claim to comprehend how that can happen, or if it actually did. You asked for what I believe to be the truth, and this is it.”

Her father’s theory was an astonishing one, and probably an idea that no one, including herself, would have taken seriously, had he mentioned it in this house while Colton had been hurt and healing. He had been right about that.

She was different now.

“How can a spirit identify someone they’d never seen before?” she asked. “It would have to mean that whatever kind of life that spirit manifests actually continues on. Not just instincts and urges, but actually able to recognize something beyond itself.”

She was feeling strange, and went on in a rush. “Wouldn’t that theory suggest that not only is a Banshee inside me, it’s possessing me? Driving me toward what it wants?”

Her father countered, “Would you otherwise believe in love at first sight? A love so strong that you’d be willing to give up your life for a stranger ten minutes after laying eyes on him?”

“I don’t believe this,” Rosalind stated firmly.

“I can’t blame you,” her father said. “It is, however, the only explanation I have. And after accepting it as a possibility, however remote, and aside from the dangers now presenting themselves like a bad case of déjà-vu over what happened to your mother and I…I see no better way to explain what you so desperately want to understand.”

Rosalind's stomach was churning. Although she wanted to discount her father's explanation, she was, at that moment, aware of Colton's thoughts. He was going to come in after her. She'd been away from him for too long.

The explanation her father had given her suddenly seemed viable. She felt as though a ray of moonlight had reached down inside her to help lighten the load, but it was actually the sensation of sudden enlightenment.

Inside her, in the dark space where the unknown hovered, some of her fear began dissipate. A small portion of it, anyway. For whatever reason, she had found her soul mate. The real one. The only one. And who cared, after all, how she had found Colton?

It was a game of sacrifice and give-and-take and spirits merging. That's what this larger-than-life love was.

Had her mother known about any of this? Foreseen it? Her mother had sacrificed herself for her family, with hopes that when the spirit rose within her daughter, if indeed it did, Rosalind would have the time to find her true love and explore her options.

Her father had other ideas.

A Banshee was probably the closest thing to real darkness on the planet. A monster magnet. Her father had maintained the hope that the creatures seeking a resting place for their black-hearted leader might never find it, and that his daughter might break the link of the Banshee spirit, who had changed the fates of so many, by being protected from all that.

By never meeting a mate.

By never setting foot outside their gates. Nothing like her mother's wishes.

But how tricky fate could be. Landau had invited them here. She had escaped her father's net. And in doing so, she had found Colton…setting the entire scenario into action.

Colton, a member of the same family as the Lycan male who had mated with the woman the Banshee had saved all those generations ago.

God help them.

Serendipity? Fate? She had found Colton in the park, and two families had been reunited by the spirit rising within her. The spirit who had recognized Colton from afar.

"Colton," Rosalind said as her knees finally began to give way.

He was there in a flash of taut, tense muscle, with a face strained paler than hers. His facial welts gave him an edgy, hungry look. She had never really seen him in the light.

But Colton Killion had always been dangerous.

What would have happened if the vampires hadn't attacked? If the bloodsuckers hadn't killed his family that night?

Would she have found Colton eventually, anyway? Would fate have taken care of the details, ensuring she would, and that the two families would again be joined together?

A date with destiny?

"We have to kill them all," she said to Colton. "All who know about me, and about you."

Colton glanced past her, to her father, who stood up as if he were well enough to ready for the next necessary fight.

"We have to stop them from making me one of them,

completely. We can't let them put a black heart inside my chest."

"How do we do that?" he asked.

Rosalind started for the door, pausing when she reached it. "I call them," she said with absolute certainty. "And hope they all show up."

The intensity of their bond made Rosalind look longingly at him one last time from the doorway. She wasn't seeking permission to do what she had said she would; she was letting him see her feelings.

There were plenty of questions still unasked and unanswered, Colton thought, and yet he had to go on trust here. Trust his gut. Trust her. Rosalind had unselfishly, and at great risk, led the demon away from him and the Landau pack that very night. Her motives had been pure. Thoughts of a black heart inside her chest, and what that might mean, were unthinkable.

More than any of them, Rosalind wanted to give a shout to all of the monsters in the area, sensing that culling monsters with a taste for blood was the only way to have any kind of peace, if only for a while.

If the creatures in this area that knew about them were removed from the equation, maybe no others would take up the scent.

He followed Rosalind outside. She walked to where the judge stood with the rest of his family and his pack.

"It's my problem," she said, and Colton knew how much effort it took for her to face them and to speak. "I'm sorry to have brought this sad doom to your doorstep. I know now that they won't go away or back off for any length of time. Though I'm not certain why they want us so much, or the actual specifics of that kind of lust, Colton and I have to face them."

She paused only to draw a breath. "I have no right to ask you to help us. You've been told what I am, and can see what Colton has become because of the vampires. It's against my better judgment to ask for your aid, but I just don't know what else to do."

"We're in." Dylan Landau spoke up first, with a giant step forward.

Judge Landau looked to his son.

"We cleaned up the park a year ago. Now look at it," Dylan said. "Monsters think it's their personal playground and that they can come out whenever they want to."

"We don't know what to expect," the elder Landau cautioned.

"Vampires," Rosalind said. "And demons. Definitely more than one of each. Supernatural creatures out of nightmares. But then, so are we, really, when it comes right down to it."

Colton noticed Dana Delmonico's brief grin. Delmonico would know about those nightmares firsthand, since she likely hadn't known about werewolves until she was bitten by one.

His gaze moved to the others present. Every single one of those Weres nodded to him, in accord.

A small twitch in his chest made him bow his head.

"We're sure as hell not going to let you face them alone," Matt Wilson seconded, with the auburn-haired female by his side.

"It seems that my pack has made up their minds," Judge Landau observed. "But this night's almost over."

"Has it only been one?" Colton muttered, because it already felt like years since he'd last stood in this yard.

"Tomorrow," Rosalind said. "I'll call them then. I can't presume to see what will happen, but it's the only option open that I can see."

Jared Kirk had followed them into the yard. He said, "The approaching sunrise will keep them down and give us time to prepare."

Judge Landau turned to his pack. "Tomorrow is Saturday. No one who counts will miss us at the day job." He turned back. "Jared?"

"I plan on being better by then," Rosalind's father said.

Landau looked at his son. "You understand how dangerous it's going to be."

"And how dangerous it'll be across the board if we don't take care of this new pest problem," Dana Delmonico added.

Colton almost smiled. Dana Delmonico was a tough cop and a tough Were. Not Lycan, but a perfect match for Dylan, all the same.

Again, facing this pack, he realized how much he had missed in the past by being a loner.

"We'll need police presence," Matt Wilson advised. "So others don't come wandering in."

"Adam Scott can arrange a perimeter," Dylan said. "With the help of a neighboring pack."

"There are other Weres on the force, outside the city?" Colton asked.

"Several good ones," Dylan replied.

"We can't take this fight to the park here," another Were said. "Besides being too close to home, outside police presence would be noted."

Colton looked more closely at the large brown-haired young man who added, "It's way too risky."

"Then we can bring them to the hospital grounds," the auburn-haired female who was Wilson's mate suggested. "No one hangs around a psychiatric ward, especially after dark."

"Good one, Jenna," Dylan said to the female before turning back to Rosalind. "Does this work for you, Rosalind? Will you be able to bring them anywhere you choose?"

Like the Pied Piper? Colton thought.

"I'm not sure if I can bring them anywhere," she replied with a tired, sober face.

She continued to shake, part of that no doubt from being so close to this many others. But she continued to maintain her stance.

Although no one allowed their gazes to linger on her long, Colton read in their faces how uneasy they felt in her presence. They were equally as uneasy with him.

He didn't blame them. Two strange Lycans needed their help. They didn't have to go out of their way to oblige, but this was their territory, and Weres were nothing if not protective of their space.

If all went well, and that was a big *if*, what would happen afterward? They'd all return to their respective packs and homes and mates, and he and Rosalind, with or without her father, would be left to themselves.

The location of Rosalind's home had been compromised. He couldn't take her back to his apartment, and the thought of reclaiming his city life made his muscles quiver in distaste. Also, and the biggest what-if of all, any future depended on the premise that he and Rosalind would survive the next night.

"Thank you," he said to Landau and his pack; two simple words denoting a gratitude that couldn't actually be expressed to the proper degree.

"I'll stand guard until dawn," he announced, afraid to go back into the house with Rosalind bunking inside it, and especially afraid to go anywhere near her if this was to be his last night. His and hers.

Not the way to think, he chastised sternly. *That last-night business.* There might just as well be more nights. Someday he and Rosalind would be able to meet again, flesh to flesh, with no clothes to get in the way, and not a black heart between them. They would take up where they had left off.

He'd confess how much she meant to him as he entered her blistering heat, feeling her arms wrapped around him and hearing her murmur of approval. She'd be his, and he hers, their bodies and their souls finally free to fully explore an almost mystical union unfettered by the chains of DNA that had tangled things up.

Believing in that future seemed to be the only way for him to get through the next twenty-four hours.

Rosalind's eyes met his. Gray eyes that were bottomless and seductive. The pull of that seduction was like a soft tug on his wounded soul.

Meet me, her eyes invited. *Find me.*

And in that instant, Colton's heart, mind, body and soul, despite all the arguments to the contrary, and with the full backing of his beast, agreed that he would.

Rosalind rubbed at her ankle, free now of the chain, thanks to the Landaus. The livid red ring of burned skin had already faded in the past hour, though the spot still stung.

The bruises on her shins were a dark blue, and gave her the speckled appearance of a leopard, rather than a wolf. She'd forgotten about the pain already.

Filled with barely contained energy, she circled the rug on the floor in the room the Landaus had given her. Colton hadn't come inside. He was supposed to be standing guard, but other Weres were sharing that job, setting up a physical wall of muscle and bone and grit around her.

Colton's restlessness beat at her, adding fuel to her own anxiety. "Come on," she whispered to the window, insanely expecting the white wulf to reply.

She tore at her borrowed clothes, stripped to naked skin and tossed the discards in a corner, needing to be free and to breathe. The sun would soon rise. She guessed there was less than an hour of darkness left in what felt like an endless night. She dreaded the coming of daylight. She had never seen Colton in the sun. Both of them were somehow tied to darkness.

Would he still love her when that darkness had fled?

"Colton. Where are you?"

Close to the windowsill, and with the memory of what use she had made of a window the last time she had been a guest in this house, Rosalind peered out. She stayed there until her shoulders complained and her head began to throb.

"White wulf, do you hear me?"

Would the monsters ignore her, if Colton could? If she didn't have the ability to call a lover, what chance did she have against the rest of the world?

Something like anger stirred in her stomach. Her beast, maybe. Possibly it was the Death-caller she imagined to be like a beast and taking up space.

Scared of what that might mean, Rosalind clamped her teeth together so that the fangs would have no room to expand. Anger was the providence of vampires. She wasn't one of them.

Again, there was movement inside her, and she swore out loud. If the Death-caller was trying to tell her something, she didn't want to listen. If she knew ahead of time how this would turn out, and how many good Weres might lose their lives, she might not follow through.

The skin on the nape of her neck prickled and chilled up. Balmy Miami breezes exerted an unusually weighty pressure that made her nerve endings burn.

She blinked slowly as her heart began to rev.

Her muscles went rigid.

And she knew instinctively, as her legs finally crumpled beneath her, that Colton had come.

Chapter 28

Her white-haired lover appeared on the sill, looking like a real ghost; a fierce, feral werewolf in man form. The look in his eyes told her of his desire to swallow her whole.

He had somehow reached the third-floor window and wasn't breathing hard from the effort. He was half in and half out of the window, crouched in the space he crammed his generous bulk into. They stared at each other in silence. The tension building between them made Rosalind sway.

"I hoped you would come," she finally said in a husky tone.

He didn't move.

"You have doubts," she said, having to put that out there to get things he might be feeling that they'd never actually faced into the open.

"Yes," he said. "Doubts."

"You're not sure about the vampire traits I've adopted, or that have adopted me. Is that it? Fangs like mine hurt your loved ones."

He leaned into the room, closer to her.

"Because I have fangs and can perceive monsters with similar ones doesn't mean I can read their thoughts," she explained. "If they even have thoughts."

He waited for her to go on, probably sensing she would.

"I've been a rebel in most ways because of an energy too boundless to contain. It's there now, pushing me, encouraging me. Beast or spirit, that energy tells me that I must be near you."

She watched a muscle in Colton's right cheek twitch.

"It could be that the monsters simply sense my attraction to you and want you out of the way, as my father suggested. And it also might be that you were their target all along by belonging to an old Were family, and I'm the one in the way. Since we can't ask the monsters about their objectives, there's only one way to find out what their agenda is."

"By going after them," he said.

"Yes. I'm not really like them. You know that. But I can't have this hanging over me, and over us. I hate it all. Don't you imagine I'd like to be normal, like the rest of the Weres out there?"

Her confession moved him, and also possibly hurt him in some way. Her ghost unfolded himself and stepped into the room with an understanding light in his pale eyes. In spite of his formidable size and the fact that he now bore signs of the same strength and power she had first noticed in that blasted park before his injuries, his expression softened. When he looked at her lovingly, a groan of relief escaped through her lips.

"If I didn't care so much," he said, "none of this would matter. Can it be fate that brought us together? Some sort of metaphysical trick that we aren't even aware of? Something in me has found something in you that I've been searching for, and vice versa, that runs as deep as our DNA? Hell, I'd like to think of it like that. Who wouldn't want to believe that spirits continue on in the ones we love, and that true love can find us in a world this large?"

Although Colton hadn't touched her, Rosalind felt the heat of his gaze. Warmth had never seemed so close, while at the same time unattainable. If they were to physically meet tonight and she were to become more like him than she already was, her unique connection to the monsters might lessen or be lost altogether. If she couldn't key in to the bloodsuckers' location, everyone here would be at a loss.

As she saw it, she stood at the edge of a cliff with her toes hanging over, wanting Colton desperately and knowing how desperately he wanted her in return. The short distance separating them hummed with the frantic energy of withholding themselves from having what they needed most. Physical contact, and the signal to go ahead and take what they could, while they could.

"Can't you sleep?" he asked gently, looking to the bed.

"I'm afraid to shut my eyes," she confessed.

"What if I'm here beside you?"

"Won't that be the ruin of us both?"

"I'm your guard dog, Rosalind. Tomorrow will test

our strength. You need some rest before tomorrow arrives."

"I have never been stronger," she whispered. *Another confession, and something you might not know.*

She went on before he could address her remark. "I'm attempting to contain the power surges that rise and fall inside me without my permission. I'm not sure where these surges are coming from or where their origins lie. Maybe all the different parts of me—all those monstrous traits—are vying for dominance. I have a war going on inside me, Colton, and can't take much more. Moving eases the urge to throw myself out of that window."

"Then I will have to distract you," he said.

She replied earnestly, "I wish you could." *But you can't. You won't. You're honorable, even now.*

Breath had become the thing uniting them lately; his warm breath on her face that shouted to her of how close he was. Her slow, exhaled sigh mingled sensuously with his in the open, and without their mouths having to meet.

As she faced him, the moment seemed suspended in time. Both of them wanted to give in to the urges. Just one move would crash the barrier they had erected, whether by accident or on purpose.

"Rationalization versus needs," he said. "We can't even console each other properly. But we're here, together. We're alive and surrounded by allies, and tomorrow might be a turning point. That will have to do for now."

He didn't believe this. His eyes told her that. They were wide, shining and surrounded by dark circles that were remnants of a pain that would never fully leave him. She had become a part of that pain.

Yet she looked deeply into Colton's eyes, tilting her head back to do so. "That's the difference between us," she said. "I've always been greedy, and have required more than what my life had to offer me."

Howl to howl. That's what had brought them together and sealed the deal, Rosalind thought. *Spirit calling to spirit.* Those spirits were wresting the willpower from them both right here. Right now.

The dark thing in her soul did a slow turn, bringing up the image of an ancient memory she couldn't quite see. Was it this Were's image, and what lay inside him? Is that what the spirit in her was trying to tell her? That it was all right to give in, and that neither of them had to be strong all the time?

"It won't let up," she said, breaking off eye contact and hanging her head. "If you stay, it won't be in that window. Not for long."

His lips were inches from hers. She knew the feel of their fullness and the moistness within; knew she shouldn't do what her heart told her to do, and that there might be consequences. But the dark thing nestled inside her urged her to rebel this one last time. When joined with the wishes of her own spirit, that urge was too great to ignore.

She stood, and rose onto tiptoe.

Reaching up, taking hold of Colton's soft white hair with both of her hands, she pulled his lips to hers.

Chapter 29

Rosalind was liquid fire, blazing flames, raging desire in the shape of a woman. How could he stand against that?

The animal in Colton wanted more. The spirit in Rosalind demanded it. Through her tantalizing lips Colton felt the core of heat that awaited him. He had never experienced anything like this, not even with her, and was willing to accept the damage that might result.

It was absolutely necessary to reach that heat.

He closed his eyes, giving in to the shape and texture of her with all of his senses. Below his waist, he was already erect and aching. His beast was excitedly calling to hers. *All due to a kiss. This kiss. The culmination of so many withheld feelings.*

Their hands met near his thighs. Her fingers brushed over his. As she slid her tongue between his lips, her hand moved between their bodies to the hardness pressing against her. The murmur of her pleasure turned him on, drove him on, made him realize that he loved her with a fury that bordered on obscene.

She was already naked. Sensuously, seductively naked.

As the kiss deepened, Rosalind's sharp nails tore at his shirt, scratching his chest, leaving a sting. As if his partial bareness wasn't enough to satisfy her, her hands then sought the waistband of his pants. He heard the buttons pop.

Riled up and unable to wait much longer for what was going to happen, and what was inevitable, Colton pushed her hot hands aside and lifted her up. He'd always had this same compulsion to hold her.

Their bodies, locked together, crashed to the carpet. He rolled her over onto her back, reveling in the slender angles so sharp beneath him.

Her sinewy arms wrapped around his rippling back, hugging him close, assuring he wouldn't change his mind.

Never in a million years would he have changed it.

She gasped once, and growled low in her throat as if she needed air, but he didn't want to let up or let her go.

He took his mouth from hers for a span of seconds to allow her that breath, and looked into her eyes when she took it. White lashes made the gray irises seem lighter. Masses of tangled white hair framed her face. Long white strands spilled across the floor like rays of moonlight. These were ghostly signs. Symptoms of their intimacy.

They were his fault.

He came back to her when she flashed a smile, but

he couldn't smile back. And when Rosalind ran her tongue across his chin in a slick downward slide that ended at his neck, then lightly bit into his flesh with her little white fangs, waves of surprised pleasure shot through both man and beast that made thoughts about promises and honor useless.

"Is that all you've got?" he asked as he stoked the curve of Rosalind's bare thigh with his fingers, inching them toward the heavenly place he would soon lose himself in if anything in the world would allow it; thinking that if he didn't get there soon, he might lose his mind.

"Not all I've got," she whispered with her head thrown back. "Not nearly everything."

Her voice was thick and incomparably sexy. Colton spread her legs with his. *For good or ill, we have jumped that boundary.* Whatever happened next, they were both equally to blame.

Her thighs were inferno-hot. He reached her soft, feminine folds without taking his gaze from hers. Dipping one finger inside her to test her readiness was nearly his undoing.

Just as it was hers.

Rosalind arched her back, lifting her breasts precariously close to his mouth. Her smooth skin was luminous in the darkened room and as pale as the meager light slanting through the window.

Soon, Colton thought fleetingly as he ran his tongue over the valley between her breasts, the moon would hand the sky over to her golden competitor. Sunrise was fast approaching.

They had so little time left. Not enough for taking one delicate pink bud of her nipple into his mouth, or removing his pants. "I'm sorry about that," he said.

Rosalind's eyes widened when he unleashed himself and settled between her legs. She opened her mouth as if she'd cry out when he pierced her petal-soft folds and slipped his cock inside her. But she didn't make a sound.

She writhed beneath him, sending her hips upward, and he had to withdraw, wait, hold on. His muscles shook with the effort.

Rosalind held him tighter.

His slight retreat shook him to the marrow, and made him colder. This isn't what they wanted. *No retreat.*

"More," Rosalind whispered, as if she had read his mind.

Harder. Faster. Now, she was demanding.

He sank into her again, knowing he belonged there and that he was claiming her for his own. His next thrust shot through her with a burning intensity that robbed them both of breath. He pulsed inside her, feeling her rush of sweet, blistering heat rain down to meet him.

Again, he plunged into her soft, warm silk. And again after that, caressing Rosalind from the inside out, each stroke more potent than the one before.

Deeper he went, feeling impossibly hard and long, until all thoughts about time vanished—blown away by the way Rosalind openly and unconditionally accepted him and the smoldering power in this union.

She met the beating of his hips with thrusts of hers. The sound of their bodies meeting filled the room with dull slapping echoes. Her heated legs wrapped around him like a fleshy velvet vice, making it more difficult for him to pull back.

Her hands were again in his hair, and on his shoulders. Her fingernails, like claws, raked his upper back.

He felt their wulfs connect in that mystical union

that took them down to another layer of being. The soul of the wulf and the soul of a man were together and meeting their match, their refuge, their sanctuary, in Rosalind. The sensation was overwhelmingly complex, and had to be even more unimaginable for her, since she housed not only two spirits, but also a third.

If he was lost, so was she.

She came back for a kiss, and sucked his lips between hers. Her canines pinched his tongue, so that he tasted blood.

Colton squeezed his muscles and plunged in and out of his lover with a demonic force. He had been seeking this all his life, and perhaps, if the whole spirit theory was true, even longer. They weren't just two bodies merging; they were starving souls bringing life back, full circle.

Their spirits were anchored by an intimacy beyond the imagination…in a place where hunger was everything. Theirs was a relationship that wove mind, body and spirit into a braided whole.

Too soon, he found that place in her he had desperately needed to reach. *So hot. So very tight.* With a final push backed by all of his need and condoned by his wulf, he hit Rosalind's molten core and burst, drowning that core with a heat of his own and feeling as if the night had swallowed them both.

Rosalind, her mouth still clamped to his, screamed. That scream went on and on as her climax hit and stretched, and as he held her there.

God, was Colton's final oath when he could breathe again. *I'm home.*

The room had grown quiet. No breeze stirred the curtains or ruffled his hair as Colton stood at the foot of the bed like some sort of angelic sentinel, observing Rosalind.

He had counted every ragged breath she took in, and noted each flutter of her eyelids, until her eyes finally stayed closed sometime after dawn.

He talked to her then, whispering tender endearments as he kept watch, and fighting the constant yearning to lie down beside her.

The room smelled of open windows, warm sheets and hot, spent bodies. It smelled of wulf, of sex, and hardly like anything human. Rosalind's heat still warmed his veins, though his muscles were stiff from standing.

He waited until the sun rose before finally flexing his shoulders. He crossed to the window to see if Weres still roamed in the yard, knowing that daylight hours would allow them an overdue rest in preparation for tonight's show of strength.

Eventually, he'd also have to sit down, eat something, shut his eyes. But he didn't see how he could do any of those things when Rosalind looked so small lying there. In sleep, it was difficult to see the brave, supernatural entity she had become in the outline of a young woman curled up in a fetal position.

She smelled like him, he thought as his lips hovered longingly above hers for what seemed like the millionth time. But with the rising sun came a warning protest from his beast.

It was time to leave her.

He looked at her again, wishing for just one more minute. Her face was healing with incredible speed. Only a smooth pink line hinted at where the shard of glass had penetrated her cheek.

"There's enough Lycan left in you to access our healing powers. You'll be glad to know that, my love," he crooned.

Rosalind's face and hands were the only naked parts of her visible. A blanket covered the rest. The heady allure of those small areas—the length of her slender fingers, the sculpted edge of her jaw—drove him crazy. That same madness brought his beast in and out of focus as all parts of him lusted for the woman on the bed.

"Oh, yes, there has to be a next time. We'll see to it."

For werewolves, sex wasn't taken lightly. But slowness, carefulness, tenderness required discipline that only real love necessitated. And he'd come to love Rosalind with every fiber of his being.

"There's no mistake about that."

He ignored the knock at the door that came a few hours after dawn, and murmured a stream of assurances to Rosalind to cover the sound. Twice, he layered her with more blankets to calm her shudders, unable to close the window that was his only means of escape.

In Miami, chills like the ones covering Rosalind, if she were human, would be an indication of illness. In her, it was a manifestation of her internal tug-of-war.

"If I have hurt you, I'm sorry," he said.

She moved a leg, and made a troubled sound. Time, for Rosalind, was speeding toward what lay ahead.

When her father called out from the hallway, Colton glanced up from his place at Rosalind's side, surprised to find that the sun had again set, and that he had somehow missed an entire day.

"Open the door," Kirk said.

It was almost time. How many Weres would fall, in their honor, a few hours from now? he wondered.

The jangle of keys in the hallway made Colton wince. “Rosalind,” he murmured.

Whatever spirit forced her to open her eyes gazed up at him with deep black pupils. The intensity of her dark-eyed scrutiny caused his internal pressure to expand and his wulf to utter a growl through his too-human throat.

“Go now,” she said, moving bloodless lips.

Rosalind was now whiter than white. He saw that clearly now, where he hadn’t before. She’d become an albino, like him. Their lovemaking session had drained all remaining color from her. Every last bit.

He swore again, though he couldn’t allow himself to feel guilty. The night had been necessary on so many levels for them both. They had both known there might be consequences.

“Eat something,” he said, wanting to keep this news from her, and fighting the necessity of a parting. He wished more than anything to see her smile, and hear her laugh. “Eat for strength,” he said. “And I don’t mean little children.”

He took the fact that her lips upturned as a good omen, sure it would be a terrible thing for them all if Banshees didn’t have a sense of humor.

With a last lingering look at her, a heartfelt glance, he cleared his throat and said in a gravelly tone, “I’ll be close.” Then he headed for the window and passed through it, to the night beyond.

Colton landed on the grass in a crouch, both hands and one knee on the ground, and waited to hear the sound of bones breaking. When that didn’t happen, he stood up.

Daylight had indeed passed. The light at the front of

Landau's house hurt his sensitive eyes when he rounded the corner.

Someone was on the porch. He was glad to see that it was a female, and not Landau or Rosalind's father. Matt Wilson's mate got to her feet. "Jenna James, in case you missed my name last night," she said, holding up a plate covered by a dishcloth. "I saved this for you."

Colton glanced to the door.

"Some of them are inside, and some are on the walls," Jenna explained. "Landau can't leave the place unmanned when we go."

"We?" he said.

"You can read wulf minds a little, right?" she countered.

"What would make you assume that I can?"

"I'm a doctor trained to read facial expression and body language. I'm also a Were, and a female. We're better at knowing these things."

He took the plate gratefully and sat on the step, not sure he'd be able to keep anything down, but aware of the fact that he needed sustenance.

"I can't read minds," he said. "Sometimes I hear thoughts if they're loud enough. The more I heal, the more I hear, if I try."

"Then you probably know they're waiting inside to speak to you."

"Loud and clear," he said.

The door opened behind him with a crack of its metal bolts. He didn't whirl or greet the newcomer.

"She's gone," Jared Kirk announced angrily. "Rosalind is gone."

The crash of the plate hitting the step was the only other thing Colton heard as he faced Rosalind's father.

Chapter 30

Wildness had encompassed her. A violent impulse to surrender to the darkness rose in Rosalind's chest, throat and mouth. *Give up*, those impulses commanded. *Give in.*

She was pure spirit, but also a mixture of several things. At the moment, she felt like a creature of the air as she fled the need for food, for company and the ravenous desire to belong to Colton, body and soul. Once she had let go of those things, she became lighter, freer. As she walked, her feet barely touched the ground.

Without a trailing parade of Weres, she headed toward a foreign place. She veered far from the park and the Landaus, following the bits of information she had gleaned from the mind of one of the she-wulfs present on the lawn the night before.

"Fairview." That's what the place was called. It was

an odd name for a building that housed mental anomalies, but that's where she'd call the creatures that had been seeking Colton or herself. That's where she'd make a stand, and find out what was behind everything that had happened so far.

She hadn't showered or dressed. The bloodsuckers would smell her lover on her bare skin. Would they come flying out of the shadows? Spring up from hidden fissures underground? Would several more of them mean that hordes of vampires were heading to the city every day, drawn by whatever ruled their nasty appetites?

"Tonight, Death calls to only a few."

Rosalind hesitated when those words came out, surprised. The thought hadn't been hers. The Death-caller had spoken through her.

She swallowed an oath and kept going, already feeling the attention of the monsters that likely sensed her just as easily as she had them. After experiencing Colton's beautiful warmth, the chill of vampires made her stomach turn over.

She flowed through the grounds of estate after estate, silencing hounds with a glare and evading security systems with no setting for spirits. She had outwitted the Weres and had gone off without them, leaving behind the men who were grounded by the heaviness of their beasts that had no full moon to free them.

Those Weres had been chained to the assumption that she'd wait for them because of their offer to help. None of them understood that it was for precisely that reason—their honor and the offer of aid—that she had left them behind.

On the sidelines, Weres did their best to help everyone. They fought secret battles so that humans and decent werewolves could walk openly almost anywhere they chose to. Landau and his pack were prime examples of those selfless few. Colton and Dana Delmonico, as police officers, were exemplary souls among them.

Colton…whose love gave her wings.

Yes, she sent to the monsters in the shadows grabbing hold of her trail. "Come to me," she beckoned. "Follow."

The building she had been searching for finally came into view. Fairview Hospital was a tall brick square emanating a faint odor of disinfectant. It sat in the middle of a large expanse of forested acreage, by itself, at the end of a long, winding road.

The building and its small courtyard looked to be immaculately cared for, and was surrounded by a six-foot chain-link fence. Frosted lights on posts near the entrance and farther down the driveway were the only sources of illumination, other than the moon.

There was no doubt about Fairview's strangeness and the necessity of it being removed from the city proper. Spirits inside the building wanted to answer her calls for monsters to follow. Though most of the beings inside were human, their minds temporarily expanded by trancelike states, a very small percentage were only humanlike, and bothered by demons of their own. And in there somewhere a Were male watched over them all, tending to lost souls with the calmness of a guardian angel.

Fairview wasn't a bad place, in spite of the pain inside it. Too bad that didn't make her feel any better.

Rosalind stopped with a hand on the fence to listen before moving on. She took in great gulps of air, processing its components.

Gone now was the salty smell of the ocean, so prevalent at Landau's house. A musty green odor of uncut grass and old trees took the place of swaying palms and manicured parkland. Aside from those things, and removed from the hospital's smells, she detected an undercurrent of stale blood.

The vampires had arrived.

Moving clear of the fence, Rosalind turned her face into the sour bloodsucker scent. Her claws and fangs sprung simultaneously as she tossed off a shudder of distaste.

She walked toward the trees, not half as scared as she supposed she should have been when whatever happened here would determine the fate of so many.

The vampires' closeness rolled over her until her teeth began to chatter. Her heart amped up its rhythm, thundered; that beat as loud as if it were planted inside an echo chamber.

She stopped with a hand on her chest, startled by what felt like a new dual beat, and spun in place, searching the dark for the cause of this phenomenon. She zeroed in on a stretch of grass near the gnarled trees lining an unused dirt road.

No. She shook her head as an intimately familiar scent reached her.

"No!" she shouted, her body quaking as if something inside her was trying to break loose. "Not you!"

There was no time to focus on who else was heading her way. The surface of her skin began to chill. Her throat felt full. It was an all-too-familiar reaction, telling her that the beast and the other thing inside her also recognized the scent.

It was the fragrance of wulf.

The dark thing inside her moved. It wanted to become lost in that scent as much as she did, and began to heave its way upward, its darkness seeping out of her pores.

Rosalind growled and clenched her teeth. She shook her head to ward off this aggressive spirit's rise. But it was too late. Darkness had colored her white skin a deep, glossy black.

A cry escaped her, and there was no withholding what she had in the past so forcefully tamped down. The spirit she housed sought freedom, needing that freedom to proceed with whatever it had in mind.

The Banshee, the Death-caller, took her over with a terrible swiftness, forcing Rosalind to open her mouth wide. The sound she made filled the night—an awful wail that was both hers and the Death-caller's flung outward in unison. That shrill cry went on and on, creating waves in the air that shook the leaves on the trees.

It was a prediction. The Death-caller, long dormant, had come forth to do what it had been created to do... and that was to announce the coming of Death.

Trembling, Rosalind turned in time to watch the first batch of bloodsuckers reach the field. Their gaunt, corpse-pale faces shone like dry bones under a moon that wasn't theirs to blaspheme.

The walking dead rushed toward her, attracted to the darkness of her freed spirit, ignorant that the call had been an invitation to their final repose by an entity that knew this for a fact.

Rosalind whirled and tried to focus, but her attention was shattered by an intensifying acknowledgment of a wulf closing in.

From beneath the overhanging branches of the

nearby trees, a white blur raced toward her, moving so fast, Rosalind couldn't track it. She knew what it was.

Ghost.

Half wolf, half man, Colton came on in all his silver-white werewolf glory, fully muscled up and growling fiercely.

"I would have saved you from this," she whispered to him.

He looked like fury personified, and moved like liquid motion—as fluid as mist, and raging silently with an incredible power that made his fur stand up. Like a battering ram, the ghost wulf plowed into the ragged line of oncoming vampires, snapping his teeth, cutting them down.

He kept running as the bloodsuckers he met disappeared in storms of black blood and ash. The sound of his heartbeat filled Rosalind's ears. His rage burned in her breast. She wasn't alone. Colton had come here, not because she needed saving, but to stand by her side.

Again, she became buoyant. A rush of heat replaced the ungodly chill. Her bones realigned in one smooth wave. Sinew snapped a new shape into existence. Her skin began to melt away, leaving fur in its place. White fur. And then she was running with a rhythm in her legs that kept pace with the hum of fast-approaching cars.

The white werewolf hit vampire after vampire with incredible force. Cries of rage went up as the vampires were scattered, now aware of the ghost whose presence was like a swinging hammer among them.

Shouts answered their cries, along with the awful sounds of bodies hitting bodies that made Rosalind hesitate in the middle of a vamp-killing strike. The Weres had come, had found her, and were taking up her fight.

Landau's pack had jumped from their cars, ready to rumble, but she sensed the curiosity that made them turn their eyes to her and to Colton—two white werewolves who had changed without the help of a full moon; ghostly beings, lethal, and weaving through the vampires as if they had been born for fighting.

Rosalind felt the brush of a hand at her throat. That slight touch made her melt again into another shape. A human shape with a fanged mouth, her skin blackened by the Banshee's second rise as a dominant force.

It was a new bit of insight that the Death-caller inside her wanted no part of the wulf.

She bit at the vampire next to her, ripping the hand from its arm, and moved in time to duck a deadly blow. There was fighting all around her. Without a full moon, the Weres stuck in human form were slashing at vampires with knives and loosing arrows from crossbows that took the place of wooden stakes.

Strike after strike hit home. Vampires went down. But it didn't matter to her what they did around her. The spirit inside her didn't see the deaths of those Weres tonight.

Only her own.

Stunned by this realization, Rosalind paused in the center of a vortex of fighting. She felt Colton's heartbeat tune to hers, then noticed that he'd also stopped moving. He lowered his claws. In slow motion, he turned to face her.

Chapter 31

Rosalind was looking at him with large unblinking eyes, Colton realized. Her outline wavered between wulf, vampire and human, failing to settle on any one thing.

She was confused.

He knew the feeling.

But Rosalind seemed to be lit from within, as if going through so many changes at once had created an energy flux that manifested as electricity. Blue sparks hugged her body in a sparkling aura. Against the darkness surrounding her, Rosalind looked like some sort of supernatural light show.

The only feature that didn't morph was her face. That face was damp and strained by exertion, and more beautiful than anything he had ever seen. So damn beautiful, he wanted to fall on his knees before her.

She opened her mouth. From her throat came a sound that was low-pitched, unearthly, and it made Colton turn from her. She had wailed moments ago and the vampires had come for her. Now, he realized, she was announcing a newcomer.

A mixture of tastes hit him. As if he'd taken a bite of something nasty, dirt, ash and the fire of what might have been mythical brimstone stuck in this throat; a terrible, poisonous concoction that had no place on earth.

Rustling sounds on the grass beat at his nerve endings. The Weres who had made good headway against the vampires had also noticed the newcomers and were gearing up for a second battle.

But demons had to be infinitely harder to get rid of than a nest of vampires on the rampage, Colton thought. And demons were up next.

"Rosalind," he said.

She heard him. When he looked, her body was swaying from side to side. Her long hair, reaching to her waist, blew in an unnatural wind caused by the fury of all those sparks she was giving off.

One lone, dark strand, however, had survived the color change to white. Crossing her pale features from her forehead to her chin, the darkness accentuated the line between her wulf's will and the lure of her other spirit.

She looked strong and courageous, angry and demented. But it wasn't Rosalind who looked at him with big black eyes.

"Who are you?" Colton asked without closing the distance that lay between them. "What did you do with Rosalind?"

The entity turned her head to glance past him. It...

she…closed her eyes, shook her head and shifted shape into the blackest thing he could have imagined. His enemy, and Rosalind's. The kind of monster that had changed them both in the short span of one bleak night. *Vampire.*

She didn't attack, or run. She raised her face to search the night sky. From her fanged mouth came an ear-shattering sound that sent her blue sparks outward, and hurt Colton's ears.

Only peripherally aware of what was going on around them, Colton noticed that the fighting had slowed. There were less than a handful of vampires left, and all of the Weres who had ventured to stand against them remained. He saw none of the demons he knew slid through the shadows in the periphery. For some reason, they were keeping well back.

The vampires stopped fighting suddenly and without warning. Had Rosalind called them off with the awful sound she'd made?

Would they run to her, if they could? Would they run away, recognizing the hammer about to fall?

In their confused hesitation, those bloodsuckers were felled by the Weres, down to the last bloody fang. Without registering the carnage around her, Rosalind shapeshifted again. In place of the vampire hybrid stood a creature Colton had seen only once before, in his parents' backyard. *Demon.*

It felt to him as though there were only two of them in the field—he and Rosalind in her current incarnation—when in actuality they had an audience. Colton sensed the Weres warily gathering around them. Ragged and bloodstained, they were waiting to see if any other devilish creatures would turn up, and holding their breath.

Rosalind was a sight, and as scary as anything else that hell had spewed up tonight. She looked like one of the absent demonic brood, with skin that was yellow, withered and cracked. A ribbon of blood, black against the sallow face, ran down her chin. Her eyes were bloodred.

"Where are they?" Colton asked, knowing the demons had to be close. Rosalind's effervescent sparks had turned crimson.

Everyone readied for a new onslaught, though no one actually moved. And then Rosalind did. She lifted an arm in a gesture that invited the demons to join her, and they obeyed, pouring in from every direction at once.

But there were only six scaly, two-legged nightmares. A meager showing. They appeared to be part human, part reptile, and several things that Colton didn't care to think about. The ugly bastards had no eyes, and seemed to be bound together by the evil purpose they served.

The demons flocked to Rosalind like rats to the Piper, attracted by the voice, the sight of her, and her dark scent. Unable to resist such darkness, and seemingly mindless in their bedazzled state, they were extremely vulnerable. They were fools.

The Weres attacked with a force that filled the silence. Shots were fired; so many gunshots that Colton couldn't keep count. The demons hadn't been prepared for sabotage, when evil was their master. They had to have believed that Rosalind was one of them.

Muffled vibrations of leathery flesh being rent in the dark produced the rumble of an oncoming storm system. Colton could not watch. He had eyes for only one entity, and wanted Rosalind back.

Rosalind's demon spirit's eyeless gaze rose to meet

his. Brilliant scarlet sparks reflected on the surface of skin that again began to morph.

He felt the tension and anxiousness of the Weres sidling closer. There was no time to tell them about the information they didn't have. He knew better than to expect another round of creatures this night. Rosalind had been visited by two species of monsters lately, and she had used two shapes to call them to their deaths. Two species. Only those. The spirit inside her had accomplished what she had come here to do. She had rid the area of harmful creatures, and in doing so, had seen to it that Rosalind was safe.

Maybe, Colton rationalized, this Banshee wasn't an evil spirit at all. And maybe this Death-caller didn't want to harm the Lycans.

If Jared Kirk's story had been true, this spirit had saved the woman she had been slated to call to her death so that that woman could mate with a Were.

What did that mean for Rosalind now?

He had to use every brain cell to work that information to his advantage.

"I believe you have one more in there," Colton said, facing Rosalind and nearly breathless, his arms raising in an open invitation. "And if truth be told, I prefer no colorful, sparkling auras at all, other than the ones created by what I'd like to do to you, and with you, in the near future."

He wanted to shout when the sparks wafted away and Rosalind's outline returned as if she had simply faded back into existence.

Colton wanted to close his eyes and give thanks for this brief sight of his lovely, wounded lover. But this wasn't over yet.

She was separated from him by less than ten feet. None of the Weres who had fought by her side, and for her, dared to go near her or get any closer, now that the night had again grown quiet and their enemies had been vanquished.

Rosalind continued to stare at him soundlessly.

"Also," he went on gently, "I have a soft spot for fur. Any color might do, really, though my favorite lately has been black. A deep, true, midnight black that's silky and exotic to the touch, and quite rare. Do you know anyone that description might fit?"

"Not anymore," she whispered.

Colton's heart stirred in his chest. They had made contact. It was a good sign.

"Second to that, I like werewolves with white fur," he said. "I could easily make do with someone who looks like that, as long as she had large, expressive green eyes. But mark my words, Rosalind, it has to be a Were. My mate has to be a she-wulf, and not any other kind of creature. We have to be a perfect fit, you see."

"That's a long list," Rosalind said tonelessly.

"Yes, well, I have looked Death in the eye on a couple of occasions, and want the time I have left to be special until I have to face it again. I want that time to be shared with someone special. That person is you. Who else would have me, like this?"

Fearing to move toward her, Colton opened his arms. *Rosalind*, he silent called. *Please come.*

He saw that she couldn't, and felt what was holding her back. The black presence that had wailed and called to the freaks who wished her harm still sat within Rosalind, on guard and carefully watching him.

"Can I speak to the Death-caller?" he asked, dropping his hands to his sides. Without waiting for a reply, he said, "I'm told that you know me, spirit."

Rosalind lowered her gaze. Her cheeks were hollow, her face haunted.

His eyes fixed on her. "We have you to thank for the warnings, Death-caller. We've heard your story and have seen what you can do. But it's time to let Rosalind go. It's time for her to live her own life."

The black eyes again looked up.

"Rosalind is flesh and blood," he said. "Though you might have loved her family, and might love her, you must see that she needs to be with her own kind. If she isn't allowed to be what she is meant to be, what's left for her?"

The spirit was listening, and hopefully understanding. Colton watched with fascination as a single tear slid down her pale cheek.

His heart stirred restlessly as he continued, groping for the right words to express himself. "I'm sorry. I don't know if you can leave her. I have no idea what leaving Rosalind would mean for you as a spirit. But I'll help if I can, and if that's possible. I love her, too, and will do whatever it takes to care for her. You know my feelings are true because you also recognize the blood that runs through my veins. Isn't that right? We supposed that's why Rosalind and I found each other—because you made sure that we did."

Rosalind's head shook. It was her voice that said, "Yes. She knows you. But she can't leave me. Being tucked inside my family's bloodline is her penance for disturbing the natural flow of life and death. She will pass through my line for an eternity."

"Then I don't care who is in there if you, Rosalind, are with me. I'll take all of you. Every last part."

She shook her head again. "I can't touch you like this." Sadness rang in her remark. "What sort of life would we have?"

"Try," Colton suggested. "Reach out to me and see what happens."

"If I do, I might see things I don't want to see. I might know the time and place of your death. I have already seen mine."

"Yours?" he repeated. "What do you mean?"

"I die tonight. I've seen this."

Colton processed that, refusing to allow the confession to make sense. A streak of pure agony nearly derailed the next idea that came to him. He was grasping at straws, with the odds stacked against him. But he could not lose Rosalind.

He had to try everything, and study every angle.

"Maybe," he began, moving toward her, "you only think you will die. Maybe what you think of as Rosalind will be gone, while the real Rosalind will continue to breathe. Couldn't the death you saw merely be a metamorphosis of some kind?" He added after a breath, "Like going from a potential Night Wulf to a… ghost of one?"

Though Rosalind hadn't lowered her gaze, he sensed another energy fluctuation going on inside her. She was considering what he'd suggested.

"You're already no longer in danger of becoming a real Night Wulf, even if you were destined to be such a thing," he said, gambling on that in order to hold her attention. "There's no chance of a black heart taking over your chest, not with the spirit's presence inside you."

Colton cleared his throat to rid himself of the lump making speech difficult. He was desperate to have his theory proved right. He had to remain calm.

"I'm not afraid of you, Rosalind, or of any information you might turn up."

Stepping closer to her, Colton searched for the trace of moistness that had tracked down her cheek, sure that former hint of sadness had come from the spirit, who had to understand exactly what was going on.

"I've already walked Death's line, Rosalind. I may be living on borrowed time. What I want is to be with you for a while longer without running and fighting and facing our demons."

Rosalind didn't advance or take him up on his offer to test what remained between them. She appeared to be frozen in place.

"Please," he said, addressing the Banshee still present in the color of Rosalind's eyes. "If you can't let Rosalind go, at least let her have the love she deserves. You have the power to do this. You have done it before."

Probably he hadn't been meant to be a ghost wulf, he reasoned, since it had taken trauma to make him what he now was. But he was growing stronger with each passing night, and no longer felt pain in the same way. The only real pain he felt came from the possibility of losing Rosalind.

What did he have left to go back to, without her?

His changes had been radical. Because of that, it wasn't likely that he would be able to go back to the city and his job. And after what had happened here, fighting crime might seem elementary and mundane.

Still, he saw the folly of his former thought patterns now, surrounded by other Weres who had witnessed the unveiling of his secrets and Rosalind's secrets, and had aided in this fight with no questions asked. Like true friends. Like family.

He allowed his attention to momentarily drift.

Dylan Landau was there, his clothing torn and his expression one of concern. His mate, Miami PD's Dana Delmonico, was beside Dylan and naked, preferring, he supposed, to give in to her animal nature now that she had stumbled upon it.

Detective Matt Wilson stood behind Rosalind with his hand on the shoulder of the auburn-haired female who had offered Colton a plate of food and the use of her field.

Farther back, away from the rest, a furred-up Lycan female's stunning red pelt glowed in the moonlight, patchy with the dark blood of the two monstrous species she had helped to take down. That she-wulf's eyes glowed with green fire.

He had to stare at that red wulf, who was in wulf form without the moon guiding her to it. He shouldn't have been surprised about he and Rosalind not being the only Lycans with this gift.

He couldn't think now about the many surprises that had rocked the night. What he was feeling, in that moment, came darn close to sudden enlightenment. He had learned something here: a big lesson about trust, honor and the need for friends. And he had learned that one terrible sorrow didn't necessarily have to piggyback on another.

He accepted the fact that he had, so far, made good on his vow as Rosalind's protector, and therefore might even be well on his way to redeeming himself. Surely that had to score him some points with whoever was watching this from above…or through Rosalind's eyes?

"Try, Rosalind," he repeated, taking another step in her direction, and hoping she would meet him halfway. "Trust me, my love. Touch me."

The will of all the others present aided his request. The night virtually hummed with their hopes for him, and for this. Beneath the fierceness, werewolves were romantics at heart.

When Rosalind took a step, the buzz of ideas and hopes in Colton's head ceased. His heart nearly stopped beating. Having her so close was both frightening and reassuring. His ravenous hunger for Rosalind hadn't lessened one bit.

Rosalind took a second wary step, her expression blank, her eyes downcast, as if she were afraid to look at him.

"Please," he said. "Do this for us. Take a chance. Prove me right."

Her heartbeat began to quicken, matching the swift rise in his. Their gazes reconnected, and through that meeting of their eyes, their thoughts melded together.

This was proof, Colton wanted to shout. The proof of a true connection. She had to feel it, as he did. She had to know what it meant.

"Rosalind," he whispered, barely moving his lips. "Please."

Chapter 32

Rosalind couldn't escape the heartfelt plea in Colton's voice. She couldn't avoid his expression of need.

Torn, she wanted to shout to all the people whose eyes were trained on her. *I'm torn by what you say, and what I fear.*

Yet there was a sudden calmness spreading inside her where there had been only darkness. Although she still felt sick, that sickness had become less of a burden. She had, she now realized, always experienced this same momentary lightness when Colton was around.

The monsters were gone, though she barely remembered what had transpired. She had killed a few, but this was still a fight for her life. She wondered if Colton's theory was correct, and she wasn't going to die. Not in the way she had thought.

He wanted to believe that. So did she. And since she

was still standing after the creatures that had come after her had been taken down, and the spirit she housed had faded to allow her the time to test a love that waited for her if she were able to grasp it, Rosalind accepted the rise of former strengths she hadn't dared to use.

She was Lycan above all. Colton had told her that. And Lycans, early on, had to learn to be masters of their own destinies. She was young in terms of Lycan years, and was part darkness as well as wulf. Learning to control the dark parts was going to be a lesson hard-won. Still, she had a reason to live with what she had been given. Love shone from the eyes across from her. Colton's love, strangely accrued from a series of misfortunes, was not false or feigned.

God, how she loved him back.

She had loved him from the start. At first sight.

The spirit inside her had made this happen. That spirit had wanted it to happen. Maybe, in light of that… she should be thankful. She'd be all right. She'd make this trio within her work out, with her own wishes coming out on top.

Colton held his breath as Rosalind ran the rest of the way and flung herself into his arms. Or maybe it had been the other way around and he had rushed to gather her to him. He couldn't be sure.

His trembling arms closed around her slender body, enfolding her, pulling her tight. As they met, chest to chest and thigh to thigh, he whispered to her with his mouth in her tousled white hair. "I love you, little ghost."

She didn't wail or writhe or violently shift into something else. She didn't fall to the ground in the kind of death she had wrongly foreseen. Yes, it could be said that the old Rosalind had died inch by inch in his arms, he supposed, and that this last embrace was the culmination of that. But if that was so, and the black wulf had ceased to exist, it was not really a death but a transition, a passing from one kind of life to another, and from being alone to having found a soul mate.

He had been right about her ability to survive the many transitions. Maybe the spirit of a Death-caller had bolstered her and then backed off to offer him a hand in gaining a bright, shiny new future. If that were the truth, there was no clear way to thank that spirit directly. And yet that spirit, deep inside Rosalind, would know everything he felt, he supposed, if it was part of her. That spirit would take part in whatever events their future had in store.

He claimed Rosalind's waiting mouth hungrily, greedily, endlessly. Their hands traded explorations that were only the starting point for burning needs finally about to be appeased without interference...at least for now.

The sleek white she-wulf who would always have another strange entity compressed inside her returned his ardor. Her full, pale, quivering mouth clung to his in the manner of a drowning person in need of a lifeline. Like a woman who had to have this one last thing in order to find true happiness. And as though the spirit within her was finally getting what it also deserved and wanted so badly: a shot at happiness.

Then again, maybe those were his own feelings he was projecting onto the she-wulf in his arms.

Gratefully, gladly, aggressively, Colton's hands stroked Rosalind. They would be on the ground in a minute, or up against a tree, but right then he was content to devour her mouth, savor her taste, become lost in the familiar burn of a love that had spanned the ages.

Rosalind was, hands down, the bravest creature of them all. He vowed never to stop kissing her, ever.

He had no inkling of how much time passed before he rose from her prone body onto his hands and knees, covered with sweat and panting from exertion. Sometime during their wild lovemaking session, the Weres had gone and the night had again grown eerily calm. Not even a breeze stirred the silence. Above them, the moon shone with a silver gleam, but it wasn't full, and its lure came nowhere near to the powerful longing for what he held in his arms.

They were ghosts. Alike. And temporarily, at least, free from marauding monsters that might in the days or months or years ahead return for reasons no one had yet actually discovered—other than dark seeking dark wherever they could find it.

With the ease of a sigh, punctuated by a symphony of bones simultaneously cracking, he and Rosalind, with their limbs still entwined, flowed from one shape to another. With their coats glistening and their muzzles quirking, they leaped to their feet.

But they didn't run to shed the excess energy that made them twice as strong as their human counterparts. Because their wulfs knew what to do with that energy, and were ten times as needy.

Colton growled his pleasure. Rosalind howled once. Raising their faces in unison, they bayed at the moon like their ancestors had done once upon a time, long ago, as they backed into shadows they had once feared for round two…or was it round ten…and to make good on their dreams.

* * * * *

MILLS & BOON
Two superb collections!
40% OFF!
One Night with a Regency Lord
One Night with a Tempting Playboy
One Night with a Seductive Sheikh
Olivia Gates Fiona McArthur Meredith Webber
One Night with a Gorgeous Greek
One Kiss in... Paris
Robyn Grady Myrna Mackenzie Dara Marton
One Kiss in... Miami
One Kiss in... London
Carol Marinelli Helen Brooks Jessica Steele